Praise for A

A RELUCTANT MADONNA

CALUMET EDITIONS

Minneapolis

First Edition August 2023
A Reluctant Madonna © 2023 by Alan Miller.
All rights reserved.

This is a work of fiction. All of the characters, names, incidents, organizations, and dialogue are either the products of the author's imagination or are used fictitiously.

10 9 8 7 6 5 4 3 2 1

ISBN: 978-1-960250-91-9

Cover and book design by Gary Lindberg
Author photo by Wannapa Raker

A RELUCTANT MADONNA

ALAN MILLER

**CALUMET
EDITIONS**
Minneapolis

My candle burns at both ends;
It will not last the night;
But ah, my foes, and oh, my friends;
It gives a lovely light!

– Edna St. Vincent Millay, "First Fig"

To the brave people of Ukraine who
treasure freedom and democracy

and

As always, for Sharon

Also by Alan Miller

FICTION

Holding Court

NON-FICTION

You Can Make a Difference
My Name Was Toby

One

Alison Powers impatiently glanced at her watch as she stood on a deserted platform overlooking a single track running in both directions past flat, sparse prairie. She ran her fingers through her auburn hair. An attractive woman in her thirties, she toted a carry-on and a PC in a leather case that hung from her shoulder. Wearing a black suede jacket and two-inch heels, she studied a one-story depot with a sign proclaiming "GRAND FORKS."

"I should have taken the Delta flight from the Twin Cities," she muttered, "instead of the scenic route." The Amtrak had arrived two hours late, and there had been little to see on the overnight trip.

Alison had not imagined that her first big opportunity would surface in Grand Forks, North Dakota, half a continent away from her desk at the *Washington Post*. Mort Ahrens had suggested her for the story as he was about to leave on a belated honeymoon, and she relished the chance. *Life takes strange bounces*, she thought, acknowledging that her introduction to Mort had come with sharp edges—*her* sharp edges—and he was giving her a chance for the big story.

Grand Forks was a far cry from the New Orleans home where she had grown up with two brothers and a sister. As the pampered youngest child, Alison had comfortable memories of a home where her mother was a stay-at-home socialite and her father a prominent cardiologist. She had majored in journalism, or, as Tulane called it, media studies. Her 4.0 average and the publication of an article in *The Atlantic* had earned her a junior position on the *Times Picayune*, which

1

led to a job at the *Atlanta Constitution*, and now—as she neared thirty with a broken relationship only months behind—to the flats of North Dakota representing the investigative desk of the *Washington Post.*

A muddy Chrysler Ram 1500 pulled into the small parking area, and a lean, weathered man eased out of the driver's seat. He wore a red and black checked jacket, jeans and a bronze belt buckle emblazoned "Deputy Sheriff." The stereotype was completed by Western boots, a large wide-brimmed hat pushed back on his forehead and dark aviator glasses masking his eyes. She couldn't guess his age but noted his scruffy beard, high cheekbones, cleft chin and, as he pulled off his shades, intense brown eyes. Not exactly the Marlboro man, but ruggedly handsome.

He strode over and said, "Miss Powers?"

She glanced around the empty platform and said, "Yes, by default. Mr. Comfrey?"

"Sorry I'm late," he said. "Did you have a good trip?"

"Well, so much for scenery on an overnight, and I couldn't believe we stopped every few hours to let the smokers get off and destroy their lungs. Anyway... I'm here." She stuck out her hand, which he engulfed in his.

She swept her arm around the landscape where industrial buildings some distance away were situated and said, "I envisioned oil wells, or fields of growing crops."

Comfrey ignored her and asked, "Did you get any sleep? Or anything to eat?"

"No, and no. I'd kill for a cup of coffee."

"We can do better than that," he said, picking up her overnight bag and slinging it into the truck. "And it's Richard, not that mister or sheriff stuff."

"Fair enough. I'm Alison."

* * *

Darcy's Café was a throwback to another era—a wooden Quonset hut look-alike with screen doors flanked by two large Coca-Cola signs. The parking lot was filled with dusty trucks, SUVs, a large dump truck, several motorcycles and a shiny Lincoln Navigator that looked very out of place.

Comfrey found an empty booth in the back under a logo featuring a huge cup of coffee and the claim "Better than your Grandma's / As good as your Mom's."

Everybody in the place was staring at Alison, who immediately felt out of place. The patrons, almost all males of varying ages, were in work clothes—boots, flannel jackets, baseball caps—except for the adjacent table. There, three middle-aged Asian men in dark suits were conversing with a younger Asian male in a sweat suit and sneakers.

Comfrey glanced at the Asians and whispered to Alison, "Damn Chinese."

She was startled and he noted her shocked look.

"That's a little harsh, isn't it?" Alison said. "And bigoted to boot."

He shrugged and said, "Might be, but they're the reason you're here. A bunch of vultures buying up our land. And once they've got it, then what? Force us out? Even though the law says they can't, they have phony corporations fronted by locals. They're getting too close to the air base. Long range bombers. Missile silos not that far away. That's why you're here, no?"

"Well, yes and no. I've been assigned the story, but my job is to take a fair, impartial look at the dispute. I didn't realize you'd be law enforcement."

"Don't let the belt buckle fool you," he replied. "Only part time when needed. Do I detect a southern accent?"

"Born and raised in Louisiana."

A bearded, dark-skinned man of about sixty entered the café and worked his plump body over to them, gladhanding the patrons and exchanging pleasantries before easing into the booth beside Comfrey.

"Earl, this is Alison Powers," Comfrey said. Turning to Alison, he added, "Earl Raincloud is the leader of the NDFC, the North Dakota Farmer's Cooperative. He's the boss man." They shook hands.

Raincloud's dark eyes sparkled as he said, "They sure grow 'em pretty back east. A pleasure, ma'am."

"She's a real southern belle," Comfrey said.

Raincloud pushed his girth away from the table, stood up and bellowed, "Hey, folks, this here pretty lady is the reporter from the *Washington Post* who's going to write the story about the land grabbers."

Several of the patrons stood and clapped. Alison blushed, and the older Asian men stared silently into space. The younger Asian, though, nodded and then winked at her.

Comrey caught the wink. "Don't let the young one fool you with that smile. He's the worst of the bunch. Born here."

"I just made you a whole passel of friends," Raincloud said.

"So much for anonymity," Alison said.

Comfrey leaned in. "Folks around here are suspicious of strangers, especially with the land grabs and them foreigners, so Earl just opened a lot of doors for you."

Darcy, the sixtyish, solidly built owner of the café, approached the booth, menus in hand. Looking at Alison, she said, "Welcome. Anything you need while you're here, just ask. Breakfast today is on me."

Comfrey's head snapped up. "How come you never offer me free vittles?"

"Cuz you never get us a story in the newspaper. I mean, except the local, when you're puttin' somebody in the drunk tank."

* * *

A half-hour later outside the café, Raincloud shook Alison's hand again and said, "Them Chinese sittin' there so nice and smug. With that Tang character, an American-born. Makes me sick."

"I don't expect there are a lot of Chinese in North Dakota," Alison said. "I think it's not so unnatural to want to be with your own people."

"Cept he's a turncoat. An ABC."

"ABC?" Alison said.

"American Born Chinese," Comfrey explained. "Works with the corporate Chinese who come over here with loads of money to buy our land illegally."

"Don't state laws prohibit foreign ownership of farmland?" Alison asked. "I did my homework before coming out here."

"Laws are meaningless," Raincloud said. "They buy up land with a front man—a local like Tang—and then turn the land against us. We got laws—here, in Minnesota and some of the other states—but they're useless when the owner is only a figurehead controlled by the Chinese and their government."

"Is that why some members of Congress are trying to change those laws?"

"Damn right!" Comfrey exclaimed. "Minority ownership of the land can kill us when the wheels are turned by the real owners."

"The two biggest meat producers around here are now owned by the Chinese," Raincloud said. "They're trying to build a billion-dollar data center in Becker, Minnesota, to get control of our farmland, our economy, run food prices through the roof, run the locals off. My people were the *original* owners here. Look where we are today. Live on reservations. Third-class citizens. I ain't gonna let that happen. That's why they hate me."

"This thing has international proportions," Alison said. "Looks like I have a lot to learn."

Raincloud leaned in and whispered, "That's what I've been doing for you. Getting the information. Not sharing with no one but you. Everything's written down at the farm. Reams of it. Names, purchases, the works. You get some rest, then we'll go over it."

He turned to Comfrey and said, "Rich, let us have a minute in private, okay?"

Comfrey looked confused for a beat but agreed and walked away.

Raincloud spoke quietly to Alison. "I know this sounds paranoid, but there's a leak somewhere, and some of the information I've got is only for you. No one else has seen it, except one lady I trust and one of the elders, *Waeinyepica* Oyate—means honest and trustworthy—one of the Spirit Lake Tribe, a daughter of Charlie Black Bird—*Wicaka*, truthful, and has *Woksape*, wisdom. She knows everything."

Alison scribbled some notes by hand instead of hauling out her laptop.

Raincloud kept talking. "These Chinese guys have set up operations around here, even Chinese police to frighten people.

And while this here Peking Group might be legit, I can't be certain they're not an undercover operation by the Chinese government. And it's happening all over. Not just here in the USA. They get people here, Chinese-Americans, to do their dirty work by threatening to hurt relatives back in the old country. Got more tentacles than an octopus."

"I had no idea it was this big. I think I'll hit the university library for more background," Alison said.

"Good idea. Chester Fritz Library, best in the state. Ask for Alice White. She's a librarian and the lady I mentioned. You can trust her. You sure you can find the farm? There's a porta potty right at the edge of the road—we were doing some construction, and the place is all tore up—but I'll meet you there tomorrow morning... eight o'clock. Get ready for a full day. Sure you won't have any trouble getting there?"

"GPS on my phone. I'll rent a car, get the lay of the land, spend some time at the library, and see you at eight."

"Much to see, people to meet," Raincloud said. He walked to his truck and left.

Comfrey rejoined Alison. "If you don't mind my asking, what was so secretive?"

"Personal stuff. He's nervous because I'm a young woman alone."

"Well, you're not alone. We can be as close as you want. By the way, can I ask if all your clothes are like the ones you're wearing?"

"Not casual enough?"

"Not if you want people to get comfortable with you. And loosen up. You got to look like you belong here, not like a page out of a fashion magazine. I think we best head over to Ross."

Ross Dress for Less was a short walk down South Columbia Road. Inside, Alison was surprised by its size and the quality and variety of clothes, at prices up to 60 percent less than she would have expected. She left with a large shoe box and a stuffed plastic bag of new clothes. Comfrey toted an even bigger bag.

* * *

Exiting the Best Western Harvest Inn wearing jeans, boots, and a colorful blouse partially hiding a bandana tied around her neck, Alison manipulated the screen of her phone—setting her GPS— then got into her rental Prius and drove off.

The young Chinese man who had winked at her in the café stood by a car across the street, watching.

Two

At sea, two hours out from Panama City, the ocean liner passengers stood at their assigned assembly stations on deck, massive lifeboats and tenders swaying from davits over their heads. Excited that the journey had finally commenced, they wore bulky orange life jackets as crew members, clad in yellow ponchos and holding loudspeakers, shouted safety instructions. A glorious sun prepared to disappear on the horizon.

At thirty-two, Danni Rose, a diminutive brunette with an athlete's toned and well-shaped body, was a woman who turned heads—not a raving beauty, but a stunner who caught one's attention with her disarming dimples, intense blue eyes and by the confident way she moved. She turned to her thirty-year-old husband, Mort Ahrens, who stood about six inches taller at five-eight but looked shorter because of his paunchy build. Bubbling with uncharacteristic effervescence, Danni said, "I can't believe we're finally getting away."

Mort adjusted his glasses and replied, "Only a year late, Panama Canal instead of London, and I only had to kill one guy to get us here."

"My husband, the downer," Danni said, pinching his arm.

* * *

Dressed casually, Danni and Mort stood in the line for dinner seating in the cavernous main dining room.

"Do you mind dining with another couple?" the concierge asked. "Or there will be a short wait."

Mort started to speak, but Danni quickly said, "That's fine. We don't know anyone."

On the way to their table, Mort and Danni took in in the large, ornate dining room embellished in gold and purple. They were led to a table for four already occupied by two attractive women in their thirties, also casually dressed and both heavily made up. One was a blonde and the other an African-American. They both wore blouses with plunging necklines that revealed a lot of bosom.

"I'm Lynette," said the African-American, "and this is Kimberly. First cruisers?"

"I'm Danni Rose, and this is my husband, Mort Ahrens." They sat down, and Danni finished her answer. "Yes, our first cruise. Is it that easy to spot? And you?"

"No, no," said Kimberly, "but this is the first one where Simeon is actually the artist on board. We collect him. We're overboard for him. His artwork, that is."

"Not good to be overboard for anyone on a cruise ship," Mort said, and received polite laughter.

Lynette was staring at Danni. "I know you from someplace," she said, and then snapped her fingers. "I know—television. Last year. That debate about water. And you kicked his ass! A law professor, right?"

"Guilty as charged," Danni said, embarrassed. "And my husband is with the *Washington Post*."

Suddenly catching up with the drift of the conversation, Kimberly pointed at Mort and said, "I saw your picture on TV. You're the one who rescued that kidnapped judge, right?"

"A justice, actually," Mort corrected.

Kimberly grew more excited. "And you killed a kidnapper, right?" She turned to Lynette. "We're in the company of celebrities."

"I only acted in self-defense," Mort clarified, "but here we're just a couple finally getting away for a quiet honeymoon. What's past is past, better left unspoken for the sake of a peaceful cruise."

Kimberly replied, "Your honeymoon? How exciting." Putting her fingers to her mouth as if locking her lips, she said, "Our lips are sealed. What deck are you on?"

"Ninth, 9052," said Danni.

"That's great. We're 9064. We'll be shipmates. You've got to do the art auctions. You'll love the art. You'll *love* Simeon."

"We live in DC, in Georgetown," Danni offered. "You?"

"We're practically neighbors!" Lynette said. "Well, almost. Our office is in Baltimore, and we live in Timonium."

"Which is in what state?" Danni asked.

Lynette answered, "Maryland, a stone's throw from Baltimore."

"Timonium sounds like one of the elements," Mort said. "You know—lithium, plutonium…"

"Cute," Kimberly said with a slight smirk, "but it's a great community. Spiro Agnew lived there."

"I wouldn't brag about that one," Mort said.

"He's so quick," Kimberly said, looking at Mort. "A great sense of humor."

* * *

Back in their stateroom, Mort opened the door to the balcony and let in the warm Atlantic air. Danni turned off the air conditioning. Mort stripped down to his shorts.

Soft through the middle, Mort was clearly not a regular exerciser even though he had been taking a martial arts class for months. He stepped onto the balcony and sat in one of two deck chairs.

Staring at the vast expanse of sea, Danni teased, "Aren't you afraid the neighbors will see you?"

They both laughed. Danni slipped on a robe and joined him.

"So, what did you think of our dinner companions?" she asked.

"In what respect?" Mort asked.

"I don't know. Any respect."

"Interesting pair. I don't really know. Informed and self-assured. Certainly not shy. Shall we check out this artist they're raving about at the auction?"

"I noticed you couldn't get your eyes off their breasts."

"Let's just say they were hard to miss. But what you have is perfect for me."

11

"It *better* be. About the auction, I don't know. But it's probably a safer bet than going to the casino." She sat down on Mort's lap, draping her arms around his shoulders.

"On second thought," Mort said, pulling her close and nuzzling his head into her chest, "maybe we're in for the night."

Three

Alison exited the Chester Fritz Library with copies of several newspaper articles. As she walked toward her car in the multi-level garage, Tang, the young Asian man, approached her. She noticed that he was taller than she expected, quite muscular, and very handsome.

"Before you get prejudiced by the other side," he said, "do you want to hear our story?" He exuded self-confidence and spoke fluent English.

"Did you follow me?" she asked sharply.

"Pure coincidence," he said unconvincingly. "My name is Tommy Tang, by the way."

"I already know who you are, and I'm—"

"Alison Powers from the *Washington Post*. I'm sure what you heard from Raincloud and that deputy wasn't very flattering."

"What else do you know, Tommy Tang?"

"I know that you're a reporter and are known to follow stories fairly. And I'm guessing that you don't know the best restaurant in town for dinner. Fortunately, I do. Would you care to join me? I dare you."

"How do you know I'm a good reporter?"

"We have our ways. Now, what about dinner, unless you've got plans with the locals—or have a closed mind." He winked again, which she found disconcerting, but in an attractive way. He moved close.

"I don't have plans, but we go Dutch. I'll hear your side of the story."

* * *

Alison pulled up in her rental car at a three-story building circa 1800 that had a sign with a frog in a top hat: "Welcome to The Toasted Frog." Tang was waiting outside the entrance in black jeans and a polo shirt. He grinned, swept his hands in a grand gesture and bowed as she alighted.

"M'lady."

Inside, the plain-looking interior offered simple and unadorned plank tables and booths. Tang chose a booth, but rather than sitting across from her, he sat beside her. The restaurant was deep, with pizza ovens in the rear and a huge, enclosed display of wines. An adjoining room featured a long bar. Despite the lack of ambiance, the menu was extensive and inviting—everything from burgers to venison.

"Best food in town," he said, moving close enough to her that their hips touched. She slid a little farther away.

"I think you got wrong information on my people," Tang said over drinks.

Alison looked at him skeptically. "I got a lot of material at the library today, so I think I have a pretty fair idea of what the problem seems to be. The local people are very concerned about foreign interests—Chinese interests in particular—not only buying up farmland through sham corporations, but trying to establish data centers and other businesses that will eventually push out the locals. It's a pattern that's occurred not only in the States, but in other countries. Gain a foothold, and then suddenly they're running the show. And there are suspicions that not all of these business people are on the up and up—the ones working for the government."

"That story comes from prejudice against us Chinese. Did you know that because China is such an economic threat to the US, Bill Gates is buying tens of thousands of acres here?" Tang asked. "And yet the locals don't seem to object to that."

"But at least he's interested in the environment and ecology. If corporate farms are the result, the local people will still have jobs and security—perhaps even prosper, which they certainly haven't been able to do around here lately."

"Our interests are the same," Tang said, "but some of these folks won't even give us a chance. Like that old buzzard Raincloud. A troublemaker. It's an ethnic bias with him as well. And yet he complains about prejudice against the Indians."

"He was certainly nice to me," Alison said. "You speak perfect English. Were you really born here? And if so, who is this 'us' that you refer to?"

"I plead guilty of being born here. My folks are Cantonese. Moved here, then moved back a few years ago. By 'us' I mean the Chinese businessmen—the Peking Group—here legally, by the way, and not out to break any laws. We just want the same chance everyone in this country wants."

"And just what do you do in this operation? Are you their Chinese Chamber of Commerce?"

Tang smiled. "Sort of, and I get very well paid for it. Do whatever they want. But tonight, not the Chamber of Commerce. Tonight I'm here on my own."

"I'll hear your side of the story, but tomorrow morning I'll get to see some of the voluminous material Mr. Raincloud has apparently gathered. I promise everyone will get a fair shake."

After a delightful meal, Alison grabbed her check just as Tang was reaching for it. Tang followed her to her rental car and opened the door for her.

"Your evening sounds dull," he said. "You sure you don't want company?"

"Positive."

He gave her shoulder a squeeze as she got into her car and then walked to his own.

She watched him pull away with a wave, wondering just how sincere he really was, what exactly his duties were with the Chinese businessmen and what he meant by "Do whatever they want."

* * *

Alison arrived at the farm about fifteen minutes early. As she was parking, she glimpsed a tall man in the distance jump into a blue car and speed away. The man, whose build was similar to Tang's, had a peaked cap pulled down over his eyes.

She waited for fifteen minutes but Raincloud didn't arrive, so she exited her car and walked toward the porta potty. Because of a bountiful spring rainfall, corn stalks that would normally be pushing through the soil were yet to surface. There was a slight wind, just enough so she held her hair down with one hand.

She noticed a dark liquid seeping from the bottom of the porta potty. Out of curiosity, she slowly opened the door. Earl Raincloud sat there, blood oozing from his neck, which was garroted. His hands were frozen in mid-air as if grasping for the wire that had almost decapitated him.

Alison stumbled backward and screamed, hitting her head on the pavement, and suddenly the nearby farmhouse at the end of the dirt road exploded.

Four

The art gallery on the ship was on the seventh deck. The auctioneer's team had set out hundreds of paintings on easels. Mort and Danni walked among the rows of artwork. Some rows represented just one artist, others had a half dozen or more paintings by different artists. Like walking brands, Mort wore a blue tee with the *Washington Post* logo, and Danni, in white running shorts, wore a tight orange Syracuse Law T-shirt, which emphasized her muscular physique and firm breasts.

"I probably should have showered and changed after my run," Danni said.

"I give you credit," Mort said. "Seven times around the deck to complete a mile. And how many did you do?"

"Only four miles," she replied. "Can't interest you at all, huh? Even walking?"

"I'd end up dizzy and falling overboard," he said. "And you know I hate jogging."

"Also walking, and bicycling, and hiking, and…"

"To each his own," he said. "You're the athlete in the family. I concede that. But I now have *my* martial arts class."

Danni nodded and said, "Krav Maga. Jewish karate. Like that's really *exercise*, killer."

"Strictly defensive," Mort said. "But I enjoy, and it *is* exercise. I've been practicing the moves every day."

Danni grinned. "You can be the poster boy of the *Post*." With that she slapped his stomach with a resounding whack.

Mort had become intrigued with the Israeli technique of Krav Maga about seven months before the cruise after reading a feature article in the Sunday Magazine of the *Post*. He thought it sounded tailor-made for him—training that pushed both the mind and the body to its limits. Even if his body was lagging, he had been a multiple winner on *Jeopardy* some years back and was ready for anything that challenged his mind. When he'd learned that Israeli instructors taught Krav Maga to US Marines and Special Forces, he made up his mind.

Fitness had always been an issue dividing Mort and Danni. She had been an All-American basketball player in college—an agile but diminutive point guard—and would jog, run or work out in the gym at least five days a week, which Mort thought was boring. He always preferred something competitive. After reading the article, he sought out a *dojo* near the paper, met the instructor (his *sensei*), purchased the required grey KMG training T-shirt and black training pants, and went twice a week for lessons. He surprisingly enjoyed it, especially the one-on-one with his instructor. Even though he thought some of the customs were hokey, such as bowing on your way in and out of the *dojo*, he had quickly dropped seven pounds and felt more fit—even if Danni didn't seem to notice.

"This show is really incredible," Mort said to Danni. "So many well-known artists…"

Lynette interrupted him from behind. "But there's only one Simeon, and he's on this cruise. We've got him all to ourselves, and we want you to meet him."

Lynette and Kimberly were together, both wearing skimpy shorts and halter tops. Kimberly looked at Mort and said, "You missed last night's auction, but maybe at dinner, or definitely at the next event."

"Are you two like a tag team?" Mort asked. "Do you ever travel individually?"

Lynette laughed. "You're such a cutey." She turned to Danni and said, "I love his sense of humor."

"A regular Steven Colbert," Danni replied sarcastically.

"Have you checked out Simeon's section?" Kimberly asked.

They shook their heads, and Kimberly wiggled a finger as if to say "Follow me."

"Is this Simeon guy affordable?" Mort asked. "I think he may be out of our price range."

"You'd be surprised."

Simeon's paintings were all of women, beautiful nude women tastefully rendered and partially covered with sheer silk or lace that didn't really hide their physical attributes. The paintings were embellished in gold, and the models—some seated, some standing—were young, well endowed, all with winsome eyes and the slightest of smiles, which made them very fetching and inviting. Mort looked intently.

Mort turned to Kimberly. "This one looks just like you."

"That *is* me," she said, smiling. "And there are some of Lynette here as well. Actually, more of Lynette. He *really* loves to paint Lynette. You know, black is beautiful."

"So you're models?" Danni asked.

"Not professionally," Kimberly replied. "In real life we're interior decorators, but if we pose for Simeon, we get a free serigraph of the original."

"How does he make money if he gives them away?" Mort asked.

"He paints multiples, sometimes giclees, lithographs, serigraphs—and he's also into different mediums like pastels, acrylics, impressionist abstracts—"

"Whoa!" Mort said. "You lost me at giclees, whatever that is."

Kimberly was just about to give Mort his first art lesson when Danni interrupted. "Doesn't leave too much to the imagination," she said, studying the painting of Kimberly.

Kimberly replied, "Old Hawaiian expression—'For free, take. For buy, waste time.' Much better than paying seven to ten thou a painting for the oils."

"*I'd* pose for him at those rates," Mort said.

"He's so cute," Kimberly said to Danni while touching Mort's arm. "But Simeon only does female nudes at the moment. He goes through phases, and we've got some of his florals, some impressionistic paintings as well."

"Maybe he'll call you when he goes through his Buddha phase," Danni said, looking at Mort's tummy.

They all laughed.

"Anyway, you'll meet Simeon at the next auction," Kimberly said. "He's a teddy bear."

An announcement came over the ship's public address system. "This is the captain speaking. Mr. Mort Ahrens, if you could report to the bridge as soon as possible. Any member of the crew will assist you with directions. Mr. Mort Ahrens."

Mort looked at Danni. "Oh, shit," he said. "What did I do now?"

* * *

The size of the bridge astounded Mort. One of the junior officers introduced him to Captain Gunnar Thornberg in a large room with a glass window revealing the operations area of the deck.

"This is almost as wide as a football field," Mort said. In front of him, the large windows of the bridge ran the width of the ship. The bridge, manned by about a dozen uniformed officers and crew members, contained multiple screens, monitors, and more electronic equipment than he had ever seen. "I'm dumbfounded," he confessed.

Captain Thornberg replied, "It takes a lot of state-of-the-art materiel to keep almost three thousand souls safe." At almost six feet and dressed in a white shirt with epaulets, the graying captain towered over Mort and gripped his hand with a firm grasp. "A pleasure to meet you. Your reputation, I might add, precedes you. I really apologize for intruding on your holiday, but your newspaper was trying to reach you. They said it was really important, and they were getting no response from your cell phone."

"I buried it in our room," Mort said. "We were hoping to escape Washington for a week."

"Well, it must be urgent for them to contact us by satellite," Thornberg said.

"I'll go right down and give a call," Mort said. "I've got a sat phone."

"No need, you can call from here if you don't object to the lack of privacy. Follow me into the inner sanctum."

The officers and crew on the bridge looked on with curiosity. The captain led Mort to a table for four in the operations room and handed him a headset. A technician placed the call.

"Mort," a voice on the phone said. He recognized that it was Steven Ginsberg, his managing editor. "We tried reaching you but got nothing. Sorry to intrude on your vacation, but—"

"Honeymoon," Mort corrected. "The one I *never* got to take last year."

"I know, and I apologize," Ginsberg said, "but I'm going to have to screw up your plans again."

"What's so urgent, Steve?"

"Alison Powers is in the hospital with a concussion," Ginsberg said. "She's a mental case because the guy you set up for her to interview was murdered. Garroted—and almost lost his head—practically in front of her. I really need you to get to North Dakota ASAP."

"Steve, I'm in the middle of the ocean," Mort said.

"I know, I know, but this *is* your story, and you picked her to handle it. We've got no choice. It's now a *blockbuster* with the murder. Your specialty, I might add. I need you, buddy. And she needs you. Just straighten things out and then you can continue your trip."

"Honeymoon," Mort corrected again.

A year earlier, Mort had been a reporter on the Investigations Desk of the *Washington Post,* one of eight hundred on staff, when J.J. Richter, Senior Associate Justice of the Supreme Court had been kidnapped. Using his intellect, Danni's connections to the Supreme Court, and by being in places that he shouldn't have been in, Mort not only solved the kidnapping but also a scandal that had led all the way to the White House. During the investigation, he had killed one of the kidnappers with a shotgun fired in desperation as the kidnapper had tried to run him down with a van.

As a result, Mort had received a lot of unwanted national notoriety and was given a promotion and the responsibility for leading a small group of four reporters tasked with investigating stories of interest.

Alison Powers was a member of that team. He had chosen her despite a first meeting that was less than harmonious, but he respected her impressive talent. Mort had assigned her to the North Dakota story.

"I don't even know where to begin," Mort said to Ginsberg.

"Everything's arranged," Ginsberg explained. "Thank Captain Thornberg for me. Unfortunately, the ship doesn't have a landing pad, so a limo will be waiting when you dock in Puerto Limon in Costa Rica. As soon as the ship clears customs, you'll be first off and taken to the airport to board a forty-minute flight to San Jose on Sansa Airlines, a commuter. Your ticket will tell you the connecting flights to Grand Forks. If there are no delays, you can be there by tonight."

Mort was silent.

"Did you get that?" Ginsberg asked.

"Jesus," Mort said, "you've been busy. Danni will kill me. You know I'll be leaving her alone for the whole cruise on her honeymoon."

"Thornberg said the crew will look after her. And she can have dinners with him or the other officers. Have you met anyone on board you're friendly with?"

"A couple of interesting people," Mort said, "but the cruise is just getting started."

"Good," Ginsberg said. "Danni will be fine. She's a tiger! We'll make it up to both of you, I promise. Bring me back a great story, Mort. But please, don't kill anybody this time."

The call disconnected and Mort stood there speechless. Finally, he turned to the captain. "Now comes the hard part," Mort said. "Telling my bride I'm abandoning her on our honeymoon."

Five

"I can't believe this," Danni said angrily, standing with arms folded in the middle of their cabin as Mort was packing an overnight bag. "Eight hundred reporters and Ginsberg only has *you*?"

"It's my story, my responsibility. I'm the one who assigned Alison."

"That *cute* Alison, which I recall you said you never noticed."

"That *cute* Alison is in the hospital, Danni. Pretty shaken up, plus a concussion. I don't know if she was attacked or what."

"It's the *or what* that gets me," Danni said.

"Steve said he'd make it up to us. You know what that probably means. All expenses paid for our next trip. And you can still enjoy this one."

"Right," she snapped. "A honeymoon alone. And I'm ovulating. Just what I always dreamed of."

"You'll be looked after. Meals with Captain Thornberg, which is quite something."

"Is he young and single? No. I saw his photo—I don't think so. I hope some of the ship's officers are cute, at least. Maybe I can get one of them to step in and take your place. We'll just name the baby Cruiser."

"Are you trying to make things harder?"

"Damn right," Danni said.

"At least we met Lynette and Kimberly. They'll be great company."

"Just what I always imagined. A honeymoon without a husband but with two women who like to pose nude. Wrap that around your imagination."

Mort dipped into his pocket and pulled out his wallet. "Look, take my American Express card," he said. "And here's most of the cash I brought on board— four hundred dollars."

"I can't be bought that cheaply."

He reached out and pulled her close. As he leaned down to kiss her, he saw a tear.

"Promise me one thing," she said. "That you won't do anything foolish. And you'll stay safe."

* * *

As promised, Mort was the first passenger off the ship. Danni stood next to him with the tag team of Lynette and Kimberly. Danni gave him a peck on the cheek.

"See you soon," Mort said.

"The road to hell is paved with good intentions," Danni said.

"Don't worry about Danni," Lynette said. "We'll take good care of her and keep the wolves away."

"Please, leave the wolves alone to do what they will," Danni said, smiling.

"We're all taking a tour today," Kimberly explained. "They say that Costa Rica is magnificent."

"Can't be as pretty as North Dakota," Mort said. "But take some good pictures anyway." Mort followed one of the ship's officers down the gangway.

Six

Grand Forks International Airport was located about eight miles from the downtown area. When Mort stepped off the Delta flight after three connecting flights and numerous airport hassles, he looked tired and haggard. He carried his overnight bag, his laptop and a fleece-lined jacket purchased in Chicago at O'Hare. After exiting, he looked around for his contact.

Richard Comfrey, in a denim shirt and bolo tie, waved and approached him.

"I'm Richard Comfrey, deputy sheriff. You're Mr. Abrams?"

"Almost right. It's Ahrens, Mort Ahrens." They shook hands. "How's Alison? What the hell happened?"

"A real shitstorm. Alison's much better. Will probably be released from the hospital later today or tomorrow."

"Was she attacked?"

"Doesn't look like it. Apparently, she found Earl Raincloud, the deceased, moments after he was killed. A pretty grisly scene. She stumbled backward and hit her head on the ground, best we can figure. His house went up in smoke about the same time. Arson. Total destruction."

"When I called from Chicago, they told me the sheriff would meet me."

"Sheriff MacCauley is at the hospital. If Alison is well enough, we want her statement. Couldn't get it earlier—doctor's orders. Let's get you to the hospital to see Alison, then I'll take you to the hotel."

As they exited the airport, Mort looked back at the terminal. "Very impressive building. Looks new and modern." He looked up at the sign over the entrance: "GRAND FORKS INTERNATIONAL." "Is this really an international airport?"

"About a dozen years old," Comfrey said, chuckling. "Truth is, nobody flies from here to Europe or Asia, but we get a lot of traffic in and out of Canada. That's the international part. Most of our business comes from UND, the University of North Dakota. They got a big air program—pilots, engineers, air traffic folks. The works. Makes us the busiest airport in the state."

A few minutes later, Mort and Comfrey entered the five-story Altru Hospital and immediately went to the information desk. They got Alison's room number and found an armed and uniformed deputy outside. Clete MacCauley, the sheriff, was at Alison's bedside with a stenographer nearby.

Alison was propped up in bed fully conscious. When she spotted Mort, she cried out, "Mort! I'm so sorry."

"About what?" Mort asked. "How are you doing?"

Sheriff MacCauley signaled for the stenographer to leave the room. "Clete MacCauley," he said, extending his hand to Mort. He was about fifty with a ruddy complexion and cheeks that looked like freshly picked apples. Shaking hands, Mort noticed the sheriff's hands were big for his size, and he was about the same height as Mort. He also noticed the Glock holstered at the sheriff's belt.

"What are you doing here?" Alison asked Mort. "You're on your honeymoon."

"*Was*," Mort said. "But duty calls. Actually, it was Steve Ginsberg who called. But here I am anyway."

"I'm such a *wus*," Alison said. "I fell over and hit my head."

"Excuse me, Alison," MacCauley said right before turning to Mort. "Can we talk out in the hall?"

Comfrey stayed with Alison as MacCauley and Mort left the room. In the hallway, MacCauley said, "You were on vacation?"

"In the middle of the ocean, three hours out from Costa Rica. On my honeymoon. A day I'm not anxious to repeat. How bad is she?"

"Slight concussion, but otherwise okay," MacCauley said. "But frightened. I don't even know if she's aware of the arson. We just finished taking her statement, but there wasn't too much she could add. She found poor Earl yesterday morning, saw a guy running away and jumping into a car, but couldn't give a positive ID. We put out an APB for a tall guy in a blue car of some sort. Not much to go on. But I have my suspicions. Earl Raincloud, the dead guy in the biffy was one of the nicest guys you'd ever meet. Didn't have an enemy in the world… well, I guess one. This murder has to be tied to the story you guys are doing. That's what brought her out here. You her boss?"

"She's in my group, and a crack reporter. The land-grabbing story, or acreage grab, or whatever it is—that's what Alison was investigating."

"Well, Earl was giving all sorts of hell to those Chinese guys or whoever—the people trying hard to get a foothold here, sweet-talking the locals with wild promises and such, buying up land with phony corporations and phony promises. To me, Earl appears to be a targeted hit. She was going to be meeting with him to get some information. His house was torched about the same time. Old Earl's throat was cut. Definitely arson. But now I'm concerned about Alison's safety. She couldn't give a positive ID, but the killer doesn't know that, and she was the only witness."

"I'll get her back to DC as soon as possible," Mort said.

After calmly reassuring Alison that everything would be all right, Mort waited for the doctor and found that she was ready to be released. He accompanied her back to the Great Western Harvest Inn in one of the sheriff's vehicles chauffeured by the deputy who had been seated outside Alison's room. Mort registered at the front desk and asked a few questions about visiting Chinese businessmen. He learned several had just checked out. Mort got a room across the hall from Alison's, then called Steve Ginsberg at the *Post*.

"The Marines have landed," Mort said.

"How is she?"

"Shaken up, frightened and nervous, naturally, but otherwise okay." They talked briefly about what the sheriff had told Mort.

"I think you'd best get her out of there," Ginsberg said.

"Already arranged a flight tomorrow morning. I'll take the car she rented, stick with the story for a day, go over Alison's notes, then try to catch the end of our cruise so Danni doesn't divorce me. The story is certainly more interesting now. I can be back here by next week."

"I can ask them to assign a deputy to watch over things," Ginsberg said.

"I don't think that's necessary. I'll hang out until she falls asleep, maybe even sleep in the chair in her room. Should be okay. But try to find out something about these Chinese businessmen the sheriff mentioned. Strange that they happened to check out the afternoon before Raincloud was murdered, but we know who they are, so I'll follow up on that."

* * *

By nine o'clock, Mort was exhausted. Sitting in a chair in Alison's room, his eyes fluttered several times and he started to doze. The television was on with the speaker low.

"Mort," Alison said, "you're tired. Why don't you go to your room. I'll lock the door."

"Until I get you back on that flight to the Twin Cities, I'm not leaving you alone."

"Then lie down here on the bed. It's a king. I'll probably be asleep as fast as you."

Fully clothed, they lay on the bed.

"I feel so guilty," Alison said. "Your honeymoon. I can't believe you came all the way here."

There was no response. Mort was already asleep. Alison looked at him, smiled, and leaned over, kissing him softly. "Thank you," she whispered, then went into the bathroom, changed into pajamas, came out wearing a robe, and turned out the light as she slipped under the covers. She got up and fastened the chain lock on the door, returned to the bed and draped an arm over his sleeping body.

* * *

At three o'clock the door opened quietly until the chain drew taut. With a soft clicking sound, a wire cutter cut through the chain, and it fell away. A man slipped into the room illuminated by a faint light from the bathroom, and the man softly walked to the bed and looked down.

"What the hell?" he muttered, startled at the sight of a man in the bed.

Alison's eyes fluttered open. She saw the shadowy man hovering over the bed. Thinking it might be Mort, she called out his name at the same time she reached out her hand to find Mort sleeping beside her.

She screamed!

The man reached down and put his hand over her mouth.

Mort rolled over. Still groggy, he said, "Wha…?" just as the man hit him with his free hand, momentarily stunning Mort, who rolled off the bed onto the floor.

"Shit!" the man said, diving across the bed to find Mort.

Despite Alison's thrashing beneath the man, he leaned down and wrapped a wire around Mort's neck.

Mort's hand found a brass lamp on the night table and smashed it on the intruder's head, stunning him momentarily. The lamp's cord pulled out of the base but stayed plugged into the outlet. Mort's hand found the frayed end of it.

As the intruder started tightening the wire, Mort grasped the lamp wire with his free hand.

Alison, pinned by the intruder's body, screamed and pummeled him with her fists, but his grip on the garrote held fast.

Mort smashed the intruder's nose with the heel of one hand and then pushed against his neck with the one grasping the electrical wire. Suddenly, he pushed the frayed copper end of the wire into the intruder's neck.

The man stiffened as a jolt of electricity shocked him. He relaxed his grip on the garrote, reaching for the lamp wire, but Mort continued to press the end of the wire hard against the man's neck. After a sizzling sound, the intruder went limp.

Alison ran to the door, turned on the light and threw open the door, screaming for help. Mort moved around the bed and reached down and felt for the intruder's carotid artery. The smell of burnt flesh hung in the air.

"I think he's dead," Mort said without emotion. "Electrocuted."

Alison came into the room. "My God, it's Tommy Tang!" She burst into tears and started shaking uncontrollably.

Seven

At about four o'clock, the corridor outside Alison's room was filled with people—sheriff's deputies, Grand Forks Police, EMTs and several men in business suits. Mort and Alison sat in Mort's room across the hall with Sheriff MacCauley, Grand Forks Police Chief Matt Nielson, and the stenographer who had been in Alison's hospital room a day earlier.

Chief Nielson, a solidly built six-footer with close-cut greying blonde hair, was talking to Mort. Alison, wide-eyed and still shaking, was wrapped in a blanket.

"Never seen this before," Nielson said. "Electrocuted by a lamp cord."

"I was just trying not to be killed myself," Mort said. "He gave a jolt when I touched his neck with the wires, so I just kept pushing against his neck."

"He must have been trying to get to Miss Powers," Sheriff MacCauley said. "Most likely he killed Raincloud and wasn't certain if she could ID him or not."

Nielson looked at Mort. "So, I'm wondering what you were doing in Miss Powers' bed," Neilson said.

"I was so tired after that day of traveling and switching planes to get here that I just zonked out."

"He was asleep before his head hit the pillow," Alison said.

"So much for my future as a security guard," Mort said.

Nielsen gave an insincere nod, indicating his skepticism at the exhaustion story.

The coroner, seventy-year-old Dr. Elijah Cummings, walked into the room holding a wristwatch. "Damndest thing I ever saw," Cummings said. "This watch has a garrote wire built into it. High-tensile kevlar. You just pull out the wire and it's a killing machine."

"James Bond," Mort said.

"James Bond?" Cummings said.

"*From Russia With Love*," Mort said. "Bond used one just like that in the movie."

"Where the hell did this guy get a James Bond watch?" Cummings asked.

"I read somewhere you can buy them," Mort said. Within seconds he had found a website on his cell phone. "There! *Woingear*. Available for two thousand bucks."

"Well, I'll be damned," MacCauley and Nielson said almost in unison.

"Like we don't already have enough weapons to worry about," Nielson added.

"Two thousand bucks, huh? Those Chinese must pay pretty well," MacCauley said.

"He said they did—when we had dinner," Alison said. "And when I asked him what he did for them he said 'Whatever they want.'"

"Including murder, apparently," MacCauley said.

"I'm not setting an inquest," Cummings announced. "Everything is pretty clear to me. Mr. Ahrens is innocent due to self-defense under section 12.1-05-03 of the criminal code."

"Which makes Mr. Ahrens a hero," Chief Nielson added. "The *Herald* is going to love that one."

Mort moaned. "Just what I needed."

Alison was still very shaken, but the authorities took her additional statement of the night's events. Tang's body was now being removed from her room. Mort decided to stay in Grand Forks, for a day, to follow up on what Alison had learned about the land dispute and do some investigation about Tommy Tang and his corporate employers. He'd report to the *Post* in the morning, get a new room and then sleep. A female officer stayed with Alison on another floor.

* * *

Morning came quickly. At the airport, Mort waited until Alison went through security at the airport and then turned to Clete MacCauley, who had driven them there with Chief Nielson.

"I'm glad to see her safe and on her way," Mort said. "She'll be okay."

"Went to check on Tommy Tang's employers first thing," MacCauley said. "Damned if they hadn't already checked out. Gone with the wind."

"How could they possibly have known about Tang's death?" Mort asked.

MacCauley rubbed his eyes. "They actually checked out yesterday afternoon. A little too coincidental for my money. But they'll be easy to track."

"Well, I'm going to nose around a bit today," Mort said as the three men walked out of the terminal. "I'll head back first thing tomorrow. I can get a flight out at seven and go through the horror of airport adventures again. With luck, I can meet our ship in Colombia and finish the cruise with my wife."

"Buy your wife somethin' real nice as a peace offering," MacCauley said.

"Good idea. Any suggestions?"

"Jewelry usually works," MacCauley said.

Nielsen shrugged his agreement.

* * *

Over a breakfast of Danish and coffee in the motel, Mort decided it was time to check in with Steven Ginsberg, his managing editor. Seated in the lobby after he ate, he placed a call on his cell phone.

"Mort," Ginsberg answered, "what's the word? How's Alison?"

"Well, there's good news and bad news, Steve. The good news is that she's in the air as we speak—on her way home. Still shaken up, but I'm sure she'll be fine."

"I'm almost afraid to ask about the bad news," Ginsberg said.

Mort's introduction to Ginsberg had been his role in the kidnapping of Justice Richter. He not only had solved the case last year but had also uncovered a conspiracy behind the kidnapping that led all the way to the president's chief of staff. Every time Mort called, Ginsberg shuddered, because each call was usually accompanied by a traumatic event.

"You'll see it on the wire services within the hour," Mort explained. "They caught the guy who murdered Earl Raincloud, the man Alison was going to interview—head of the farmers' group. They torched Raincloud's house too."

"That's the bad news?"

"No, but the murderer broke into Alison's room early this morning to kill her because he thought she could identify him."

"And?"

"And I electrocuted him. He's dead."

"Oh, my God," Ginsberg said. "Not again." After a long silence, Ginsberg asked, "Did you say electrocuted?"

"Long story, but he didn't expect to find me in her room at three in the morning."

"In her room? Do I want to hear more?"

"I'll explain when I get back, but you'll have read about it by then. It was just pure luck—and a Krav Maga thrust with my hand. I'm going to try and pick up the pieces of the story she was working on, then try to catch the last few days of the cruise. I'll be back in the office next week, then I'll head back to North Dakota to find out what's going on with these land sales."

"Mort, you're going to have to do more explaining to Danni than me. In Alison's room at three in the morning?"

"Guard duty. Good thing I was there."

"I'll take your word for it, but Mort…"

"Yeah?"

"You can't keep going around killing people. It's bad for our reputation."

Eight

Danni awoke to a noise in the hallway. She glanced at her watch. Three o'clock.

"Mort?" she said. "I think I heard something in the hall." But there was no Mort. She had forgotten that Mort was gone. She got up and walked to the door, opening it cautiously with a shoe in her hand, heel-out like a weapon.

Walking down the hallway, she spotted a stocky, middle-aged man about six cabins away. He was shoeless as he turned the corner and disappeared into another corridor. Judging from the photos plastered around the ship, the man looked like Simeon, the artist.

* * *

At breakfast on the tenth deck, before leaving the ship for a tour and shopping in Cartagena, Danni sipped her coffee with Kimberly and Lynette. Danni wanted to talk about the man in the corridor, but she wasn't sure how to broach it. Finally, she summoned up the courage.

"I saw a man creeping down the hallway near your cabin at three this morning," she said. "Was he coming from your room?"

Kimberly and Lynette exchanged glances.

"I guess our secret is out," Lynette said. "The answer's yes."

"At three in the morning?"

"You might as well know. The fact is we do more than just pose for Simeon. After all, his paintings command a steep price. So, we let him have his little favors with us."

"Is it what I'm imagining?" Danni asked.

"Depends on your imagination," Kimberly said. "He's harmless. A quick threesome really gets him going. Enhances his creativity, he says. He loves our black and white aspect. I think the black more than the white."

"He likes us both the same," Lynette said.

"You know he favors you," Kimberly said. "Admit it. But we all manage to have pleasure."

Danni looked shocked. "Oh, my god," she said. "He's no youngster. Doesn't his age concern you?"

"Thinks young, acts young," Kimberly said. "That's all that counts. He's already had heart attacks, years ago, he said, but he takes care of himself, and he's always popping pills. We take it easy, and he says he can handle anything. Even the two of us, and he says if that's the way he has to go, it'll be with a smile on his face."

"Join today's world," Lynette said. "He really *is* harmless, and he makes it worth our while with his paintings. Actually, it keeps us from getting bored with each other as well. A little variety is not a bad thing. We've been together over a decade now. Besides, he's a patriot."

Danni shook her head. "A patriot? I don't understand."

"A 'minute man,'" Lynette said. "A minute and he's finished."

Lynette and Kimberly convulsed with laughter. Danni just stared at them.

"To each, his own, I guess," Danni said. "Or her own. But I think I'll stick with Mort and monogamy."

"I hope you don't think less of us," Kimberly said.

"I don't make value judgments about other people's lives," Danni said. "It's hard enough to find value in my own."

* * *

At the end of their excursion, Danni, Lynette and Kimberly walked up the gangway wearing shorts and newly purchased Costa Rica tees. They all had the tired look of a busy touring day.

"The three of us look like a reverse Oreo cookie," Danni said. "Or the Andrews Sisters in black and white."

"Who are the Andrews Sisters?" her companions both asked.

"Before your time. But Mort loves some of the old songs and TV shows. The Andrews Sisters were a popular singing group in the '50s or around then, I think. Swing singers."

"Way before my time, luckily," Kimberly said. "Now Adele and Billie Eilish..."

"Any songs we'd know?" Lynette asked.

"Let's see. 'Don't Sit Under the Apple Tree,' 'Rum and Coca Cola.' Mort got addicted to those old swing songs because J.J. loves them."

"J.J.?" Lynette asked.

"My father-in-law, J.J. Richter," Danni explained.

"What's his racket?" Lynette asked.

"He's a judge, or to be accurate, a justice."

"Where?"

"On the US Supreme Court."

Kimberly stared for a minute and then said, "Jesus, I knew you and Mort were famous but didn't realize you were that well connected."

"Richter," Lynette said with a puzzled look. "Isn't he the one who was kidnapped?"

"It's a long story," Danni said. Uncomfortable with the way the conversation was heading, she said, "I can't believe that Cahuita National Park—so magnificent. Unbelievable foliage. And those incredible monkeys."

"Not a bad day for a hundred bucks," Lynette said. "But those lizards were gross."

They reached the passengers check-in, getting appreciative stares from the officers at the entrance.

"I think that cute one wants you, Danni," Lynette said.

"Wish not, want not," Danni said. "All this girl wants is a shower and some relaxation before dinner."

"Then we'll head up to the gallery," Kimberly said as they stepped into the elevator. "Because Simeon will be there, and you'll finally get to meet him."

"Whoopee. Don't know if I'm ready for that."

* * *

The three women entered the art gallery after dinner wearing colorful dresses, coiffed hair and fancy makeup ready for an evening of ship's entertainment beginning with a visit to the gallery. Danni was hoping for a night with some quiet music. Last evening, they had tried the casino. Danni, who had pledged to herself not to lose more than fifty dollars, played blackjack for the first time, coached by Lynette. She had won six hundred dollars and for the first time understood how gambling could become an addiction.

The front of the gallery featured eight of Simeon's paintings on easels. Four were his specialty, draped nudes. The others were from different periods of his career—a still life, an abstract, a Paris street scene and a watercolor. Simeon was conversing with several other passengers and one of the auctioneers. When he spotted the three attractive young women, Simeon spun away and rushed over to them.

"My dears," he gushed. "I've been waiting for you." With that he planted a wet kiss on Lynette and hugged Kimberly. The artist wore a leather vest, shirtless, showing off muscular arms and copious chest hair that supplied a background for a gold Star of David on a thin chain. He sported a long ponytail and a twirled, waxed moustache and goatee and a leather cap. Danni guessed him to be in his late fifties, perhaps sixty, with an accent she thought was Middle European, perhaps Hungarian. His deep-blue eyes stared at Danni for a moment before he reached out and took her hand, saying to Lynette, "And this is your new friend?"

"This is our new *best* friend, Danni," Lynette replied.

Simeon looked at Danni almost hungrily. "You must turn around for me."

"Excuse me?" Danni said.

"Turn—spin around so that I can appreciate every aspect of you."

Danni looked uncomfortably at Kimberly, who spun her hands around in a circle.

Danni did a full 360.

"Exquisite!" Simeon said. "I must paint you."

"Glidden or Sherwin-Williams?" Danni asked, smiling.

"And quick witted," Simeon gushed. "Perfect. No, I must paint you before this trip is over. Perhaps you misunderstand. I am an artiste, not a house painter. But you jest."

"I'm certainly flattered," Danni said, "but I don't think so. I've seen your paintings of Lynette and Kimberly, and the last thing I need is leering law students in my classes."

"You are a teacher?" Simeon asked.

"A law professor," Lynette interjected. "And her father-in-law is a judge."

"A justice," Danni corrected. "I don't think he'd approve either. To say nothing of my husband, Mort."

"I promise you, we will be discreet," Simeon said. "But you are perfect—just the model I have been looking for. A perfect nose, soft eyes, slender, petite. God has been kind to you. Perfection." He stared at her breasts. "*C'est magnifique!* No, I must paint you."

Danni almost blushed. "Well, I'm certainly overwhelmed, but to coin a phrase, 'It ain't gonna happen.' Besides, you've got Lynette and Kimberly right here. Nature has been much kinder to them, if you get my drift."

Simeon looked crestfallen. "They are my loves, but *you* can be my Madonna."

Lynette and Kimberly flashed a knowing look between them. Clearly, they had not anticipated Simeon's gushing reaction to Danni.

Uncomfortable with the conversation, Danni diverted. "Simeon. That's a unique name. What's the lineage?"

"Born near Budapest," he said, hoping to engage her and cause a change of mind. He reached out to take her hand, which she discreetly moved away.

"Simeon is one of the twelve tribes of Israel," he explained. "Later they became the Jewish people. Simeon was the second son of Jacob and Leah. My father was named Jacob, my mother Leah, so it was ordained."

"And who was the first son?" Danni asked, hoping to keep the conversation flowing in that direction.

"My brother, Mordecai," he answered, "who lives in Tel Aviv. You are Jewish?"

"By birth, yes," Danni said. "But religious, no. We're secular, but we respect the culture. Not necessarily the Israeli government, however."

"We?"

"My husband and I. He got called away on business, and I assure you he'd say 'No' to my posing."

"A *shanda*," Simeon said. "What man could leave *you* for business? We have so much in common, it seems. I give you time, perhaps, to reconsider." He turned away to speak to another guest.

Lynette said softly to Danni, "I've never seen him gush like this. What a great compliment. And you'll leave with a painting worth a small fortune."

Kimberly whispered to Lynette, "Don't encourage her. We don't need competition."

While staring at the loquacious artist, Danni said, "I'll have to struggle by on my salary, I guess." She turned and walked to another spot in the gallery that featured tranquil nature scenes by Schaefer-Miles.

As they continued around the gallery, Simeon moved on with the auctioneer to another couple but kept glancing back at Danni.

"What's a *shanda*?" Kimberly asked.

Danni knew the meaning. "A Yiddish expression meaning 'It's a great shame.'"

As they continued walking around the gallery, Lynette said, "I didn't realize you were Jewish. Not that it makes any difference."

"Well, Simeon is Jewish, as he mentioned," Kimberly said. "Somewhat of a religious fanatic about it. Doesn't eat pork or shellfish. Won't paint on Saturdays. Something about no work on the Sabbath."

Danni responded, "He's way more religious than I am. There are multiple branches of Judaism. Mort and I are secular, humanistic. We respect the history and some traditions, but that's about it."

After another fifteen minutes of perusing the gallery's paintings, Danni said, "Let's get out of here. He's creeping me out, and I think I saw him taking a picture of me with his phone."

"You should be flattered, Danni," Lynette cautioned. "He's one of the most popular artists in the world, and he really came on to you."

"I guess I'll have to learn to live with the pain," Danni said. "You two can live with the pleasure."

"Mort would probably love a painting like that."

"Mort can have the real thing. I assure you that's a better deal."

Nine

The justices of the Supreme Court conduct their private conference and deliberations in a room in which only they are present—no clerks, no attendants, not even cell phones. It's just the nine members of the Court discussing or arguing their positions on cases, with the chief justice determining who will be assigned to write the decisions for the majority. If there is a dissent, the most senior dissenting justice determines who will write the dissent.

The Court had been rocked by scandal the previous year, not only by the kidnapping of Justice Richter but upon the discovery that one of the Court officers had hidden a recording device in the deliberation room—the Black Box as it was described by Court employees and often by the justices themselves. Their deliberations had been shared by an unwanted tenth party, and the resulting scandal had reverberated all the way to the White House.

That term of the Court had ended much as this one was ending, with several of the biggest decisions left to be released on the last days of the term. The previous autumn had also seen the addition of a new justice, Julius Gallagher, who had replaced J.J. Richter's close friend and philosophical adversary of twenty-five years, Anthony Battaglia, who had resigned because of failing health.

Julius Gallagher had joined the Court after a contentious battle in the Senate and had received only one vote over the mandatory sixty necessary to be named to the Court. Also a conservative, as was Battaglia, Gallagher was much more of an activist and presented

43

himself as an "originalist," meaning that he strictly adhered to the original intent of the Founders when they adopted the Constitution. At the age of forty-seven, he had already crossed swords with J.J. over several cases, notwithstanding the decades of age and experience on the bench that separated them on so many levels.

As usual, the justices shook hands and took their assigned seats to begin the conference on this late June morning. J.J., as the senior associate justice, sat opposite the chief justice at the other end of the gleaming, polished table. Chief Justice Constance Treller, in her seventh year as chief, sat at the head of the table, and Gallagher sat closest to the entry door, since it was the function of the most junior justice to act as doorkeeper if there were any interruptions.

Of the several major cases remaining to be decided, unquestionably the most controversial was *Oregon v. Gluckstein* to determine whether Congress had exceeded its authority in passing a national assisted suicide law, which the president had reluctantly signed. It was an election year, and in a closely divided country the president, an avowed conservative, needed progressive votes for his reelection.

The progressive left, and the nation's leading newspapers, including *The New York Times,* had editorially endorsed the law. The conservative press and media had opposed it based on the theory that the question was best left to the individual states to determine. Speculation was rife as to how the Supreme Court would rule.

There had been no public leaking as to how the Court would rule, as there had been the previous year when an early draft of the decision that reversed the half-century ruling in *Roe v. Wade,* concerning a woman's right to abortion, had been leaked, provoking national outrage.

But this was not to say that Gluckstein, as it was known—the assisted suicide case—would not be of national import. A non-profit organization, named A Compassionate Death, had challenged Oregon's ban of assisted suicide on the grounds that the act was protected by the Due Process Clause of the 14th Amendment to the Constitution claiming that it deprived those seeking an assisted death of the guarantees "of life, liberty... and the equal protection of the law."

Several states permitted assisted suicides but the majority forbade it. The case had been argued successfully for the plaintiffs in the United States District Court in Oregon but had been reversed two to one in the Ninth Circuit Court of Appeals. The final word was now to be decided by the Supreme Court.

J.J. Richter had resumed his status as the senior associate justice after the summer, during which he had been recovering not only from the kidnapping and a skull fracture but also from an induced coma following his rescue. His recovery had been capped off by his marriage to Helene "Chickie" Rosen, who was Danni's mother. Danni had been the Cupid who had brought them together.

Often referred to as the "Lion of the Court," J.J. Richter, known to his peers and those close to him as "J.J.," had in more than thirty years on the bench firmly entrenched himself as the leading liberal, or progressive, on the bench. Now approaching eighty, he had lost none of his passion. With roots in Wyoming, he was literally the curmudgeon of the Court, an individualist, never willing to accept the pomp and décor traditionally ascribed to Supreme Court Justices.

As usual, J.J. was dressed casually in a denim work shirt and Western boots, a forever reminder of his roots. Rumor had it that his mode of dress was the same under his black robe. Even though he stood only five-foot-eight with a slender build, J.J. managed to dominate the room.

Much to the surprise of his peers on the Court, J.J. had adopted the position of the circuit court on the assisted suicide case and had drafted a majority opinion in which he had agreed that the choice of assisted suicide should be left to the states and was not within the purview of the Constitution. He had the support of six of his colleagues, in what appeared to be a 7-2 decision.

Julius Gallagher, the originalist conservative, agreed with J.J. in principle and had drafted a concurring opinion that related judicial history as far back as the Magna Carta and included several references to the Bible.

Heads snapped up when J.J. said, "I think you should reconsider your concurrence, Julius. My opinion sustains your beliefs, and bringing in the Bible and religion only adds fuel to a fire, which we don't need."

Gallagher straightened in his chair and said, "Perhaps you could add a line or two to *your* opinion stating that suicide was a grave sin equivalent to murder just as Exodus proclaims."

"No biblical material in my decision," J.J. responded. "We've drifted too far away from the separation of church and state, which was the vision of the Founders. As one preaching the originalist doctrine, that seems logical to me. Perhaps you might consider the wisdom of *Terminiello v. Chicago.*

Gallagher, his full cheeks and jowls shaking as he jerked his head, seemed perplexed. "That doesn't spring to mind," he said.

"337 U.S. at 37," J.J. said, looking down at his notebook. "To quote, 'There is danger that, if the Court does not temper its doctrinaire logic with a little practical wisdom, it will convert the constitutional Bill of Rights into a suicide pact.'"

J.J. paused, then said, "Suicide—that certainly seems appropriate here. Bill Douglas, who wrote the opinion, was a great justice, and I think he might have been talking to you, Julius."

Chagrined, Gallagher said, "Well, I always felt that Douglas was wrong more often than he was right, so I guess I'll have to live with my concurrence."

The discussion was interrupted by a loud knock on the outer door. Gallagher, as the junior justice, moved to open it a little more than a crack and asked, "Yes?"

The door was pushed open wider, forcing him back. Travis Anderson—the Marshal of the Supreme Court Police who headed its 145-person complement—stood in the doorway and abruptly addressed the justices.

"We've had a credible bomb threat, Your Honors, and I'm clearing the building until the issue is resolved. Sorry to intrude like this."

Anderson, a six-foot-two African American and a close friend of J.J.'s, had formerly headed the Montgomery County Police in Maryland and had been seriously wounded in the successful rescue of J.J. a year earlier.

The Chief Justice rose from her seat and said, "Please follow the chief's direction and vacate the building as quickly as possible. We'll pick up from here, hopefully, by tomorrow." Most of the members referred to Anderson as "Chief" even though his actual title was "Marshal."

The members quickly exited the room, returned to their chambers to dismiss their staffs and left by the underground garage.

Ten

In Travalah, Maryland, that same afternoon, J.J. decided to inspect the grounds around his well-tended, single-story house, with two dogs trailing him. The house was situated on a plot of several acres. In the three decades he had lived there, the young saplings he'd planted along his long driveway had become sturdy evergreens, and the emerald arborvitae hedges that surrounded the property had grown thick and high, offering cherished privacy. There was now a new, large flower garden next to a fenced-in patch of vegetables, a touch of Chickie's, tended by Lupe, the housekeeper.

J.J. was dressed in the same blue work shirt, jeans and Western boots that he had been wearing earlier in the day when the Court was cleared. "I used to do a much better job on the groounds," he said, talking to the dogs, "but that's Chickie's influence on me."

The dogs seemed more interested in the treats he kept in his shirt pocket than in checking the condition of the grass. One of the dogs, an aging golden retriever, hung close to him, while the other, a brown and white springer spaniel, seemed much more interested in looking for "varmints," as J.J. called them. He took a treat out of his pocket and handed it to the golden retriever, who gobbled it eagerly.

"Good girl, Connie," J.J. said, patting her on the head. The springer realized she was missing out and came racing up. "I've got one for you, too, Katie," he said, reaching into his shirt pocket again. The springer took the treat, ran about twenty feet away and laid down to eat it before rolling in the grass on her back. "You're going to get covered in cuttings," J.J. said to the springer, "and Lupe will have a fit."

J.J. had become a resident of Travalah over thirty years ago when it was still a sleepy suburb of Washington, DC. Travalah was now a wealthy and sought-after location, no longer sleepy but affluent and desired. He had purchased the property with his late wife, Meg, who had died of cervical cancer a dozen years ago. Lupe had been her caregiver and the housekeeper, and now she ruled the kitchen and the household. She resided in a small apartment that had been added on and attached to the main house. A barn stood a distance from the house, and J.J.'s latest vehicle, a red Ford F-150 was parked inside near Lupe's Subaru Forester.

On his way back to the house, followed by the dogs, J.J. wistfully looked at the spot in the barn where his Harley had been housed. After marrying Chickie, she had finally convinced him— or rather insisted— that his motorcycling days were over. But he still savored his biking memories.

A black Audi Q-4 e-Tron slowly pushed down the driveway and entered the barn. Chickie climbed out and went to the charging station in the barn, plugged in the car and walked over to J.J. and the two dogs. Chickie, who deceptively looked in her fifties, was now sixty-two and cut a powerful figure in her dark business suit. She gave J.J. a peck on the cheek, and he gave her waist a squeeze. Chickie was CEO of one of the nation's media giants with headquarters in Virginia.

"How was the drive from Alexandria?" he asked.

"Not bad now that half of DC, including you, is getting ready to desert for the summer," Chickie said. "Took less than an hour. I relaxed a bit and listened to Sirius. How was your day and why are you home so early? For the anniversary?"

J.J. looked perplexed. "We got married over Labor Day. What anniversary?"

"Just a year ago today you were kidnapped."

"Forgot all about it. Probably pushed it out of my mind. I tend to do that with unpleasant things. Anyway, for starters, I can tell you that I did a much better job on the grass than your expensive gardeners."

"Poor boy," Chickie said. "When the Court recesses, you'll have three months to grouse about all the things that are making your life easier. By the way, I got a text from Danni today."

"How goes their honeymoon?"

"*Their* honeymoon? Tough to call it a honeymoon anymore," Chickie said. "Mort got called by the *Post* and apparently scooted up to North Dakota on an emergency. Danni is left hanging out with a couple of women they met on the cruise."

"On their honeymoon? That's a colossal bummer. Must have taken heaven and earth to get him to leave."

"Or a call from his managing editor, as I understand. Something about a murder that happened on a story he's in charge of."

"Another murder? Mort's got to stay away from them before they become a specialty."

"If it wasn't for the last one, you might be dead. Don't forget that."

"Touché."

* * *

As they ate dinner in the dining room, J.J. leaned over and gave the springer a piece of chicken. Chickie said, "You've got to stop feeding Katie from the table. You trained Connie." The larger dog just watched from her spot on the floor.

"Mort feeds her from the table, and I don't want her to get lonesome until they're back," J.J. said.

"It drives Danni crazy."

"Well, once she's back, you won't have to see it."

"Tell me more about this bomb threat," Chickie demanded. "Seems to be happening far too often."

"I haven't heard the last word, but Travis interrupted our conference—highly unusual—and gave us all the afternoon off."

"Must have sounded serious. Travis is not one to panic."

"Probably not the last one we'll get. There's lots of crazies out there. Some of them are even my associates."

"That's unkind."

"The truth hurts."

"It's past time that you retired, as I've been urging. You can't save democracy by yourself. And then we could do some serious traveling, just like the kids are doing."

"The kids, as you describe them, are in their thirties. When they carry me out, that's when I retire. I've got a good staff, and there are still some folks in the media who are responsible, thank God. Somebody has to fight to protect the Constitution. I wish Anthony was still on the Court. At least I could reason with him, and things were civil. He recognized individual rights, the Bill of Rights. With this present majority, I can't turn my back. And Anthony's replacement is an arrogant doofus."

"Quite a rant. Doesn't all this make it difficult to work together day after day?"

"We can be collegial, but I sit with my back to the wall so I can't get knifed."

"Joseph John…" Chickie said.

"Joseph John," J.J. said. "I only hear that from my mother in my dreams. Or when I'm in trouble with you. No, I can't save the country alone, but there are a few patriots left. This too shall pass—or so history has taught us. Until it does, until we return to respecting the Constitution, the Bill of Rights, precedent, common sense and the rule of law, I'm hanging in."

"You're frustrating, and stubborn, J.J.," Chickie said. "But I guess that's why I love you."

Eleven

The ship docked in Cartagena, Columbia. This aspect of the cruise—
different cities, different countries, a chance to experience different
cultures that had only previously been geographical places and
names—was something Danni really enjoyed, even without Mort. The
cruise also gave her time to think about her life and how different
it was from that of Lynette and Kimberly. Danni was shaken by the
disclosure of their relationship with Simeon. She had assumed *they*
were a couple—certainly not unusual today—but the threesome with
Simeon had caught her flat-footed. Still, they were fun to be with, and
without Mort there was still laughter and most of all, companionship.

Danni was no prude. She had endured two broken engagements
before her relationship with Mort had surfaced after a hiatus of three
years. She and Mort had met originally when they were both at
Syracuse University. He was a junior, and she was in her final year of
law school.

Her life with Mort was more settled than her life before him, even
though he sometimes got emergency calls and went off on dangerous
stories. But she wouldn't trade it for anything. And besides, now that
they had Katie, the springer, what more could she want? Except,
perhaps, being a mother. She knew her biological clock was ticking.
They had been trying to get pregnant, but so far, no luck. At least it was
fun, so they kept trying.

* * *

During the late afternoon, Danni walked down the long corridor to her room, pushed the door open, walked in and stopped cold as she spotted a man's legs on her balcony.

At the sound of the door opening, Mort emerged in the open balcony doorway and saw a surprised Danni standing there with a shopping bag under her arm and a baseball cap pushed back on her head.

"Ah, so the warrior returns from the hunt," Danni said, her voice dripping with sarcasm.

Mort looked at his wife in skimpy shorts and a tight blouse and said, "Wow! You look… I mean, in that outfit… so sexy. I'm surprised you made it back to the ship."

"You're assuming that I turned down all the offers I got. Don't assume."

Mort entered the cabin and kissed her. She gave him her cheek. He dug into his pocket and handed her a wrapped package.

"I can't be bought," she said as she unwrapped it. The wrapping dropped to the floor, and she pulled out a green and gold emerald necklace.

"Mort!" she shouted excitedly. "It's gorgeous. Okay, maybe I *can* be bought." She gave him a passionate kiss. "What did you do now, rob a jewelry store? And how bad was this crisis in North Dakota?"

"Pretty bad," he said. "But it's well covered in this *Chicago Tribune* story I picked up during a layover." With that, he picked up a newspaper from the bed and sheepishly handed it to her.

She took the paper and asked, "And the flight?"

"Not nearly as bad coming back as going. Delta to Chicago, Chicago to Atlanta, and Atlanta to here. But maybe it wasn't so bad because I knew you were at the other end."

"Charmer," she said.

Danni unfolded the paper. As she started reading, her eyes widened as she read out loud: "Reporter kills assassin trying to murder colleague." She looked up at her husband and said, "Morton—you didn't…?"

"He was trying to strangle me," Mort said weakly. "Read on... you'll see I had no choice."

Danni continued reading and then her head popped up, eyes flashing.

"You were sleeping with Alison? You slept with her on our honeymoon? Jesus!"

"Not like that," Mort said. "I slept in her room, like a guard dog. She was terrified. I almost got strangled."

"It says here that you were asleep in her bed. In her *bed*?"

"Fully clothed, honest. I fell asleep because the damn trip took so long. All those airplane changes, and the layovers, the waiting time. And then rushing to the hospital, dealing with the sheriff and all. I was wiped out."

"In her *bed*? And she was fully clothed too?"

"I think... I think..." he stammered. "She changed into pajamas after I fell asleep."

Danni stared at him, then down at her emerald necklace. "This thing better be worth a fortune. On our *honeymoon*?"

"Read the rest of the story," Mort pleaded. "It's a pretty good recap. Then you'll understand. And the necklace? It only cost a year's salary."

"It better *not* have," Danni said, "or you'll be in worse trouble. I'm taking a shower. I don't believe this is my life. Or my honeymoon."

"Room for me to join you?"

She stared at him incredulously, saying nothing. Then, clutching the bracelet in her hand, she headed for the small bathroom. Mort could hear her mutter, "In her *bed*."

Twelve

As they were dressing for dinner, Mort said, "How'd the cruise go? Did the captain really come through with dinners and handsome officers for companionship?"

"No and no," Danni said. "But he offered. I spent a lot of time with the girls, Kimberly and Lynette. We had some good times, had some fun, saw some great sights in places I never thought I'd visit."

"So, you really didn't miss me?"

"Don't fish for a compliment. Actually, they were great companions. They're a *couple*, you know."

"I assumed as much. I couldn't care less, as long as they didn't hit on you."

"They didn't have time. They have some interesting threesomes going with Simeon."

"No shit?"

"Mort, you know I love when you're so articulate. Yes, no shit!" Danni said. "It's part of their deal with him to get paintings, I guess."

"Sounds like they're getting more than paintings. And so is he."

"You'll see him tonight. He's having a big unveiling of his latest masterpiece, although frankly he creeps me out. In a lecherous sort of way. But I told the girls we'd be there."

* * *

The fifty gallery seats were filled with more watchers standing in the background. The chief auctioneer, John Lock, a fiftyish man in a black sports jacket and pants, looked almost formal except for his open-necked shirt. Behind him, a large painting on an easel was covered by a black canvas. Simeon stood near him, beaming and wearing his signature leather cap, sandals, dark slacks and open-necked pink chambray shirt with mother of pearl buttons, sleeves rolled up halfway. A heather-purple vest completed the eccentric outfit. Simeon oozed self-appreciation.

Nodding to Simeon, then to the gathering, Lock said, "You are exceptionally fortunate on this cruise to have one of the world's greatest contemporary artists. You have seen some of his work here in the gallery. His art graces the walls of numerous museums. He was the official artist for both the Super Bowl and the World Cup, among other events. He has decorated one of the major ocean liners, although not this one. He escaped the confines of communism at an early age and refined his talents in Paris.

"Simeon's story is unique. Born in Hungary to a family of meager means, his talent as a painter was recognized by the time he was twelve. Repressed under communism, he escaped to Paris as a teenager, before the Hungarian revolution, where he honed his skills and where he was first acknowledged for his talent and unique style. He challenged himself to be the greatest artist in the world, came to the US in the '80s, and has since been awarded numerous prestigious recognitions in various mediums.

"One of the unique talents of Simeon is that he has worked not only with oils and watercolors, but he has worked in metal, created etchings on copper, and conceived amazing sculptures. His unique ability allows him to create these extraordinary works of art in a matter of days, and so it is tonight that we proudly unveil his latest, which he has titled *The Reluctant Madonna* and has painted here on the ship in the last few days. We are proud to offer at auction this unique painting, seen for the first time tonight."

With that, Lock pulled off the canvas covering of the latest masterpiece, revealing a beautiful young woman painted in soft colors and burnished in gold. The subject had the slightest of dimples, a pert nose and firm chin, with full upturned breasts and erect nipples.

"Good God," Danni blurted out, "that's me!"

"You posed *nude* for this guy?" Mort sputtered in a hoarse whisper tinged with anger. "You forgot to mention *that*!"

"I *did not*," Danni said, in more of a hiss than a whisper.

Lynette and Kimberly, who had been sitting several rows away, walked over. Kimberly asked Danni, "When did *you* have time to pose? You never said anything."

Lynette echoed, "Why didn't you share with us?"

"I *did not pose*," Danni said emphatically. "That son of a bitch was taking pictures of me in the gallery, as you may recall, and the rest must be his imagination."

"Well, we knew he was a great painter," Lynette said.

"*Hell* of an imagination," Mort said.

Several of the other passengers turned at the noise of this conversation and then cast their eyes on Danni. Among them was a well-dressed couple in their fifties who turned back to the painting and scrutinized it more closely before speaking quietly to the auctioneer. Among the other passengers seemingly transfixed by the artwork was a fortyish man with thinning, sandy hair and sandals. He kept staring at the picture and then back at Danni.

Danni jumped up and stormed to the front of the gallery, where Simeon and John Lock were talking with several other passengers. She pushed her way into their faces.

"How dare you?" she hissed at Simeon.

He gave a benevolent smile. "I'm a painter. I paint, and I use my imagination."

"This couple," Lock said uncomfortably, indicating the well-dressed man and woman, "have already made an offer of ten thousand dollars. This is an auction, though, and we haven't officially opened for bidding. The Enrights have also made a prior bid, so we may have a battle on our hands."

The man turned to Danni. "You are a beautiful young lady," the man said. "We would treasure this painting. Even more so, now that we have met the model." He turned to Mort, who had joined the group. "You are a very lucky man."

Danni spun to Simeon. "I'm going to sue your ass off."

Mort stepped in and pushed Danni away. "It's not the fault of these people," Mort said, gesturing to the man who had made a bid. To the bidder he spoke directly. "And I *am* a very lucky man. Interested in selling if your bid is successful?"

"Sorry, but no chance," the man said. "We have the spot already picked out for it."

Danni, still fuming but much calmer, said to Simeon, "I'm not kidding. I will start a lawsuit. You can't capitalize on my image."

"My reluctant Madonna," he said softly with a saccharin smile. "Just between us, I have made you immortal. But proving in court that it is you is an exercise in futility. I am a painter, I paint. I combine reality with my imagination. And how could it be you? Remember, as you yourself said, you never posed."

Thirteen

The last night at sea featured the captain's dinner for which several passengers were selected to join the captain and other crew members at their tables. At this dinner, Danni and Mort were two of the captain's guests along with Harvey and Betsy Enright, the older couple who had earlier expressed interest in the painting. After the bidding had opened earlier that afternoon, Mort turned to Danni and said, "I'm going to make a bid."

Danni said, forcefully, "No you're *not*. Not with *our* money. If you buy it, I promise you I'll get it in the divorce."

The opening bid was the ten-thousand-dollar bid, but Harvey Enright immediately upped it by five hundred, and the bidding went back and forth in five-hundred-dollar increments until the first bidder dropped out. The Enrights were successful, purchasing the painting for fourteen thousand dollars. The Enrights, as Mort and Danni learned, were prominent stockholders in the cruise line.

"Did you enjoy the cruise?" Captain Thornberg inquired of Danni.

"The cruise was wonderful," Danni said. "I even made some friends, although I would have rather my husband didn't get called away." She nodded toward Mort. "And, of course, one other unfortunate incident, which shall remain undiscussed."

"Your favorite part of the trip?"

"Going through the Panama locks was fascinating."

"I was away for that part," Mort said. "But generally I prefer my lox on a bagel."

Smiles all around.

"You mustn't let that unfortunate incident spoil the cruise," Harvey Enright said. "Frankly, we'd love to have you visit us anytime to see that marvelous painting."

Captain Thornberg asked, "I'm sorry, but what was this unfortunate incident? Is there anything I can do?"

Mort said, "That artist, Simeon, painted a nude woman who had an amazing likeness to Danni."

"I see," the captain replied. "But isn't that a great compliment to you?" he asked Danni.

"I never posed for him," Danni said, frowning. "And he took liberties with his imagination that will probably end up in court. Frankly, I could kill him."

Thornberg smiled. "Not on my ship, I hope."

* * *

Early the following morning, farewells took place dockside. Kimberly and Lynette promised to visit in the DC area. Danni and Mort promised to reciprocate and view the couple's collected art. Danni didn't have any inhibitions about viewing others nude, but she drew the line when she was the subject.

On the flight home, Mort asked, "Do you think you can sue him?"

"I guarantee you that I'm going to research it. And talk to J.J. The Supreme Court recently had a case involving the estates of Prince and Andy Warhol—somewhat similar. That case was just decided, so J.J. will now be willing to discuss it. And I can get a look at the briefs of those parties, which are now public records."

"Well, you certainly made clear your anger," Mort said, "and your threat of what you'd do if he ever painted your likeness again. But it *is* a great painting."

"I may have gone a little overboard with my threats. I was probably upset as much about how his imagination made me prettier than I am. Flattering, yes, but—heat of the moment."

Fourteen

After an uneventful flight home, Mort and Danni arrived for dinner with J.J. and Chickie the day after the bomb threat at the Supreme Court.

Following their marriage the previous summer, J.J. and Chickie had split their time between his home in Travalah and the luxurious quarters that Chickie maintained at the Watergate in Washington. When Court was in session, they generally opted for mid-week days in Washington. Weekends and warmer weather found them in Travalah where J.J. was far more comfortable.

The Travalah home was initially a simple one-story ranch with two bedrooms. As Meg, J.J.'s first wife, was dying of cervical cancer, J.J. added a two-room apartment for Lupe, the towering Mexican who took over management of the household and now reigned as cook, housekeeper and member of the family. During the renovation, he enlarged the master bedroom and guest room and then added an *en suite* to each. A grand porch ran from the front door to the kitchen, which was the nearest room to the end of the driveway. Most people entered the house by way of the kitchen. Last year, when one of J.J.'s kidnappers had entered through the kitchen door, he had been knocked unconscious by Lupe wielding a frying pan.

Mort and Danni entered through the kitchen and were greeted with great excitement by Katie who spun in circles and then peed on the kitchen floor. They all gathered in the dining room and Lupe, who felt that her place was in the kitchen, reluctantly joined them at Chickie's insistence.

"You never posed for this artist, but he painted a partially nude portrait that appeared to be you?" Chickie asked.

"Not *appeared* to be me—it *was* me," Danni insisted. "And *very* nude, with a lot of liberties taken with my body."

"Guy was a hell of a good artist though," Mort said, smiling.

Danni shot him a drop-dead stare.

"How big was it? A normal-size picture? Portrait-size?" J.J. asked.

"It's not the size," Danni snapped, "it's the indignity. The nerve of him! I told him I'd sue his ass off. And I intend to do just that."

"It was an oil, about two feet by four feet," Mort said. "Didn't show her feet."

"But apparently, just about everything else, from what you say," Chickie said.

"In *vivid* detail," Danni said.

"But draped with some sort of see-through fabric," Mort said. "A couple bought it for fourteen thousand at auction."

"Fourteen thousand dollars?" Lupe said. "Ay, *caramba*! Must be one good painter."

"I'd think twice before I climb the litigation tree," J.J. said.

"Because?"

"Because those cases are extremely difficult to win, as with the Warhol case. Tough to prove that it's you, despite the likeness, especially because you never posed for him—and because a case against a famous painter, such as this guy Simeon, is sure to get a lot of publicity and call attention to something you don't want to draw attention to. There are many First Amendment cases in which painters prevail because of freedom of expression. Be flattered and angry—then forget it. It's one portrait in a world of eight billion humans, and it's not like he's selling copies."

"Well, I'm going to research the hell out of it," Danni said.

The dogs were suddenly up on their feet and barking at the kitchen door.

Travis Anderson barged in, still in uniform, looking very serious.

"Travis—didn't expect to see you tonight," J.J. said.

"Didn't expect to be here, J.J."

There are few people who refer to a Supreme Court Justice other than by "Your Honor," or "Justice," or even incorrectly as "Judge." Travis's relationship with J.J. was not only unique, but their annual "Law and Order" presentations were nationally famous. Plus, they were both Medal of Honor recipients, albeit from different wars.

"I'm here on business, unfortunately," Travis said. "I've arranged to assign two US marshals to each member of the Court. Justice Gallagher's home was fire-bombed tonight, and we don't know who did it, or why, or whether it's part of a larger plot."

"My God," Chickie said. "The world *has* gone crazy. Are the Gallaghers okay?"

"They got out okay—limited damage, which can be repaired. Their cats didn't make it. After yesterday's bomb scare, we decided to act on the side of caution."

"Bomb scare? What bomb scare?" Danni asked with alarm.

J.J. said nothing, but anger appeared on his face. "Just another example of the country's crazies. It was nothing, as usual. Cowards."

J.J. turned to the chief. "We're pretty safe here, Chief," J.J. said, "and you know I don't like the security thing. It was probably someone from Gallagher's past with a personal grudge. He has an abrasive edge."

"We don't know that for sure," Travis replied. "Unfortunately, this *isn't* a matter of discussion. There will be a rotating cadre of marshals at the home of each justice until this is figured out. I know you'll grouse about this, but you'll be driven to Court and back in a federal vehicle."

J.J. muttered something under his breath. It sounded like, "Shit."

Fifteen

After Mort and Danni left and Lupe had retreated to the kitchen, Chickie said, "I'm going to call Penelope Gallagher and invite them to stay here until their place is repaired."

"You're *what*?"

"You heard me. It's the least we can do."

"What about they stay with their kids? Or hotels? Got quite a few good ones in DC."

"Their kids aren't in the area, and they shouldn't have to retreat to a hotel. Not after an incident like this. Besides, it'll be a good opportunity for you to temper your antagonism."

"I've got no antagonism. It's just that he's worse than some of the other conservatives. An *originalist*! And arrogant to boot. And since when are you so friendly with Penelope?"

"She's actually very nice. And we've had lunch several times since he was sworn in. It's the Christian thing to do."

"You're Jewish, remember?"

"J.J., you know what I mean. It'll be nice to have them."

"And I don't get a vote? What else don't I know?"

* * *

Two days later, the Gallaghers arrived with luggage. The damage to their home was not as extensive as originally thought and could probably be repaired in a few weeks. That first evening, the four of them had dinner together—Lupe's prime rib with all the trimmings.

"What a great meal," Julius Gallagher said. "You're so lucky to have a good cook."

"I beg your pardon," Penelope Gallagher said.

Julius blushed and stammered, "Present company excepted, love."

"I certainly hope so," Penelope said. "By the way, did you take your pill?"

"Yes, Mother."

"Pill for what?" J.J. asked. "I'm on a regular pill regimen myself."

"Heart," Gallagher replied. "I've got a bum ticker. Had my first heart attack at twenty-nine."

"Well, that does answer one question," J.J. said.

"To wit?"

"You *do* have a heart," J.J. said.

"Joseph John!" Chickie snapped.

"Just funnin' m'love," J.J. said. "Julius knows me well enough by now."

"No offense taken, Chickie," Gallagher said. "We've all felt the bite of his tongue at some point."

* * *

J.J. and Julius Gallagher sat in the back of a windows-darkened SUV, a US marshal at the wheel. Behind them, another SUV followed, driven by a second marshal. During the drive into DC, both justices were individually studying documents, Gallagher working with an open laptop and J.J. rustling through papers.

"At least the government gets to save on the cost of marshals," J.J. said, "with both of us at the house."

"And if I hadn't already said thanks, thanks. That was really a kind gesture."

"Don't thank me. It was Chickie's doing. I was against it all the way."

"You know, J.J., you put up a good front. But you're not the curmudgeon you try to be."

"Guess I'll have to try harder then."

As they got closer to the capital, Gallagher looked around and said, "This is still a great thrill for me. The sights, and seeing the Court just past the Capitol building."

"Over thirty years, and it still sends chills down my spine," J.J. said.

"It looks like we'll wind up this term by the end of the week," Gallagher said. "Do you have big plans for the summer? Most of the others have speaking and lecturing engagements, mostly overseas."

"Been there, done that. But it's a cheap way to see the world. All expenses paid. If you haven't had a free trip to London or Albania, you ain't had nothin'. Although, as we have learned, those perks can be seriously abused by some of us. These days, I settle for my end-of-season barbeques at the house, where I invite the entire Court and staff. Always on July Fourth, except last year when I was recovering from that kidnapping. I suppose that I'll even have to include *you* this year."

"Thanks a lot. It's good to feel wanted."

"Don't get a swelled head. It's because of Penelope."

The privacy panel was down, and the marshal who was driving chuckled at the by-play.

Sixteen

Danni was going over notes in her office at American University Law School, preparation for a six-week course in environmental law she was scheduled to teach during the summer term. Dressed casually in jeans, sneakers and a Costa Rica T-shirt, her routine was a morning jog, shower and then head into the office on an irregular schedule. Mort was back at the *Post* and Katie, unhappily, was home alone for the day.

A knock on the door invited her to say, "Come in."

A man she didn't recognize entered and said, "You are just as attractive dressed as you are in Simeon's painting."

"Excuse me?" she said, startled.

The man, about forty with glasses and thinning hair, was dressed in khakis and a wild, short-sleeved shirt. His arms were heavily tattooed. She noted his bulging eyes. He looked familiar, but she couldn't place him.

"The cruise," he said. "I was on the cruise with you. I was there when you lost it with the artist, and I have to say I don't blame you. Even though it was an amazing painting. I'm Devon McCarthy."

"And you're here because…?"

"I'm here *especially* because of you. I just registered to audit your class."

"You're a law student? Here?"

"No, no, I'm here *only* because of you. I was so intrigued, and so impressed, that I had to get to know you better. We'll be spending six weeks together, and I wonder if you have any tips for me. I graduated Cornell Veterinarian School a while back. I don't practice though—the luxury of coming from money."

Danni was dumbfounded. "Well, my tip is… buy the textbook and come prepared. I didn't know that we had students auditing the course."

"I'm really auditing *you*, not the course. Can I interest you in a cup of coffee?"

Danni's first thought was, *No, you can't interest me, period.* But she tried to be discreet.

"No thanks," she said. "Enjoy Washington until the course starts. I'll see you then."

She put her head down and started scrutinizing the material in front of her, but she was clearly unnerved by the interruption.

"You'll probably see me before that," the man said. "I'll be around." And then he left.

Danni picked up her cell phone and called Mort.

He picked up on the first ring. "Danni," he said. "What's up?"

"Mort, do you remember that creepy guy from the art auction? The night I lost it with Simeon? He was alone—didn't say anything."

"I don't think so," Mort said. "There was a lot going on that night."

"The creepy one. About forty, wearing that long T-shirt down to his knees?"

"Oh, yeah— him. I wondered if he was going commando under that T-shirt."

"Well, he just showed up at my office. He's taking my summer course in environmental law."

"He's a law student?"

"No, that's the creepiest part. He's auditing. Mainly because it's *me* teaching the course. He says he's a veterinarian."

"Great. Maybe we can get a discount for Katie."

"Mort! Be serious. The guy gives me the creeps. Talked about how much he loved the Simeon painting. The *nude* painting."

"Well, he's got good taste. I love you that way too. So, you've got an admirer. He looked harmless enough."

72

"They all *look* harmless. Until they're not."

"Did you get his name? I can run a background check. Even better, so can Travis."

"That's a start. I'll see you at home."

Seventeen

Mort shook his head. There seemed to be no limit on weird people in this world. What are the chances that an individual who was on the cruise would end up in Danni's office only a week later and be auditing her class because he was infatuated with her? Or with a nude portrait of her, for which she never posed, drawn by a famous artist who was also infatuated with her. Six degrees of separation couldn't explain this to him.

When his desk phone rang minutes later, he snapped back to reality. It was his managing editor.

"Mort, Steve here. Good to have you back. Sorry we had to interrupt your trip... er, honeymoon. Can you shoot over to my office now?"

"On my way, Steve."

In the *Washington Post's* state-of-the-art headquarters, the seventh and eighth floors housed the newsroom personnel. With floor-to-ceiling windows, they were bunched in neighborhoods of workstations ringed by hundreds of video monitors. Mort's small group of four investigative journalists was in the middle of the seventh floor, and he had to head for Ginsberg's corner office. As he entered, he passed a large reminder of the paper's past, a framed statement from the late Ben Bradlee: "The truth, no matter how bad, is never as dangerous as a lie, in the long run."

"What's the story on North Dakota?" Ginsberg asked. He was sitting with his feet up on the desk—Bradlee style—in shirtsleeves.

"I spent the day there after getting Alison off on her plane back to DC. Developed a good relationship with both the sheriff and the police chief, followed up on some of Alison's leads, and now I'm off to New York to interview the head of this Peking Group, the Chinese outfit that Tommy Tang—the guy who tried to kill me—was working for. I need to figure out that connection and get their story. I went over Alison's notes and suspicions about this guy. Some of the stuff is pretty far out."

"What was his name again? Tang?"

"Yep. Like the drink. Tried to kill the two of us, and luckily I, uh, electrocuted him, as you know."

"You're in the clear on that?"

"No sweat. Both the sheriff and police chief were in accord, and the coroner is not even holding an inquest. Clear self-defense."

"You're damn lucky you guys weren't killed. You didn't have a weapon?"

"I hit him with a nose chop I learned in my Krav Maga class. The electric cord did the rest."

"Well, you got your money's worth on that martial arts class. How soon will you be heading to New York?"

"As soon as I'm caught up here. I spoke to North Dakota, and they gave me the contact info."

"Check out our new digs on West 22nd Street when you're there. Long past time the *Post* had a decent office in the Big Apple."

"Today, I'm going to do some research on the Chinese and their infiltration techniques. I'll spend the day in the morgue."

"Mort, we don't use that term any more. Our records are digitized, computerized, and modernized. These days, everything is in our *library*."

"I'm just an old-fashioned guy, Steve. To me, it's still the morgue."

* * *

Mort spent the rest of the morning in the library. He was surprised to learn that the FBI had raided a building in Chinatown based on a search warrant issued for an unlisted business purporting to be a public relations firm. Apparently, though, it was conducting Chinese police operations on American soil without approval from the US, and certainly beyond their jurisdiction.

The Chinese, of course, denied the enterprise was a police operation. They claimed it was staffed by "volunteers" who merely assisted its citizens living in the US with visa applications and the like. The FBI claimed the PRC (People's Republic of China) designated these "volunteer" operations, which existed in several large cities, as "Operation Fox Hunt," in which the PRC hunted down Chinese for alleged crimes or other nefarious reasons, even nationalized Chinese in the US, and urged them to return to China by threatening harm to relatives back home. The "volunteers" were also suspected of collecting intelligence for the Chinese government.

The FBI had made several arrests, but Mort could not find information about the disposition of the cases. It was clear that harassment and pressure put on Chinese nationals by these illegal "Chinese Police" operations were an ongoing threat. Mort made some copies, took notes and wondered how, or if, this could have anything to do with his investigation in North Dakota.

Eighteen

The following day—the last Wednesday in June—Mort arrived in the Big Apple. Checking his GPS, he decided to walk the mile and a half to Chinatown where The Peking Group had an office near Mott and Canal Streets. In a brisk twenty-five minutes Mort passed the imposing New York Supreme Court building at 60 Chambers St. and circumvented City Hall, arriving at the Chinatown address— a nondescript four-story building with a red door. Surprisingly, it was next door to a six-story building he immediately recognized from a *New York Times* story he had read only yesterday. It was the location of an FBI raid looking for illegal Chinese police operations.

There was no sign on the door, but he pressed a buzzer, and a minute later an attractive young Chinese woman opened the door and said, "Mr. Ahrens? We have been expecting you. Please follow me." She wore a multi-colored silk kimono that Mort thought would look great on Danni.

Mort was led into a lavish, oriental-style room where three men awaited. There were thick velvet drapes on the walls. Two men were seated. The older man, about sixty, was behind an ornate teak desk and the other, a few years younger, sat beside it. The standing man was much younger, probably in his twenties, and wore a dark sweater over an open-necked blue shirt. Although Mort was unaware, the two seated men had been seen by Alison in Darcy's diner in Grand Forks days earlier.

The younger Chinese man thrust out his hand and said, "I'm Jai Hao, and this is Zhang Wei," indicating the man seated beside the desk. Gesturing to the older man, he said, "And that is Li Chang, who is president of the Peking Group."

"What exactly can we do for you, Mr. Ahrens?" the younger man asked in impeccable English.

"Well, as you know from my call, I'm the reporter in charge of a story we are investigating for the *Washington Post,*" Mort said. "It's about farms and land being bought up throughout the Midwest and turned into corporate properties. There is great curiosity as to where this practice is heading and who will be the beneficiaries. Many people, particularly North Dakotans, are upset. This affair has garnered national attention, so my investigative team was assigned to follow up. Alison Powers was originally in Grand Forks until that attempted murder by your employee, TommyTang."

Zhang Wei, who was seated beside the desk, spoke up in broken English. "I am the *wo shi bab la*, the attorney for the Peking Group," he said. "But I am also admitted to practice here in New York." He turned to Li Chang and said, in Chinese: "*Ā lun ssu xiānshēng fùzé guānyú tǔdì huo nóngchǎng pei gōngsī shōugòu.* Mr. Ahrens is in charge of the story about land or farms being bought up by corporations."

Li Chang answered in Chinese: "*Li hsien sheng shuo yeh hsü t'a;a ying kai ho pi erh kai tz'u;u hsien sheng t';ant;an, pu shih wo men. Kai tz';u shih mai ti te, shih t'a ts'ung che hsieh nung min na li mai liao hao chi wan ying mu te t'u ti. Wo men shih wai kuo jen, wo men pu neng chih chieh mai nung ch'ang. fa lü chiu shih che yang, kung p'ing pu kung p'ing ling shuo zhuó.*"

After he finished speaking, Zhang Wei turned back to Mort and said, "Mr. Li says perhaps you should be talking to Mr. Bill Gates, not us. Gates is the one buying up tens of thousands of acres from these farmers. As foreigners, we cannot be property owners of these farms. That is the law, fair or not."

Mort was prepared for this deflection. "The allegation is that foreign companies are using what we call 'front men'—US residents who can legally purchase these properties—to buy them under false pretenses illegally."

Zhang Wei repeated what Mort said to Li Chang in Chinese: "*Fei shuo wai kuo kung ssu cheng tsai shih yung wo men zuò wei pai shou t'ao, lai ho fa kou mai che hsieh ti, shih chi shang shih pien hsiang fei fa mai ti.* "

The older man scowled and responded: "*Chang hsien sheng shuo, wo men lai che pu shih wei liao wei fa mai ti, huo che t'ao pi chien kuan. Wo men shih ho fa te sheng i jen, wo men ho fa t'ou tzu. Wo men chao t'ou tzu chi hui, tui wo men yu li yeh tui ti fang yu li.*"

"Mr. Chang said we are not in this country to break the law. Or, I might add, to circumvent it. We are legitimate businessmen, looking to make legitimate investments for our company and for our people. We seek to invest and look for localities where those investments will be profitable, not only for us but for the people in the areas we invest in," Zhang Wei said.

"That's why I'm here," Mort responded, "to hear both sides, to dispel the rumors and report the story truthfully. That's what we do at the *Post,* and that's what I do personally."

Again, Zhang Wei repeated Mort's words to Chang Li: "*Che chiu shih wei shen wo lai che , liang pien tu t'ing t'ing, kao ch'ing ch'u tsen hui shih . wo men pao she pao tao chen hsiang . wo men yu pao ho wo tzu chi chih kuan hsin chen hsiang.*"

"But," Chang Li said in broken English, to Mort's surprise, "you are more than a reporter. You are also perhaps one who rescues a woman and dispatches an attacker. Fatally. Perhaps a government agent?"

Startled by this accusation, Mort floundered. "The last thing the government wants is someone like me working for them. I am a reporter, plain and simple. What happened that night when your employee attacked us was a reflex, a reaction, nothing more. But, Mr. Tang *was* your employee. And he came prepared to kill Miss Powers. It was just lucky that I was there. I'm sure you know that another man was killed, a man who was investigating these land sales."

Chang Li responded in Chinese to Zhang Wei: "*Cheng fu tsui pu hsiang yao te chiu shih hsiang wo che yang te jen . Wo shih chi che, hen chien tan. Na t'ien wan shang ni te jen kung chi wo men , shih pen neng, wo men ming pai. K'ei t'a shih ni te ku yuan, shih t'a chun pei sha pao erh ssu hsiao chieh. Wo tsai na li chih shih p'eng ch'iao. K'ei shih yu jen pei sha liao , cheng tsai cheng tsai tiao ch'a che hsieh ti te jen."*

He then said to Mort, "We understand that you are a married man but were in this young woman's room in the middle of the night. That seems to be a strange situation."

Mort felt his face reddening and his anger rose. He replied crisply, "She was my subordinate and had witnessed a horrible event undoubtedly perpetrated by *your* employee. I was there to protect her and get her safely back to Washington. Frankly, if this is the tack you wish to pursue, I won't pursue this any further."

Zhang Wei raised his hands and said calmly, "We are a legitimate business, Mr. Ahrens. We are seeking to build a data center nearby in Minnesota. We make other local investments—always legally—to make life better for the people in North Dakota and, naturally, to make our company more profitable. That is capitalism, no?"

At this point Chang Li picked up a small bell on his desk and tinkled it softly.

The woman who had answered the front door stepped into the room. Looking at Mort, she said, "Can I offer you some tea? Cookies?"

It broke the tension, and Mort said, "No thank you, I'm heading for Katz's delicatessen before I go back to Washington. I've heard about it for years."

"Corned beef on dark rye, thick with mustard, cole slaw on the side," the younger man, Jai Hao, told him, shaping an imaginary large sandwich with his hands as they all smiled. "And get a Dr. Brown's cream soda. You'll be in heaven."

"Advice taken," Mort said.

Chang Li raised his hands in a soothing gesture and spoke to Zang Wei: *"Na ko hsing t'ang pu shih pei p'ing chi t'uan te jen. T'a shih pen ti te , pei ta k'ei t'a chou te. Wo men pu chih tao t'a shih ko huai tan. Che shih chien fa sheng te shih hou, t'a chih wei wo men kung zuò liao chi t'ien. Wo men ying kai hsien tiao ch'a t'a te pei ching. Tan kuo ch'ü te te kuo ch'ü.*"

"You should understand," Zhang Wei said, "that this Tang person was not a regular employee of The Peking Group. He was local, from North Dakota apparently, and we did not know he was a thug. He had only worked for us a very short time when these tragic events happened. Perhaps we should have investigated his background more thoroughly. But past is past."

"How did he come to work for you?" Mort asked.

Zhang Wei turned to Chang Li and repeated Mort's question in Chinese. Chang Li shook his head and put his hands out, palms up.

"He was recommended," Zhang Wei said. "How is the young lady?"

"She'll be fine," Mort said. "Recommended by whom?"

Chang Li shook his head, and Zhang Wei said, "I am not at liberty to say."

After a few more minutes of conversation, Mort thanked them for their cooperation, although he was certainly curious about who had recommended a killer to these men. But he was not getting any sinister vibes. It would be hard to believe they were foreign spies.

Katz's delicatessen was about twenty New York City blocks away, about a mile, so he walked, arriving hot and sweaty a half hour later. His mood was not improved by a menu with a corned beef sandwich for $25.50. He thought back a few years to when he was dating at Syracuse and an entire evening out didn't cost much more than that.

As he looked around, sitting at a table in the middle of the eatery, the scene looked somewhat familiar. He called the waiter over. "Why does this place look familiar to me?" he asked.

The waiter said, "Do I get a prize if I get it right?"

"How about a good tip?"

"That works," the waiter said, and started moaning, "Oh, Aaagh, Oh my God, Oooh, Aaah. He contorted his body at the same time. People at adjoining tables watched and laughed.

Mort snapped his fingers. *When Harry Met Sally!*" he exclaimed.

The waiter pointed a finger at Mort and smiled. "You're not a regular here, are you?"

"From DC," Mort answered.

"Should have guessed. Can't wait to see my tip."

On leaving the restaurant, and paying on his own credit card because he was embarrassed at the cost of his sandwich, Mort hailed a cab and headed back to the World Trade Center. He couldn't wait to tell Danni that he had a waiter who did an impersonation of Meg Ryan's orgasmic performance. He forgot about visiting the *Post's* New York office.

On the flight home, he pondered the close proximity of the Peking Group's building to the premises raided by the FBI for conducting illegal Chinese police operations. Was that a mere coincidence? The Chinese men he had met seemed to be legitimate businessmen but refused to reveal who had recommended Tommy Tang. Could there be a connection?

Nineteen

The Justices assembled on Wednesday morning with only one major decision left to be announced—the assisted suicide case, *Oregon v. Gluckstein*. Thursday, which would be the last day of the term, also featured other matters such as last-minute motions or *habeas corpus* petitions from lower federal or state courts that had to be disposed of, admissions of new members to the Supreme Court Bar, announcements of retirements of Court personnel and, rarely, one of the justices.

The Court had also returned to the "hand-down" practice of announcing and sometimes reading opinions in open court. The practice had been abandoned during the height of the Covid pandemic but was now returned as part of the procedure on decision day. Generally, the majority opinion would be read or summarized by whichever justice wrote the majority decision. Sometimes, a dissenting justice would also read or summarize his or her opinion. Generally, that occurred only when the dissenter vehemently disagreed with the majority. On rare occasions, a justice would make a remark, inadvertent or not, using language not included in the written decision, which was always seized upon by the media as indicative of a state of mind not expressed in the writing.

Constance Treller stood as she spoke to the other justices who joined her in the conference room. As usual, she was impeccably dressed in a pastel slack suit with a colorful neck scarf. The talk amongst the members had been of summer plans, travel and teaching commitments and the like. Treller planned to spend the summer on her Arizona ranch with her husband. J.J., clad as usual in his jeans, sport shirt and boots, was consumed with plans for his traditional July 4th barbeque, which several of the other justices would be attending. One of the main attractions this year, J.J. promised, was a visit from Anthony Battaglia, who had retired from the Court last year in failing health and had regained much of his former self after multiple visits to the Mayo Clinic in Rochester, Minnesota.

The other justices were clad in business casual. Some had interviews scheduled later in the day with prospective law clerks for the upcoming term. Most had already made those selections and wanted to make certain all was in place for the summer. Their locations had to be known at all times, in case of emergency applications, which they handled individually, or in rare cases—when the vote of the entire Court was required—by long distance conference call.

"As for the order of things," Treller said, "J.J., I assume you'll be reading or summarizing *Gluckstein*, which will have the press on the edge of their seats. I think their big surprise, however, may be that you led the majority here, overwhelmingly."

"Got to keep them on their toes, C.J.," J.J. replied. His practice, not only with Treller but several of her predecessors, was to refer to the chief justice as "C.J."

Julius Gallagher arose from his seat with a pained expression.

"Justice Gallagher?" Treller asked, anticipating a question.

Gallagher opened his mouth, muttered something garbled, then pitched forward onto the table and slid unconscious to the floor.

J.J. immediately leaped from his spot, bent down, rolled Gallagher over and started pounding on his chest, shouting, "Heart attack! Call 911! Get the defibrillator!" For the most part, the justices stood there in shock, but Treller sprang to the door and shouted for help.

J.J. kept pushing rhythmically on Gallagher's chest until he gagged and started to breathe.

Court personnel trained in medical emergencies raced into the room, followed moments later by EMTs, who administered oxygen and inserted a needle into Gallagher's arm. Within a minute, they had loaded Gallagher onto a gurney and moved him out.

As the EMTs were leaving, a woman who seemed to be in charge turned to J.J. and said, "Nice work, Judge. Hopefully, that saved him." And with that, the conference came to an abrupt end.

J.J. was still on his knees on the floor as the other justices crowded around him.

"How did you know it was a heart attack?" Treller asked.

"He's been staying with us since their house was firebombed," J.J. said breathlessly. "His heart troubles came up in conversation. I kidded him about conservatives having a heart. I hope that I acted in time."

"You were incredible," Treller said. "We'll have to notify his wife."

"I'll call Chickie from chambers," J.J. said. "She'll get hold of Penelope right away."

* * *

Several hours later, Chickie called J.J. from the hospital with Penelope at her side. Gallagher was stabilized and resting comfortably.

Chickie handed Penelope the phone. "J.J.," Penelope said, choking up, "I don't know what to say... how to thank you. You saved his life."

"Just needed a little more time with him to change his philosophy," J.J. said. "Can't let a good man go."

Twenty

At the same time J.J. was saving the life of his colleague, Danni Rose was in the American University law school library. As an assistant professor of environmental law, she had access there to virtually everything a young professor could want. Only minutes from the White House and the US Supreme Court, it was situated in a city of lawyers. It was also a short distance from Alexandria, Virginia, headquarters of Rosen-Billings Enterprises, a conglomerate that owned many television and radio stations throughout the nation and where her mother, "Chickie" Rosen, served as CEO. Mort would often joke that he was a "struggling" journalist and his mother-in-law was a media tycoon.

Chickie had become CEO upon the death of her husband a decade earlier. When she took over the helm, the company's stock immediately nose-dived but crucial decisions she made quickly restored it as one of the nation's leading communications companies.

As Danni was making notes in her library cubicle, someone tried to get her attention by clearing his throat. Lifting her eyes revealed the creepy tattooed man from the cruise ship staring at her.

"Oh," she said. "Is there something I can do for you, Mister…" She pretended not to remember his name.

"McCarthy," he said, "Devon, to you."

"And?" She was already feeling uncomfortable under his gaze.

"I got the textbook listed in your syllabus," he said. "But I was wondering if there were any other lawbooks I should read over the next several weeks to help me be up to par with your regular law students."

He was either very dedicated, very persistent, or as she suspected less interested in environmental law than in the professor. His presence made her feel uncomfortable though he hadn't done anything to arouse anger.

"You might try *Civil Action* by Jonathon Harr—H-A-R-R," she said. "A classic, even though it's three decades old. Won the National Book Critics Award, or something like that. Reads better than fiction."

He pulled out a small pad and wrote it down. "Can I interest you in that cup of coffee?" he asked.

"No, but thanks. Knee deep here in preparation."

"Tomorrow?"

She shook her head. "The last day of the Supreme Court term. I've been invited as a guest. Before you get the wrong idea, though, our relationship is going to be *strictly* academic. If you have any misgivings about that, you may want to withdraw from the course."

McCarthy didn't bat an eyelash. "Sure, I understand," he said. "Trouble is I can't get over that portrait of you. It captured your true self."

"Well, I'd certainly like to forget it," Danni said. "He had a vivid imagination."

"No, he was spot on. Going with your husband tomorrow? Is he covering the Court for the *Post*?"

Danni was growing irritated by this increasingly personal conversation. "You seem to know a lot about my life. Much more than required in a professor-student relationship. Frankly, I find it annoying."

"The last thing I want to do is annoy you," McCarthy said calmly. "I'll just be the veterinarian in the class and try not to upset you. But for your dog, I'd be more than happy to offer free advice."

Danni was surprised that he knew about Katie. How much did this man know about her life? She'd have to remember to push Mort to do that background check.

"We're done discussing my life," she said crisply. "I'll see you next in class."

With that, she turned back to her computer and he left. *Damn that Simeon!* she thought. The last thing I need is an ogling middle-aged student. Or a delusional stalker.

That evening Mort said he'd ask Travis to check out McCarthy.

* * *

In Travalah, as J.J. and Chickie were getting ready for bed, J.J. made a statement in such an off-handed manner it told Chickie he had given it a lot of thought. "I think we should push off the July 4th festivities until Labor Day like we did last year," he said. "Doesn't seem right to have a party just days after his heart attack, though it looks like he's going to pull through."

"I was having the same thought," Chickie said. "But last year you were still recovering from the kidnapping."

"Same thing, different characters."

"I'll take care of it," Chickie said, climbing into bed and switching off the light. Connie was already asleep in her dog bed under the window. Clearly, she had no opinion on the matter.

Twenty-one

The Supreme Court term scheduled its last day for Thursday. Danni was invited by J.J. to be in the courtroom when the final decision of the term would be released, and the concluding ceremonies would occur.

At home on Wednesday evening, Mort was hunched over the dining room table cleaning a .32 caliber Browning automatic pistol he had purchased when he was a student at Syracuse. It was small for an automatic and held eight cartridges, seven in the clip and one in the chamber. He had bought it when he was a cub reporter looking for a kidnapped teenager. When his suspicions ultimately led to her recovery and national publicity, it had produced a job offer from the *Post*. Four years later, here he was. After moving to Washington, he had registered it with the Metropolitan Police.

Danni walked into the room and watched him silently for a moment. "You know how I hate guns," she said. "Why do you insist on keeping that thing?"

"Sentimental value, I guess. It's a special manufacture, so kinda rare. But in today's crazy world, I keep it in pristine condition. And loaded. On the top shelf of my bedroom closet. You should at least have some familiarity with it."

"I don't want to know about it. And I don't want to see it. Besides, what do you need a gun for? You're now a martial arts whiz. You kill them with your bare hands."

"Not funny," Mort said. "I want to show it to you."

"Not interested."

"Aw, c'mon. Humor me."

Reluctantly, Danni walked to his side. He turned and put the gun in her hand. She cringed and handed it back.

"See here," Mort said, "this is the safety. You click it down before you fire—otherwise it won't."

"I *said* I'm not interested, and I'm done with safety since I'm off the pill, so why don't you put down your toy, come into the bedroom and I'll let you play with something much more interesting."

Mort immediately wrapped the automatic in a towel and followed her into the bedroom.

* * *

Mort and Danni lived in the exclusive Georgetown section of DC because Danni had always dreamed of living there, and if that's what Danni wanted, that's where they would live. They had originally rented an apartment, which Mort, raised in middle-class Harrisburg, felt was much too expensive. But they managed it with their two salaries. Between them, they earned $150,000 a year, and while Mort blanched at a monthly rental of $3,200, it was doable.

When they first met, Mort didn't know that Danni came from a very wealthy family. Not only was her mother, Chickie, a big-time CEO, but when her father had died a decade earlier, he'd left life insurance in the millions. But you would never suspect an affluent upbringing from Danni's demeanor—she gave off no affectation of wealth, disliked what she described as the "Princess" syndrome and never wore showy jewelry. But she couldn't overcome that as an only child she had been raised with many advantages and much attention.

Mort, on the other hand, had an entirely different experience as a child. His parents had a simple, middle-class home in which he shared a room with his one sibling, an older sister, now married and living in Minnesota.

Mort and Danni had recently moved into their Georgetown condo, which Chickie had given them as a wedding gift last year. Near the Potomac, the unit occupied 1,700 square feet, with underground parking, fronting on the street, and a dog-friendly policy. It was a far cry from Mort's family home, or his simple studio apartment in Syracuse, or his one-bedroom unit in Lincolnia, Virginia, that he had rented when he started with the *Post*.

Mort had priced similar condos in the area—not as luxurious as their "gift" home, nor as close to the Potomac—and the near-million-dollar price had not only shocked him but made him very uncomfortable. His parents had not yet visited, and he made it a point not to discuss real estate values in Georgetown with them. He even avoided telling his peers where he lived, except in general terms.

* * *

On Thursday morning, Danni decided to make an early stop at her office. She parked in the tiered lot on Nebraska Avenue, which opened at eight, planning to Uber to the Supreme Court to avoid the traffic crunch on decision day. The Court proceedings started at ten.

The law school was virtually empty, because the first summer sessions didn't meet every day and most of the faculty was already vacationing. As she approached her office, she spotted something outside the door. Moving closer, she discovered two dozen long-stem red roses wrapped in green tissue paper. They couldn't have been from Mort. Granted, they had been unusually amorous last night, but he couldn't have gotten the flowers to her office that early.

She picked them up and read a note: "To the Madonna." She stepped back and pushed the roses away. Could it have been Simeon? Unlikely. He probably didn't even know where she taught or where her office was. More than likely they were from her soon-to-be student Devon McCarthy. Flushed with anger, she walked the roses to the main office, where a lone woman sat behind a desk and said, "Did you see who dropped these off outside my office?"

The receptionist replied, "No, but they're gorgeous."

"Well, I have no place for them, so enjoy them," Danni said and handed them to the shocked woman.

Twenty-two

As Danni suspected, First Street was closed off from Massachusetts Ave. where she had the Uber drop her off. Media trucks were parked in front of the Court with satellite dishes pointing skyward, stanchions driven into the pavement as a deterrent to terrorists, and a perimeter of steel fencing was around the front of the building. When Danni had clerked there for a year, she'd had a tendency to take the building for granted. The Marble Palace, as it was frequently referred to, stood atop a wide set of stairs with sixteen imposing marble pillars beneath the architrave on which was inscribed "Equal Justice Under Law." Looking at it today, she was once again filled with awe as she was on the day she interviewed with J.J. Richter for a law clerk's position.

There were the usual protestors and placards facing off in front of the building, as well as a restless crowd of tourists and onlookers. Danni thought she spotted Devon McCarthy, but the man quickly ducked out of her vision. The thought of McCarthy fanned the flames of her anger. She hoped the man wasn't him, especially after her episode with the roses. On reflection, though, she was certain it was McCarthy. She had mentioned yesterday that she would attend the Court's session today, and this morning roses were delivered to her office. That was not a coincidence.

Entrance to the Court was no longer available through the imposing bronze doors at the top of the stairs, so she walked around to the side portico reserved for guests and dignitaries where she had to pass through the screening devices and have her handbag scrutinized.

She knew the Supreme Court officer who conducted the search, and they exchanged pleasantries.

The small courtroom was already filled with spectators, some of whom had spent the night on the steps just for the chance to get one of the four hundred seats and view the day's proceedings. The black chairs at the front were reserved for dignitaries and officers of the Court. The red benches on the left, which faced the raised dais where the Justices sat, were reserved for the press and other media representatives who covered the Court. They were already filled. Danni and other invited guests were seated on the red benches to the right, which quickly filled up. Danni glanced at the ceiling forty-four feet overhead and smiled as she recalled her basketball games there with J.J. when the day's work was done. Basketball in "the highest court in the land."

Once the clerk had announced the opening of the day's session and the justices were seated, the clerk issued a directive forbidding the use of cell phones or recording devices. The other prerequisites of the day were completed, and the final case of this year's session was called—"*The State of Oregon v. Oscar Gluckstein, A Compassionate Death, et al.* – No. 22-214."

Justice Julius Gallagher's chair was vacant. Danni thought back to a year ago when it was J.J.'s chair that sat empty because he was hospitalized following his kidnapping. And here he was again, almost eighty years old. Although she was a student of Supreme Court history, she could not recall any other time when a justice had been absent on the last day of court two years in a row.

The chief justice announced, "The majority decision will be presented by Senior Associate Justice J.J. Richter." Danni was surprised, not only that J.J. was presenting, as the Court once again returned to the "hand-down" procedure, but that J.J. had authored the majority decision. She was convinced that he would be in the minority and would fight for the right of individuals to be allowed physician-assisted suicide, the popular progressive position, as opposed to the majority of the Court, which was more conservative. Had he convinced the Court to adopt the more progressive position? During the pandemic, hand-downs—read by the justice who authored the majority decision—were dispensed with, and decisions were handed out by the clerk at the commencement of each session.

J.J. spoke from his seat to the right of the chief justice. "The decision of the Court is seven to two, in favor of the respondents, the State of Oregon, the Court holding that there is no national right to assisted suicide, and it is a matter to be determined on a state-by-state basis."

Danni gasped loudly enough that several heads turned in her direction.

J.J. continued, "While the normal procedure would be to have me read, and perhaps comment on my opinion, I have chosen instead to read from the concurring opinion of our Junior Associate Justice, Julius Gallagher, who is unable to be present here today as he is hospitalized following a heart attack."

It was not unusual, but infrequent, to have a justice in the minority read from his or her opinion, but it was highly unusual to have the author of the majority opinion read from a concurring opinion. Nevertheless, J.J. was not one to be bound by the "usual."

"I think," J.J. continued, "that Justice Gallagher has the right for his voice to be heard, and I might say that while I do not agree with much of his expressed beliefs, I shall do so on his behalf. I know that some people will be surprised at my conclusions."

"You're damn right," Danni said under her breath.

"And while I am sympathetic to the position of the appellant, A Compassionate Death, and of the *amicus curiae*, I cannot find any constitutional reason to sustain the belief that an assisted suicide is something that is covered in our Constitution or deserves universal acceptance in the law."

J.J. then read Gallagher's opinion, which included his references to biblical interpretations about suicide from both the New and Old Testaments—Exodus, Romans, and St. Matthew among them. Gallagher quoted Jewish law which equated suicide to murder, which he stated was a sin. When J.J. finished, he shook his head.

"I think that Justice Gallagher reached the right conclusion in this case for the wrong reasons. I hesitate to utilize biblical interpretations, because I feel they have no place in the law except for their historical value. They lead us, I believe, away from the intent of our founders—a separation of church and state. It is in the Constitution that I seek my answers, not in scripture.

"I can find no reason to invoke the Commerce Clause into this case, as I quote in my decision noting *State v. Lopez*, nor do I find that prohibiting a national law on suicide violates the 14th Amendment because it neither denies a person the equal protection of the law nor deprives a person of life, liberty or property without due process of law.

"Assisted suicide, and the interpretation of it, varies widely throughout the country, and while a handful of states and the District of Columbia allow physician-assisted suicide, helping someone to die by suicide is specifically prohibited in over forty states. My belief, joined in by a majority of this Court, is that the question is best left to the states with their varying geographical divisions and interpretations.

"I understand that national polls indicate that the majority of those polled feel—by a wide majority, I might add—that physicians should be allowed to assist in the termination of life for one who is incurably ill and seeks such assistance, and yet The American Medical Association, among many others, opposes the concept. But my interpretation is based not on religion, nor public opinion, nor sympathy, but on the document that I am sworn to uphold, the Constitution of the United States, and the answer is clear to me."

J.J. looked up as he concluded, and several people rose to applaud—an act strictly prohibited. The chief justice gaveled for order, and the clerk dispatched officers to remove those whom had violated the protocol of the Court. Danni merely shook her head in disbelief.

* * *

In J.J.'s chambers, once the Court session concluded, his clerks and administrative assistants were preparing for their summer vacations and other plans. J.J., shucking his robe, was in his typical Western garb. Danni circulated among the staff to renew hellos and chat. She also sat for a short period with the law clerks to tell them what to expect, warn them never to disturb any of the books and materials J.J. had strewn around the chambers and generally just to get acquainted. Not only was she a law clerk alum, but she had been J.J.'s favorite in addition to now being his stepdaughter, one whom he still often referred to as the daughter he never had.

She finally got a chance to buttonhole J.J. about his opinion in the assisted suicide case.

"I can't believe you ended up on that side of the case," she said.

"I didn't end up there, I was there all along. It's just not a federal issue in my mind."

"But what about—?" Danni started.

"What about we hold it until tomorrow evening?" J.J. said. "We're coming over to you for dinner, right?"

"Yes, and Mort's doing the cooking."

"Mort's cooking? I'll remember to take some Tums beforehand."

Twenty-three

Although Danni was now wealthy in her own right, her money was in safe investments, and to her it was as if it never existed. She and Mort lived on their salaries. The accoutrements of wealth were for others.

The second bedroom of the Ahrens condo had become Danni's office, and the only TV, a forty-five-inch Sony, was in the spacious main bedroom where Mort spent a lot of time watching sports events—almost *any* sports event—although he did have a small desk in the corner. The condo featured a modern, fully equipped kitchen, where neither of them spent much time cooking. Their normal practice was to bring in food several times a week or have it delivered by DoorDash.

The newlyweds had acquired several pieces of art, which hung in the bedroom and living room—none by Simeon—which included a large floral by Maya Green in the living room, a gift from Kimberly and Lynette that came shortly after the cruise. There were also several sports pictures of Mort's, which hung in the hallway, since Danni didn't want them in any of the other rooms.

The furniture was an eclectic combination of modern and traditional. The front entrance opened onto the street with a small alcove separating it from the living room, which was large and featured both a small and large sofa, several comfortable armchairs and tables, lamps and a bookcase filled with law books, sports books and memorabilia, and Mort's journalism library. A hallway from the living room led to the second bathroom and a main bedroom with its own *en suite*.

At dinner, as J.J., Chickie and Danni sat around the table, Mort served.

"I still don't understand how you could end up being on the side of the conservatives in that case yesterday," Danni said to J.J.

J.J. responded calmly. "It wasn't a conservative or progressive decision, as I said. It's strictly a constitutional issue, and I went with the Constitution."

"But what about the people who need help, who are faced with that awful life or death decision, who might be afraid to act on their own?"

"There are plenty of places that offer assisted suicide," J.J. said. "Just cross a state line and you're there. I'm sympathetic to their plight, but it's not an issue that falls under the Constitution."

"Cross the state line?" Danni seemed incredulous. "That's the same illogical thing conservatives said about the abortion decision. Just last week there was a poor couple in Florida—he was terminal and begged her to kill him. She loved him and shot him in his hospital bed, and now she's being tried for murder. How do you reconcile that?"

"I don't," J.J. said, "and I understand that she couldn't bear to see his pain. But it's not a case for federal relief."

"Well, abortion is not in the Constitution either," Danni said. "And you had no difficulty fighting to retain that right last year."

"You just hit on the key word—retain," J.J. responded. "Abortion was deemed a constitutional right for half a century, and the Court took it away. Our job is not to *diminish* rights, which is what the *Dobbs* decision did. Several amendments were abused there. In yesterday's case, it's an entirely different ball game, one that's best left to the states."

"Boys and girls," Chickie said, "enough shop talk from you two. Court is adjourned. Let's just enjoy the dinner that Mort created."

They finished dinner, and Mort asked if anyone wanted coffee, tea, or anything else.

"Let's head into the living room. It's more comfortable," Chickie said. "Mort, I'll help you clear the table." She got up and began stacking dishes.

A short time later, they sat in the living room. Chickie and J.J. shared the large sofa. Danni and Mort sprawled in the armchairs. Katie was on the sofa, being petted and spoiled by Chickie. J.J. was drinking a beer, his preferred libation.

"Mort," Chickie said, "wherever did you learn to cook like that? What a great meal."

"Not bad for a writer," J.J. said. "When you said we were having beef Wellington, I thought you had invited a wrestler to join us."

"Just a little something I threw together," Mort said, in an understated manner.

"I knew there had to be a reason Danni married you," J.J. said. "I just never suspected it was because of your cooking."

"I thought it was for my looks," Mort said.

"Guess again, Martha Stewart," Danni said.

"Danni," Chickie said, "why don't you show us the pictures you took on the cruise?"

"You mean the honeymoon without a husband?" Danni said.

"Below the belt," Mort complained.

Danni got up and walked into the bedroom just as the doorbell rang. Katie leaped off the sofa and ran to the door, barking wildly.

"Who's that, girl?" Mort asked. "We're not expecting company."

At the door, he looked through the peephole but no one was there. Katie continued barking.

As Mort opened the door to look around, a pistol jammed into his neck, pushing him back into the condo.

Twenty-four

"What the hell?" Mort exclaimed.

Katie continued barking but wagged her tail at the same time, as she usually did with strangers. The intruder reached down with a syringe in his hand and plunged the needle into the dog. She yelped, jumped back, staggered and within seconds fell into a heap.

J.J. and Chickie watched in shock.

"Katie!" Mort yelled, panicked.

"Where's Danni?" the intruder demanded.

"I know you," Mort said. "The guy from the cruise."

"Where's Danni?" Devon McCarthy repeated angrily.

Mort thought quickly. "She went out for ice cream," he said.

"I've been watching the front. She didn't leave," McCarthy said.

"Out through the kitchen to the garage," Mort said.

"Then we'll wait," McCarthy said. "I want Danni."

"Who is this man?" Chickie demanded. His bulging eyes were bloodshot.

"Shut up," McCarthy snarled, "and maybe you won't get hurt. Who are you?"

McCarthy took the pistol, a semi-automatic Glock with an extended magazine, away from Mort's neck, pushed him into the center of the room and waved the pistol around. He was dressed in a black hoodie with black slacks and boots. His wispy hair was slicked back, and his eyes looked as though he was drugged. He swayed from side to side.

"You can't just walk in here like this," J.J. said. "What do you want? Money? We'll give you money."

"Ha! I don't need your damn money," McCarthy snorted. "I have more than you. I want Danni." He didn't seem to recognize J.J.

McCarthy pointed his pistol at Mort again, almost shouting. "You don't deserve her. You didn't even deck that painter when he showed that painting. Nude, but not for the world to see. I can see her beauty. She was hysterical, but you didn't even grab him, beat the crap out of him when she was so upset. You don't deserve her, and now it's all over. I can make her happy."

Danni, in the meantime, was in the bedroom closet, reaching up to the shelf that held the pictures from the trip. She had just transferred them from her phone into five by sevens.

"This is the guy who's been stalking Danni," Mort said more calmly than he felt.

"He's a screwball," Chickie said. "He just killed Katie, for Chrissake."

"She'll be fine," McCarthy said. "Trazodone and Benadryl. I'm a vet. She's coming with us."

"What do you mean, with us?" Chickie said. "You're a veteran? We can get you help. You need help." She and J.J. were still on the sofa, and Mort was standing in the middle of the room watching McCarthy waving the pistol around.

McCarthy threw back his head. "*Veterinarian*, you stupid bitch. I *know* drugs."

"Danni's not going anywhere with you," Mort said, gauging the distance between McCarthy and himself for a front-leg kick. Part of his Krav Maga training had been to maintain awareness of surroundings in times of stress, have quick reactions and use his instincts. He wasn't close enough for a take-down. The gun would take him down first.

"Wrong, pudgy," McCarthy said. "Start thinking your last thoughts. I'm leaving with her, to give her the life she deserves. You've only got about ten seconds left, so start praying."

J.J. started edging toward the end of the sofa.

"Don't move, old man," McCarthy snarled, "unless you want to die too. What are you people doing here anyway? They should have been alone." He was speaking rapidly, almost incoherently, his voice rising.

"Ten," McCarthy said. "Start thinking your last thoughts, paper boy."

"You're insane," Chickie said.

"No, lady, I've never been saner."

Standing down the hallway, Danni had recognized McCarthy's raspy voice and remained out of sight.

"Nine," McCarthy said. "No one will ever find us where we're going." He waved the pistol toward Chickie and J.J. as Mort looked for a way to cross the room.

"Eight," McCarthy said.

Danni moved quickly into the bedroom, searching in all directions. Her purse, with her cell phone, was in the kitchen. No way to call 911.

"Seven."

She plunged into the closet and stretched to reach Mort's pistol on the top shelf. It was just out of her reach. She jumped, the same way she had done during her basketball days, grabbed the towel with Mort's pistol wrapped inside and landed with a thud on the floor.

McCarthy heard the sound. "What was that?"

"Your brain rattling in your head," Mort said.

"Now I'm not even giving you those last seconds, smart ass."

"No!" Chickie screamed.

Gun in hand, Danni moved quickly down the hall. What was it Mort had said about the safety? Why hadn't she listened more carefully? She fumbled with the pistol, found the safety and released it. She burst into the living room, pistol held firmly in both hands the way she'd seen cops on TV do it.

McCarthy spun toward her. "Danni!" he shouted, suddenly smiling.

At the same time, J.J. threw his beer bottle and hit him in the chest. Beer sprayed from the bottle.

Danni squeezed the trigger and fired.

McCarthy's gun went off just as Mort spun across the room and hit him with a vertical front kick.

McCarthy staggered back, looking down at his chest. "You shot me," he said in disbelief.

Chickie softly groaned and moved a hand toward her left shoulder. "I think I'm shot," she said, slumping to the sofa.

As J.J. moved toward McCarthy, who was struggling to stand upright, Danni fired again. McCarthy doubled over. "Why did you do that?" Then he crumpled face down on the carpet.

Mort grabbed the gun from Danni's trembling hand and bent over McCarthy, his .32 pointed at the body. He turned to J.J. and said, "Chickie's shot. Call 911."

Mort reached down and felt for McCarthy's carotid artery. "He still has a pulse." McCarthy's Glock had fallen from his hand to the carpet, and Mort kicked it away.

Twenty-five

J.J. was at Chickie's side. "Chickie? Honey?" he said with tears in his eyes.

Mort, still poised over McCarthy with his pistol, shouted, "Did you call 911?"

J.J. said, "We've got the marshals outside. Go get 'em."

Within a minute, the two US marshals who had driven them to Georgetown were in the living room. Brad Pennington, the senior marshal, sized up the situation quickly and pulled out his phone, calling in an alert. "Justice Richter's daughter's house, there's been a shooting. His wife is hit, assailant down. We need backup and an ambulance!" He gave the address.

Danni moved to her mother, who weakly said, "I think I'm okay, but it hurts like hell now."

Danni moved her mother's hand away from the shoulder. There was surprisingly little blood, but her blouse was stained from the oozing wound.

The second marshal, Joe Tricano, had raced out of the condo and returned seconds later with a first aid kit. He said to Danni, "I've got it," and gently pushed her aside, bending over Chickie.

"Doesn't look too bad," he said, pressing gauze on the wound.

J.J. said, "Let's get her to the hospital in the SUV."

"No," Pennington said. "EMTs will be here in seconds. That's a lot quicker. Anyone else hurt?"

Mort and Danni said they were fine.

Pennington looked down at the unconscious body. "Who is he?" McCarthy was breathing but not moving.

"Where the hell were you guys?" J.J. demanded of the marshals.

"Outside in the SUV. We saw the guy knock on the door," Pennington said, "but we didn't know if he was another guest or not. Had the gun hidden."

He turned to Mort, who was still holding his pistol. "You did good, sir," he said, then reached out and took the .32.

"I didn't do a damn thing," Mort said. "J.J. hit him with a beer bottle and Danni shot him. When he didn't drop his gun, she shot him again. He only got off one shot and hit Chickie."

Pennington shook his head. "Incredible."

The front door was still open, and the sound of distant sirens was getting louder.

Danni turned to Mort and said, "The safety. I remembered the safety. I shot him."

"You did great," Mort said.

Within minutes, the living room was filled with EMTs, Georgetown Police, and two members of the FBI—a woman agent who seemed in charge, Monica Blizzard, and Angel Morales, a swarthy six-footer. There was a tangle of ambulances, police cars and unmarked cars with flashing lights in the street. A curious crowd had already assembled.

"We'll take jurisdiction," Blizzard said to Mort. "An assault, kidnapping or homicide of a federal employee, or member of their family, particularly relevant here, is punishable by twenty years to life under the United States Code, or in the case of a fatality, by the death penalty." She stated it in a monotone as if reading from the United States Code.

McCarthy was removed by ambulance with an oxygen mask on and zip ties strapped to his wrists.

* * *

It seemed like only minutes later when Travis Anderson arrived in jeans and a sweatshirt. He had been playing basketball with his son, at home in Rockville, Maryland, when he got the alarm. He shouted to his wife, Michele, where he was heading and covered the twenty miles in thirteen minutes. Because of his close relationship with J.J. and the family, he was consumed with dread that the shooting was worse than what he saw when he arrived.

He looked around at all the activity, at Pennington and Mort, and said, "What the hell happened?"

As Pennington started to explain, Blizzard interrupted and said, "We have his pistol," indicating Mort, "and the one the assailant used as well. We're about to take a preliminary statement from Mr. Ahrens."

"You have a pistol?" Travis asked Mort, who just nodded. "And you shot the guy with it?"

"Nope," Mort said. "Danni did. Saved the day."

"Danni? Danni who hates guns?"

"Thank God, I showed her how to release the safety," Mort said.

Blizzard showed Mort's .32 to Travis, who said, "Not exactly a blunderbuss."

"Can't the statement wait?" Mort said to Blizzard. "I really should get to the hospital to see how Chickie is."

"Chickie was shot?" Travis asked. "By the perp?"

"Yes. Can't we go to the hospital first, and I'll give you a statement there? J.J.'s there as well."

"I can take them in our SUV," Pennington said, looking at Blizzard, "and you can follow and take the statements there."

"Highly irregular." Blizzard said.

"This whole thing is," Travis said, "but I head the Supreme Court Police and I've got some jurisdiction here, so that's the best idea I've heard. Which hospital?"

"MedStar," Blizzard said. "It's very close."

Travis didn't wait for an answer and headed for the door, waving at Mort and Pennington to follow.

Reluctantly, Blizzard was the last one out the door. She glanced at Morales, who shrugged his shoulders as if to say *What can we do?* Protocol had been breached. They left Georgetown Police at the condo and all trooped out.

* * *

They traveled the two miles to MedStar, a Trauma 1 center, and headed for the emergency room. About a dozen people were in the waiting room, all of whom looked up with great curiosity when the entourage stormed in.

Pennington had led Chickie right past the desk and entered the emergency room itself. "Federal marshal," he said to the startled desk attendant. "Gun shot."

After a period of regrouping, Mort sat down with Blizzard to give a brief statement while they sat on the chairs and benches. It was another twenty minutes before a doctor in green scrubs entered and looked around, confused.

"Judge Richter?" he said.

J.J. separated from the group and walked over, Danni with him. He shook the doctor's hand and asked, "How is she?"

"She'll be fine. The bullet passed right through and didn't hit bone. She didn't even need a transfusion, but we'll keep her overnight as a precaution."

"I'll stay," Danni said.

"No," J.J. said. "I will. Just like she did last year when it was me who got hurt." He nodded his head to the doctor. "This is my daughter, Danni Rose. She shot the guy who shot Chickie... my wife. I didn't even know she had a pistol. Didn't know she could shoot."

"Beginner's luck," Danni said.

The doctor had heard more than he needed to know. "As soon as we get a room, I'll make arrangements for you to stay, Judge. And I must say, it's an honor to meet you."

"Justice," Danni said. "He's a justice."

Now thoroughly confused, the doctor withdrew with a nod.

They waited while Mort finished his preliminary statement, which Blizzard typed into her laptop. Then she asked J.J. for a short statement as well. While J.J. was relating his recitation of the events to Blizzard, Danni came over to them and said, "He's a stalker—the guy I shot. Been stalking me since we were on a cruise. Sick fantasies."

Morales, who had just reentered the room, said, "The shooter is in the OR. Looks like he'll make it—they're pretty sure, anyhow. One shot to the chest, the other in the abdomen. He'll be under guard, naturally. Then we know where his home is going to be for years after that."

Blizzard arranged for Danni and Mort to report to the FBI field office the following day to formalize their statements. She would arrange something with J.J. at his convenience.

Travis told the two marshals, Pennington and Tricano, to take Mort and Danni home and said he'd arrange for another team to cover J.J. and Chickie. "Good job, Annie Oakley," he told Danni. "By the way, I followed up on Mort's information and know who this shooter is. Devon McCarthy is a member of the family that was involved in the opioid scandal. They're worth billions. He's a psycho—been in and out of institutions for years. An addict. Was a veterinarian but lost his license. Has all sorts of delusions and fantasies. Supposed to be on meds. A really weird dude."

With thanks to Travis, and assurances that Chickie would recover, Mort and Danni left. When they got back to the condo, the forensics team was still finishing up, including digging the bullet that went through Chickie out of the back of the sofa. Danni looked at Mort and said, "How about we find a hotel for the night? I don't think I'll be comfortable here."

"How about Travalah?" Mort said. "If Lupe finds out about the shooting on TV, she'll go crazy."

"My God," Danni said, "we've forgotten all about Katie. Poor puppy. We don't even know if she's alive."

"Shit, you're right," Mort replied. "What kind of parents are we?"

They were met by Sgt. Rolando Vasquez of the Georgetown Police and before they even had a chance to ask about the dog, he volunteered, "I knew that you'd be worried. I took the liberty of calling the Veterinary Emergency Group on M Street. We've worked with them before and they're terrific. Marcy Black, one of our patrol officers, took the dog over and just called in. The dog will recover, but she's like an overdose case, so they're keeping her tonight and you should check tomorrow, probably afternoon."

"I can't thank you enough," Danni said.

They pulled together a few items of clothing and asked Sgt. Vasquez to lock up on the way out.

Twenty-six

The ringing of Mort's cell phone aroused Mort and Danni the next morning. He swung his feet over the side of the bed, threw back the covers, and moved sleepily to the other side of the room where his pants were draped over a chair. Exhausted from last night's events, he and Danni had given a quick explanation to Lupe and assured her that Chickie would be okay, and they'd have breakfast with her the next morning.

Mort pulled out his phone.

"Steve," he said into the phone.

"Mort," Steve Ginsberg replied, "you've got to get back to North Dakota. All hell has broken loose. The Chinese have a spy balloon floating across the Midwest, and the whole administration is in a frenzy. In fact, everyone is in a frenzy, the crazies especially. It ties in with your investigation. Didn't you see the news last night?"

"We had our own adventure going on, Steve. Weren't you tuned in? I was planning to head back in a day or two anyway."

"Good. Well, make it soon. This thing with the Chinese is turning into a cause célèbre. Bigger than we imagined, and I want you back on it ASAP." He paused. "Adventure? What kind of adventure? I always get nervous about your adventures."

"You'll see it on the news today. In fact, it's probably in the late editions of the *Post*."

"Why am I starting to hyperventilate?" Ginsberg said.

"We were having dinner with Justice Richter and Chickie at our place last night…"

* * *

Danni and Mort had a quick breakfast with Lupe and then checked in with J.J. at the hospital. Chickie was in considerable pain but feeling better overall. The medical staff said she would probably be released later that day with her arm in a sling.

"Miss Chickie hurt, she need me," Lupe said. "I take care of her. Don't wanna lose her like Miss Meg way back. I go hospital."

"Look," Mort said, "I have to go to the office. Danni, why don't you go with Lupe to the hospital and then I'll drive over to MedStar, pick you up and we can check on Katie at the vet. If we're lucky, I can pick her up as well."

Mort was thankful that Danni simply agreed.

* * *

At his desk, Mort fired up his computer to check on the story about the Chinese balloon. He read several articles and understood the concern was primarily that the balloon had hovered around Malmstrom Air Force Base in Montana for several days, the home to many ICBM missile silos. Googling the base, he saw that it was near Great Falls, Montana, which was at least eight hundred miles from his next destination, Grand Forks. It seemed unlikely that the "spy" balloon was tied into the North Dakota story.

Mort scrolled through his contacts and called Sheriff Clete MacCauley in Grand Forks.

MacCauley picked up on the third ring. "Mort," he said, "I was going to call you today. Thought you had forgotten about us. There are things happening here… things we have to talk about. But first, how is the young lady?"

"She's doing well," Mort said. "She took a few days off, but I don't think she'll be coming back with me."

"Probably just as well. She had a pretty gruesome experience. Did you buy peace with your wife with the jewelry?"

"I did, Clete, but she was still pissed that I fell asleep in Alison's bed."

"Probably wouldn't have been pissed if Alison was sixty-five," MacCauley said, causing Mort to smile.

"We just had an adventure back here, by the way," Mort said. "A crazy stalker tried to kidnap my wife last night and wanted to kill me."

"My God, you seem to have a cursed life," MacCauley said. "Ought to settle out here for peace and quiet. I assume he didn't kill you, unless you're calling from Heaven."

"More likely I'd be calling from a different place. But my wife shot him. Twice. He's critical."

"You guys have some kind of Bonnie and Clyde thing going? She'd definitely fit in with our culture. My sort of woman."

"She hates guns."

"Apparently, she got over it to save your ass. Anyway, there are things happening out here. The *Grand Forks Herald* has a young reporter on it, but he's way over his head. We don't have your know-how or resources. How soon can you be out here?"

"Probably tomorrow."

"Let me know and I'll pick you up. We have to talk privately."

* * *

Back at home in Georgetown, Mort looked at the living room carpet now stained with McCarthy's blood.

"Got to get this sucker cleaned," he said to Danni.

"No," she replied. "I want that carpet gone. Out of the house and out of sight. I don't need any reminders of last night." Danni was kneeling on the floor, stroking Katie's head. The dog was lying on the floor, enjoying the attention.

"The vet didn't even charge me," Mort said. "Probably because the police dropped her off, and also because they were aware of the shootings last night. Anyway, we'll shop around for a rug first chance we get."

"Whenever 'first chance' is," Danni said, "since you're apparently off to North Dakota again."

"Alone," Mort said. "But something important must be happening out there, because Clete wants to discuss it privately."

119

"Thank him for the jewelry suggestion," Danni said, "although it doesn't make up for your night in bed with Alison, innocent or not. Hope you won't be gone more than a week because I should be ovulating again shortly… matter of days."

Twenty-seven

Clete MacCauley met Mort at the airport shortly before noon. The two men shook hands warmly.

"Glad to see you," MacCauley said. "A lot has been happening around here. I think you can help us figure it out and get yourself a great exclusive."

"Have any other newspapers been nosing around?" Mort asked.

"Not that I'm aware of. But as I told you, the *Herald* put this young reporter on the farm issue right after Raincloud got killed, but they haven't been able to put it all together. Fire marshal confirmed the arson of Raincloud's farmhouse. With Tang dead, they put it to rest. But we've got a lot more to talk about. Have I got suspicions? That's why I wanted to talk to you alone. Anything concrete? No, but if it smells like a pig, et cetera."

"You're placing a lot of faith in me," Mort said. "But how about putting some food in me first. I've been traveling since six and I'm starving."

"Done."

In downtown Grand Forks, MacCauley parked in a no-parking space in front of an older, two-story building with a sign that said "Rhombus Guys."

"Looks like a mercantile business, not a restaurant," Mort remarked.

"Best pizza in the state," MacCauley said. "You're in for a real treat."

They walked in and were immediately greeted by a thirtyish barista behind the long bar. "How goes it, Sheriff?"

"Ricky," MacCauley said, "meet Mort Ahrens, the newspaper man from back east. Is there a table outside?"

"If there isn't, I'll throw somebody out. Rain just stopped, so, truthfully, you've got your pick. It's Monday—half-price on the large pizzas."

"We'll take a Deluxe," MacCauley said, "and I'll have your house brew." He turned to Mort.

"Me too," Mort said.

"Two Holy Hand Grenades," MacCauley said to Ricky.

"Coming up."

"Their house-brewed stout," the sheriff explained. "Distillery is in another building. You're gonna love it."

They walked outside to the patio, which was more like an alleyway between buildings. The Deluxe turned into a large pizza with Canadian bacon, sausage, beef, regular bacon, mushrooms, mozzarella cheese sauce and veggies. Mort stared in disbelief.

"Stomach pump for dessert?" he asked.

* * *

Following the meal, MacCauley took Mort to his office, which to Mort's surprise was located on the second floor of the Grand Forks Police station. Mort looked around—a receptionist desk in the outer office without a receptionist, another empty office, a small conference room, and MacCauley's personal office, which was large but sparsely furnished with grey government-issue furniture. The walls were adorned with animal trophies ranging from a deer's head to that of a small brown bear and several large fish. Clearly, MacCauley was an avid outdoorsman.

"I'm impressed by all the trophies," Mort said.

"Dumb luck and expensive scopes."

"I doubt that, but getting down to why I'm here and the perceived Chinese land grab and threat. I have Alison's notes, some articles, and notes about her dinner with Tang. I know she gave a statement, and I could use that too."

"No problem."

"Great, but I have to admit that cooperation with law enforcement is rarely so easy."

"You ain't in Kansas anymore, Dorothy," MacCauley said. "We work with them that can help us, and if you can get some answers, you're 'them.' We got limited resources, as you can see, and we'll take whatever help we can get if it's legit. You're legit, even if you are cursed."

"Thanks, kinda. You know, Tang was insistent that the Chinese were also legit, according to Alison's notes," Mort said.

"One—them that was here might be legit, but there's a lot more than Tommy Tang's assessment to look for. And two—Tang was only working for them a very short time, according to what we've learned so far. But he was apparently somehow involved in the land purchases before that, or whatever the hell they were. But we don't know for whom the bell tolls," MacCauley said. "Raincloud had compiled a wealth of information, according to what he said, but that went up in a cloud of smoke, literally, with his murder. So, who's behind all this? Tang knew, I'm sure, but he's not around to tell us."

Mort nodded and said, "That's the sixty-four-dollar question and what I'm here to find out. And to follow up on local suspicions about these bu.youts. Of course, suspicions need facts to back them up. What are your thoughts about this Chinese spy balloon? Was it a spy balloon or a weather balloon blown off course? The update indicates that it was a sophisticated spy balloon. But why around here? And what could that have to do with the land grabs?"

"Well," MacCauley said, "if they were spying on our missile sites in Montana, and they're looking to get close to the Grand Forks Air Base here, who knows?"

Mort was curious. He knew that the air base in Montana was the home to many missile silos and strategic to the nation's defenses. But the air base in Grand Forks was an unknown quantity.

"What's the story on the air base here?" Mort asked. "I got the impression from Deputy Comfrey that it wasn't much of a base. He said something about the air programs at UND being very important to the local economy. And it's clearly separate and miles away from your *international* airport, I see."

"International? Shit. A couple of flights from Canada. Not that much of an airport, but we got a couple thousand people who work at the air force base."

"I agree about the airport."

"As for Rich Comfrey, he sometimes talks about things he doesn't know much about to make himself sound important, plus some things he should know enough not to talk about. Not a heavy hitter to start with, if you know what I mean. And for the air base, it's part of our Air Defense Command. Used to be home to the air tankers, B-52s and missiles. Then they moved the missiles to Malmstrom in Montana. Wanted to shut Grand Forks down, I guess, which would really have hurt our economy, but then some Pentagon brain realized it would be a great spot for the unmanned Global Hawks—spy planes, if you will. Today it's home to unmanned and remotely controlled RQ-4 remotely powered aircraft. The air war of the future. Intelligence and reconnaissance. Just take a look at Ukraine and you can see how important unmanned aircraft are. And the Chinese know that too."

Mort shook his head. "I had no idea. You certainly seem to be in the loop, but as the sheriff, that's to be expected, I guess."

"My wife works at the base, a civilian employee, but I can tell you that this job couldn't sustain us without her income. And the base is only a few miles out of town. And take what Comfrey says with a grain of salt. He's a part-timer."

"Part-timer?"

"Yeah. Under the law here, I can appoint special deputies as the need arises. Comfrey is mainly a weekend deputy, and he's got other things going for himself, mostly funded by his wife, I think, and some of which I'm a little suspicious of. He loves to flash the badge, but he's not a source to be relied on. As for my staff? Look around."

"No one here," Mort said.

"Thing is, I've got thirty-three special deputies, but Grand Forks County is 1440 square miles, over 73,000 residents. Real spread out. Lot of ground to cover, and if you break that down into shifts, vacations, sick time and whatever, my office is spread real thin. So, you got it. My secretary—administrative assistant, if you will—is off today. If I need someone to cover the bars on the weekend, or there's a bad crash, or I just need a body, I appoint a special deputy."

"That gives me a whole new perspective on your situation. That information on the air base certainly would explain the Chinese interest," Mort said. "I'll get myself settled in with what's left of today and get an early start tomorrow. Probably at the university library because Alison said it was outstanding."

"Good place to start," MacCauley said. "You've got my number whenever you need me. This place will grow on you. One of the best places to live in the country. You'll see."

"And your winters?" Mort asked.

"Not nearly as bad as advertised. We were actually picked as one of the best small cities in the US by *Fortune* or one of those magazines. Just look into the future and picture yourself as editor of the *Herald*."

"I guess you can never say never," Mort said.

After a few more minutes, MacCauley drove back to the airport and dropped off Mort to get a Hertz rental. He gave him a copy of Alison's statements. Mort had a good feeling about Clete MacCauley.

Twenty-eight

At the registration desk, the clerk looked at Mort with a half-smile, or perhaps a smirk. He was a young man, probably late twenties, blonde with an open-collared shirt and a vest advertising "Best Western Harvest Inn."

"You return to the scene of the crime?" he asked.

"Have we met?" Mort asked.

"I was on night duty when all shit broke loose. I'm Reagan."

"Like the President?"

"Yeah. My folks were forever Republicans."

"Could be worse," Mort said. "Could be Trump."

"I would have killed myself already. You just in for the night?"

"I think more like the week."

"Tell you what—I'm giving you a two-room suite, bedroom separate from the living room and work area. Special price for heroes, eighty-nine bucks a night. Parking and breakfast included. That cute young lady going to be with you?"

"Don't think she wants any more of Grand Forks," Mort said, reaching for the registration card. "Nothing personal."

Reagan gripped both hands on the desk. "Too bad," he said. "That was the most fun I've had since I've worked here. Cops galore. To be honest, I didn't care for that Tommy Tang."

Mort was surprised. "You knew him?"

"Sneaky bastard. Lousy tipper," Reagan said. "He showed up that night—in the middle of the night—and asked for her room number. I figured he was in for a nightcap, if you know what I mean, and I gave it to him. Wouldn't be the first time he showed up like that. Never thought he was planning to kill her. He thought she was alone. You must have shocked the hell out of him. I mean *literally* shocked him." Reagan winked at Mort like a co-conspirator sharing a secret.

"Does the sheriff know all this?" Mort said.

"For sure," Reagan said. "It was just damn lucky you were there."

* * *

The suite was more than Mort had anticipated. The bedroom and bathroom were separate with a king-sized bed. A large living room had a sofa, desk, chair, refrigerator and microwave, along with a wi-fi hookup. He set up his computer on the desk, put away his clothes, looked at his watch and decided it was not too late to call Danni.

"How's it going, babe?" he asked.

"I'm glad you called," Danni said. "It's a little weird being here alone for the first time since... you know. And I wanted to talk to you anyway."

"You miss me?" Mort asked.

"Don't fish. Haven't had time to miss you yet. I've been composing a threatening letter."

"To who?" Mort asked. "Or should I say to whom?"

"To Simeon," she said. "The girls called me earlier. They read about your adventure in North Dakota and then what happened here, but the call wasn't about that. They joked that I actually held a gun in my hand but said they've been really busy with Simeon."

"Posing?"

"No, it's quite involved if you've got the time."

"So, shoot," Mort said.

"That's not funny either."

"I didn't mean it that way. Just an expression. What's their problem?"

"They've got their own problems, but this one is my problem. Simeon has a daughter who has been estranged from him. She told him to fuck himself and never talk to her again. Well, he got very depressed

128

because of the falling out with his daughter, really depressed, and decided he needed to see his *Reluctant Madonna* again, so he painted another picture of me. On canvas—full-sized. The girls said it was even better than the first one. This time, though, he decided to make copies, a limited edition, because it was so good."

"And because he'd make even more money from it," Mort said. "But you said he couldn't do that, right?"

"Well, I can't stop him from painting, but if it's me, or a reasonable likeness of me, I can sue. I researched it and I was right about that. And J.J. agreed, but he said that a lawsuit would just bring unwanted attention to the situation. Law schools are so skittish at the moment about political correctness, the U might just can me, or certainly stop my advancement because of the publicity. The 'nude professor' and all that. Imagine the tabloids. And Fox News. I'm trying to compose a letter to Simeon to explain all this but also to threaten—to get the idea out of his head because of what would happen if it became a court case and I won. It could destroy him! Especially after he's been put on notice. But on the other side of the coin, I don't want his breakdown on my conscience. Not over a stupid painting, nude or not."

"Wow. That's a lot of stuff. Need any help with the letter?" Mort asked.

"Well, you're the family wordsmith," Danni said. "If you've got the time, it would be great. And then I can send it registered mail, or have it served like a summons, and try to scare him into stopping."

"I'll get on it right now. I don't start on the land grab story until tomorrow. You should see the suite they gave me to work in."

"You're sure you can do this? There's more to the story, but that's for another time. I love you."

"And back to you. Or as Demi Moore said to Patrick Swayze in *Ghost*, 'Ditto.' Give Katie a kiss for me."

Twenty-nine

Mort stared at the ceiling, trying to figure out the best way to complete his Simeon assignment. He was looking for language that would assuage Simeon's depression but would also be acceptable to Danni. Finally, he concluded that the success Simeon enjoyed in the world of contemporary art probably meant that money was not his motivating purpose. Instead, it would likely be the response to his work if copies of the *Reluctant Madonna* were available and not just the original. Appealing to Simeon's sensibilities would be a far better path to follow, he decided. If that didn't work, they could take a threatening approach.

He recognized Danni's legitimate concern that a nude portrait, whether she had posed for it or not, could be damaging to her career. The notoriety of a portrait by a world-famous artist, which most people would relish, could have a boomerang effect in the academic world. The portrait was not something she wanted to have available to students for viewing. A portrait in the home of the Enrights was one thing, but multiple copies could be a disaster. With all that to consider, however, her sensitive side didn't want to send him off the deep end. The letter required finesse.

Privately, Mort thought that the portrait, whether she posed or not, was stunning, and Simeon's imagination only proved how talented and perceptive the artist was. After the kidnapping event, a year earlier, Mort had told his therapist that he was "awed," as he described it, that "a schlub like me" could end up married to such a stunning, intelligent woman, from a background so unlike his own.

He had always questioned his self-worth, and even his unquestioned success as a journalist, his photogenic memory and his winning several hundred thousand dollars on "*Jeopardy*" did not assuage his self-doubts.

He made several starts on composing the letter and ended up with:

Simeon,

Understanding both your passion for art, your unique talent, and in my particular situation, as the subject of your *Reluctant Madonna*, even though I never posed, I beseech you not to make additional copies or duplicate your efforts in any way or by any other medium, other than the original which was purchased by the Enright family. Your talent could have an adverse effect on me, and could be detrimental, if not devastating, to my career.

As an assistant professor at a law school, please understand that I am in a profession that has very high standards for the conduct of those who chose it as a career. Our lives are carefully scrutinized, and anything that can adversely affect us also reflects on the institution where we earn our livings. In that regard, your excellent portrait, whether I posed for it or not, is something that reflects on me and can damage my career, if not bring it to a halt, after many years of study and preparation. I need not say more.

I don't seek to litigate this matter, and while a single portrait is the right of the artist, making copies by whatever method, for sale or profit, is an entirely different situation. The artist does not prevail in those situations, and I can site numerous cases with that result. Your personal attorney can confirm this. I accept your outstanding talent, and we all have situations in our lives that we'd like to change, but be satisfied with your excellent portrait, and please appreciate the damage it can cause to me if you publish even a limited edition.

Therefore, I implore you, if you have any consideration for me, my feelings, and my career, not to make additional portraits, or copies of any kind, for the painting you titled, "A Reluctant Madonna." It will be the most meaningful gesture you can make.

Sincerely, (and signed)

Mort read and reread the proposed letter several times and then sent it by email to Danni, stating: "After much thought, love, I think this would be an appropriate way to deal with the problem. Your thoughts, Mort."

* * *

It was nearing midnight when Mort went over Alison's notes from the day she had spent in Grand Forks. He followed that by reading the articles she had printed out and decided to visit the university library in the morning to interview the librarian who had helped Alison, Alice White.

He washed up and looked into the bathroom mirror, disgusted by the image he saw. In his shorts, he sprawled across the large king-sized bed and fell asleep, waking up to an irritating pinging noise from his computer—an incoming message. The computer told him the time was 2:28. Groggy, he decided it could wait until morning.

At seven, Mort awoke and set out to practice some Krav Maga moves before showering—a cross body punch, a palm heel strike like the one he'd thrown at Tommy Tang, an elbow strike for an adversary behind him, and an eye strike. He graded himself on each move. After about ten minutes, he switched to kicks—a vertical front kick and a spinning heel kick. On his first attempt at a round kick sweep he lost his balance and almost fell, saving himself with an arm extended to the floor. His foot slammed into the desk, and his computer crashed to the floor, still operating. He shook his head in disgust and said, "Ahrens, you are a *klutz*."

After showering, he remembered the message he'd received late the previous evening. The message was from Danni. He was surprised and delighted that she fully endorsed his letter to Simeon:

> Mort, I knew there was a reason I married you – you are the master of words, you finessed the situation so well, while we both know I have a tendency to be impetuous. The letter is perfect, and I am going to type it on my office stationery (to emphasize the threatened profession), and send it by some method where he has to sign for it—maybe registered mail or Fed Ex. We'll find out if he has a conscience. I hope you're having a good night's sleep and hope you'll be back soon with your story in hand. I should be ovulating again shortly. Loving you in the middle of the night, Danni
>
> PS – Katie is here with me and she misses you already too.

Thirty

At the hotel's complimentary breakfast, Mort took coffee, made toast, grabbed a hard-boiled egg and sat alone pondering his day and the letter for Danni.

Mort got into his Subaru SUV and glanced at the GPS. It was just a short hop from the hotel to the Chester Fritz Library on the university campus. He parked next to Memorial Hall, an elevated parking garage, and walked past the law school to the library. The size of the brick building surprised him. Walking through the center entrance, he was equally stunned at the imposing double staircase leading to the second floor. Somehow, with his Washington mindset, he had expected something older and smaller. Typical Eastern arrogance, he said to himself. There is a large *rest of the country* beyond the border of the District of Columbia.

He mounted the stairs to a glass enclosed receptionist and asked, "Is there a Mrs. White, Alice White, available today?"

The young man behind the glass scrutinized him and said, "I'll check if she's on today. If not, I'm sure one of the other librarians can be of assistance. What's your name?"

"Mort Ahrens of the *Washington Post*." He handed a card through the slot in the window.

The young man's eyebrows went up and he made a call. After a moment, he said, "She'll be with you in a few minutes."

Alice White was about five-foot-five, stocky, with greying black hair, chestnut brown eyes and a dark, almost leathery complexion.

135

Mort guessed she was around sixty. She greeted him smiling with her hand extended.

"I assume you're Alison's boss," she said.

"Guilty."

"Lovely young woman. How is she after the ordeal here?"

"She'll be fine. In a couple of days she'll be right back in the mix."

"I read about it in the *Herald.* Dreadful. And you, I believe, are the *executioner*." She said it with just the hint of a smile.

"More than that, I hope," Mort said. "Maybe accidental murderer is more appropriate. But yes, just being in the right place at the wrong time. I have her notes and printouts, and I want to follow up to get as much information as I can."

"Let's start in the archive division on the fourth floor," Alice said, "because that's where your young lady left off. Do you mind walking up?"

Mort shook his head. "I must say that I'm blown away by this facility."

"Not what you'd expect in the 'boonies,' is it?" Alice said. "Largest library in the state—over two million volumes. Depository for patents and trademarks by the federal government, with a lot of special collections. We were just renovated a couple of years ago."

"How many librarians do you have?" Mort asked. "And *who* was Chester Fritz?"

"About four dozen of us," Alice said. "All different specialties and disciplines. Chester Fritz was a graduate, an unlikely donor of a million dollars back in the sixties. And the rest, as they say…"

"…is history," Mort finished. "Well, consider me duly impressed."

On the fourth floor, Alice led Mort to a workspace, pointed out the various archival locations, and gave him her cell phone number. "If you need anything, just holler," she said.

"I expect to be here in the archive for the day, maybe more," Mort said. "Can I at least buy you lunch?"

"I'd like that. Give me a buzz around noon, and I'll come to collect you. With most of the students gone for the summer, the Memorial Union shouldn't be that crowded."

* * *

The Memorial Union at the center of the campus was another new, immense building that housed all kinds of student activities, the student newspaper and enough food shops to rival a shopping mall. They agreed on the Dakota Deli and ordered sandwiches and iced tea. As they ate, Alice inquired about Mort's research.

"Well, I got a wealth of material," Mort answered. But there seems to be a lot of confusion about these land sales. When I finish up here, I've got to go out, roll up my sleeves, and put all these stories and rumors into some coherent form and figure out just what's going on—who is buying, and what the purpose of it all is."

Alice glanced at him. "Rolling up your sleeves is the easy part."

Mort smiled. "And the hard part?"

"Getting people to talk to you, to share their experiences, to give you the so-called lowdown on what's happening. They're not likely to open up even if you're trying to help them. Suspicion, and decades of being lied to by outsiders."

"What do you suggest?"

"Well, for starters, the usual victims of these small farm buyouts are small farmers, and more often than not, they're indigenous people, Native Americans. Always seem to be the first victims, if you look back on history."

"And?"

"I suggest that after you're done here you go to the Recorders Office and check out the land sales over the past several years. Then check with some of the farmers who sold their acreage. Why did they part with their land? You're going to be surprised at what you find. But you're going to need an entry plan."

Mort studied her. This woman apparently knew more than he had first thought. He needed her help, but first he needed her trust. Could she be the woman that Raincloud had referred to in his discussion with Alison?

"What are you getting at?" Mort asked. "Whatever it is, I'll give it a fair shake. Obviously, the *Washington Post* is already invested in this story."

"I know the *Washington Post* is one of the outstanding newspapers in the nation," Alice said. "And I appreciate what your team did concerning the scandals of that last president. Which brings me to you—Mort Ahrens, rescuer of a Supreme Court Justice and a man who solved crimes leading all the way to the White House. Plus, you dispatched that Tang character who was out to kill your associate. With an electric cord, no less. You are a straight arrow, Mr. Ahrens. What we Lakota call *Ozuye wicasta*, a warrior."

Mort could feel himself blushing. When Alice White used the words "we Lakota," he realized for the first time that Alice was Indian, like Raincloud. This issue he was investigating had deep resonance for her. But he could not accept that he was in the role of a "warrior."

"As usual," Alice went on, "the victims, are the little people. My people. And there's something else you should know. My full name is not Alice White but Alice Whitebird. I'm a member of the Spirit Lake Tribe, a sixty-year-old unmarried busybody who managed to escape and get several degrees, which is how I ended up at the Chester Fritz specializing in historical records and Native American culture. I can be your entry to people who would not otherwise give you a second look. We've lost hundreds of thousands of acres that were guaranteed to be ours by treaty, so everyone's motives are suspect. Even Mr. Bill Gates. But I suggest you dress down a bit to fit in a little more."

Thirty-one

As they were walking back to the library, Mort formulated a new plan. "There is nothing I'd like more than to have your help, Alice. Whenever you might have some time, I'd be honored."

"Well, I have tomorrow off," Alice said. "I've been saving some personal days because I wanted to spend some time at Spirit Lake. It's about a two-hour drive, and I'd be happy to go there with you, but plan to stay at least two days. Are you up for tomorrow?"

"You're on," he said. "This could add a hands-on touch to the story."

"If it can help my people," Alice said, "it's a no-brainer."

* * *

Mort revised his afternoon plans as well. He could always utilize the archives at the Chester Fritz, but the opportunity to get first-hand information at the reservation and a few photos was something he could not pass up. Checking out the land records at the County Recorder's Office could wait for a couple days.

He considered what Alice said about "dressing down" to make his appearance less intimidating, so later in the afternoon, on the way back to the parking lot, Mort passed Memorial Union and did some quick shopping—a UND sweatshirt. At Ross Dress for Less he invested in a pair of boot-cut jeans, two Farm 218 T-shirts, a Bison adjustable baseball cap, two button-down plaid shirts, a green fleece hoodie, athletic socks and a pair of running shoes. He figured Danni would be impressed when she saw the sneakers. He now had a completely new persona.

* * *

Back at his suite, his phone's "Cavalry Charge" ringtone announced an incoming call. He was surprised to hear Sheriff MacCauley's voice.

"How goes the battle?"

"Slow but fruitful. After a day foraging through the archives at Chester Fritz, I got some good background. But the best thing was meeting a librarian, Alice White. I'm going out with her to the rez to get some hands-on information," Mort said.

"Great lady," MacCauley said. "She just became an elder. Can open a lot of doors."

"She never mentioned that part."

"Got dinner plans?"

"Nothing special."

"I'll pick you up at seven. You can join Greta and me for supper. She wants to meet you, and she's also a great cook."

The MacCauleys lived in a simple, ranch-style home on the outskirts of Grand Forks. The building was about fifty years old with a front porch that ran the width of the building. Several Indian artifacts hung near the front door, which opened directly into a simple living room with a large dream catcher on one wall.

Greta MacCauley was a sturdy, black-haired woman in her forties. Mort immediately guessed that she was Lakota, and he was right.

Feasting on venison steaks, baked potatoes and mixed vegetables, Mort learned that Greta and MacCauley had been married for twenty-two years and had two teen children, neither of whom was home at the moment. The younger, a girl, was visiting a friend, and the older son was a student at the Cankdeska Cikana Community College at Fort Totten near Spirit Lake.

"Tommy will finish up there next year and head to UND," MacCauley said. "He's a hell of a hockey player, and a good shortstop to boot."

"Scholarship material?" Mort said.

"Free ride all the way. And then, who knows?"

"More important," Greta said, "is that he's studying indigenous cultures and natural resources management. Aims to learn about the background of our people, *my* people, and then bring back something that will fold right into a livelihood. Chances of making it as a professional athlete are five thousand to one, but with a solid education, he'll have a career."

MacCauley nodded. "And not end up as a small-county sheriff who needs his wife's income to make life livable."

"Oh, stop that, Clete," Greta said. "We managed fine before I was at the air base. Tell me, Mort, just what do you think you'll find about the people buying up our lands? Chinese? And what's the scheme they have?"

"If it's Chinese, or any foreigners, they can't purchase acreage under the law *per se*," Mort said. "But the buyers apparently have front men, locals who qualify for the purchases and then they allegedly run the show from the background. At least that's the rumor. The Chinese I met deny it's them. They claim just to be businessmen wanting part of the American Dream. I'm here to find out the truth. And tomorrow, with the help of Alice White, I hope to learn a lot more."

"Whitebird," Greta said. "She's one of us, a member of the tribe and now an elder. She should be a great asset."

"As you have been for me," MacCauley said to Greta.

Mort could sense great warmth between them.

Greta gave her husband a hug and then said, "Truth is, you only married me so you could get hunting and fishing rights on the rez."

* * *

Once he was back in his room, Mort decided to give Danni a call.

"I'm glad you called," she said. "I was going to call you anyway. I finished the letter and read it to the girls."

"Girls?" Mort said. "You mean Kimberly and Lynette, the salt and pepper duo?"

"Not nice," Danni said. "Anyway, they thought it was very effective, so I had it Fed Exed to them, express, and they're going to deliver it to Simeon personally tomorrow and get him to sign for it just like a Fed Ex receipt. They think it will be more effective if they add their influence."

Mort walked into the bathroom with his phone squeezed between shoulder and ear, unzipped and relieved himself. "That might be a good idea," he said. "And if not, we go to plan B."

"Plan B? What's that? A lawsuit?"

"No," Mort said, "that's our last resort. Plan B is what we come up with next. Maybe even visit him personally when I get back. Where does he live?"

"Place called Rehoboth Beach, Delaware— a resort community on the Atlantic. A couple hours from us. The Bidens have a summer home there."

"Why am I unimpressed?" Mort said.

"There's more," Danni said. "The girls were going there to spend time with him anyway, because he says he wants to change his will and leave everything to them after the blow-up with his daughter. It must have been pretty ugly."

"Family feuds are the worst. At least the girls must be happy."

"I think they're really concerned about his depression. The letter from me certainly won't help things. On another topic, when do you think you'll be back?"

"I have plans for the next couple of days and then snail work to do—searching records, interviews here and there. Maybe another four days."

"I was hoping you'd be home before that."

"Doesn't look too promising. I met an Indian woman who can be very helpful."

"I'll bet you did. They find you like bees to honey."

"Danni, she's sixty years old. A librarian and a tribal elder, for God's sake. And I'm not such a stud, except in my mind."

"Tell that to Alison," Danni said, "in *her bed*. It's a good thing I have that necklace to keep me warm."

"Kiss Katie for me," Mort said.

Thirty-two

Mort picked up Alice at her home, a small cottage near the university. Alice took a look at Mort's outfit—jeans, a Wrangler twill shirt, a Bison baseball cap and running shoes. "I was waiting for Mort Ahrens," she said. "Who are you?" Then she added, "Good look."

They piled in the "stuff" she was taking to the reservation—two cartons of food for her family plus a small bag of clothes and a bag of "whatever" for friends. Mort took his computer, a small carryon with toiletries and a change of clothes. The sun was up, and it was already quite warm with promises to reach the low eighties.

"You can thank Alison's notes for the outfit," he said.

"Smart woman."

When Mort was at Syracuse University, he had become fascinated by the treatment, or mistreatment, of Native Americans, the original owners of the land. Among the books lining his shelves in Georgetown were *Black Hills/White Justice*, *The Journey of Crazy Horse*, and *An Indigenous Peoples' History of the United States*. He had also read the horror stories about boarding schools where Indian children were placed for education but more often for mistreatment and even death. Some of those "educational" burial grounds were still being unearthed. The trip to North Dakota to unravel the question of who was buying up farm acreage and for what purpose was a bonus for Mort, an opportunity to put definition on what had been history.

As the miles rolled past, much of it flat grassland with only a small percentage of visible farming, Mort asked Alice, "Is this why they call it the Great Plains?"

"The real Great Plains, Black Hills and the Badlands, are to the south of us in South Dakota," she said. "But you'd be surprised to know that agriculture is our biggest commodity, with large farms making up most of it. Small farms and farmers are rapidly disappearing around here. We're among the nation's biggest producers of grains, especially cereal grains, and our unemployment is among the lowest in the country. The problem is that this year's tremendous snows have left the land sodden, planting is late, and the crops will be smaller."

"Why is the unemployment so low?" Mort asked.

"Probably because they discovered oil here in the fifties. The petroleum industry has flourished ever since. The downside," Alice explained, "is that despite all the job opportunities for locals, the oil industry brought in a class of workers who brought trouble with them. But that's not in this section of the state. Here everything revolves around agriculture."

"Still enough jobs for the locals?"

"Yes, but these oil folks, professionals allegedly, are from elsewhere," Alice said. "Nothing but trouble in my estimation."

They drove along in silence for a few more miles, then Mort asked, "What about your climate? And tourism?"

"Except for the Black Hills and the Badlands, mostly in South Dakota, along with Mt. Rushmore, there's not much in the way of natural attractions in the Dakotas. Maybe Theodore Roosevelt National Park. Summers can be hot and dry, and winters, with the wind blowing across the plains, get colder than a witch's teat."

Mort was surprised at her characterization.

"Why is it called Devil's Lake but the Spirit Lake Reservation?"

"The rez has had several names, but since the nineties it's been Spirit Lake. My people believed it was the home of an underwater serpent, *Unktehi*, so it was designated as *mni wak'an*, which means something like 'place of spirit water.' Early settlers thought that the meaning was Devils Lake, indicating something evil or bad—a Lake of the Devil—thus the difference."

"*Unktehi*," Mort said. "An underwater serpent. Like the *Loch Ness* monster?"

"A Scottish cousin," Alice said, smiling.

* * *

Mort figured he would check into a hotel near the Devils Lake Casino and spend the rest of the day getting familiar with the reservation. He expected Alice to line up some of the farmers who had sold to the Chinese for the interviews and then take care of her own business. Alice suggested that getting a hotel room should be last on the agenda.

As they got near Devils Lake on U.S. 2, Alice directed Mort to take a left on ND 29. As they crossed the lake, she said, "Welcome to the sovereign nation of the Spirit Lake Tribe, a member of the Sioux Nation."

"Do I need a passport?" Mort asked, jokingly.

"What you need is intellect, honesty, your computer and some good interviews."

"I can promise three of those. Not so sure about the intellect."

"I am," Alice confirmed. "The first thing I want to do is introduce you to Philip McKay, our leader, and an elder, naturally."

Even with his research, Mort wasn't sure what to expect. He didn't anticipate lean-tos and teepees, but he also didn't expect simple one- and two-story frame homes spread over a wide area.

"How large is the reservation?" he asked.

"About a quarter million acres," Alice said. She then added, "Our white fathers have been *very generous* to us with the Treaty of 1867."

She directed Mort to drive to Fort Totten, located within the boundaries of the reservation. There, Mort was surprised to find a modern industrial park with three large concrete and steel buildings.

"Bit of a shock?" Alice asked.

"Big surprise," Mort said, looking at the sign—"Sioux Manufacturing Corporation." He inquired what they manufactured.

"Bows and arrows," Alice said lightly, her eyes sparkling.

"No, seriously," he said.

"Mostly materiel for the Department of Defense," Alice said. "Kevlar helmets, panels, and now getting into aerospace prototypes. Government contracts. It's owned by the tribe and most employees are Lakota Sioux."

Alice directed him to tribal headquarters where Philip McKay was waiting. McKay had a ruddy complexion and blazing blue eyes. He stood about five-foot-ten with curly black hair. As they shook hands, Mort thought McKay looked more Irish than indigenous.

"A pleasure," McKay said before Mort had the chance to say a word. "Your fame precedes you, and I know why you're here—to investigate—but slip a good word about the reservation into your story if you can."

They retreated to the tribal offices. Clearly, Alice had already done the groundwork.

"I've lined up some people for you to talk to," McKay said, "members who sold their farms primarily outside the reservation, but one couple within it. They seem to be looking forward to great returns, as you'll hear. Coincidentally, the person they dealt with in most cases was apparently Tommy Tang, the gentleman who is no longer with us."

He said nothing further about Mort's deadly encounter with Tang.

Thirty-three

Clayton and Rose Little were seated in the tribal headquarters conference room. Mort wondered how long they had been waiting. Alice took off to run her errands. The Littles, in their late fifties, were both dark-skinned with black hair similar to the Indian stereotype Mort had pictured. Clayton was dressed in jeans and Rose in a housedress hanging limply on her body.

McKay did the introductions. "Mr. Ahrens is investigating the acreage sales. As you know, his paper is curious as to whether they're legitimate and not illegal. He is *waeinyepica, zonta.*

Mort's expression asked for a translation.

"Honest and trustworthy," McKay said.

"I try. And just call me Mort."

Clayton Little jumped in, answering an unasked question. "My family has always had the farm on the rez going back generations. It's one of the smaller farms. The Littles were very involved in governing, and my grandfather had been leader way back, long before Philip was elected. My brother Chet is the tribal chief of police and it's been a struggle on and off, but we managed."

"You chose to sell your property?" Mort asked.

Rose Little spoke up. "We didn't really sell, at least for ten years. That's the good part. That young Chinese man was very convincing. So far, we've had no reason to doubt him. He told us the corporation with the Chinese owning just a legal percentage of the land—in our case 18 percent, and other investors we don't know, legal ones—would all be part of a corporation in our names and each individual corporation, in the names of the other investors, and that we would get a guaranteed return for the next ten years."

"How would you get a return if you sold, or entered into an agreement? And when did this all take place?" Mort asked.

Clayton replied, "The company bought our farm over a year ago, with mostly Chinese money but limited Chinese control through this corporation thing. But they gave control back to us, at least regarding operation of the farm. We could continue working the farm for ten years, and each year we'd receive the amount of 10 percent of the purchase price, or whatever they called it in lawyer doublespeak. After ten years we would have received the full amount of the original price plus whatever we earned from the farming. In ten years we'd be too old to farm anyway, and our children are not interested in farming. Most of the children aren't. They moved to the cities."

"Wait a second," Mort said. "If I can understand this, after selling your land, you're continuing to work it as if you were leasing back your land?"

"Not exactly," Rose said. "It involved a lot of legal mumbo jumbo. Our first payment was due earlier this year and we received it. Thirteen thousand dollars. We sold the farm for $150,000, kept $20,000, and they reinvested the balance. In turn, we could do whatever we wanted with the $20,000. We still technically own the land, and we get the proceeds from selling the crops. But the best part is, even if it's a bad crop, or a drought happens or some other disaster, we still receive annual payment. And they pay the taxes. It was almost too good to be true. Well, it's not really taxes for us, it's fees to the rez, but those who own land off the rez pay taxes to the state."

As Mort struggled to understand this deal, he talked himself through it. "So you divested your farm for $150,000, gave them back or reinvested $130,000, walked away with $20,000 and a guaranteed income? Is that it?" He thought, *Such a good deal, it probably isn't.*

"That's right," Clayton said. "They invest the money we gave back to them—that's their business. They keep what they make on their investments, and we get our annual money plus whatever we can make from the land. We had to get permission because the property is on the Rez, and because of the restrictions on foreign ownership here in North Dakota. The restrictions are on farm acreage, but not timber or cattle or those kinds of things. The others who sold, or whatever you called it—divest? They owned their land outside the reservation, so they didn't need any permission. We got permission from Spirit Lake."

"Do you know how many farms have been transferred this way?" Mort asked.

"We knew of a few others around here. All the others were on private land. But there's a lot of farms in North Dakota, probably around 40 percent of the state's total acreage. Could be hundreds. Farmland is going for about two thousand an acre right now."

"How do you know the Chinese only own a limited percentage?" Mort asked.

"It's right there in the paper we signed. We got a copy," Clayton said.

Mort was already doubting that the Chinese he had spoken to in New York had been honest with him. He always felt he was not suspicious enough of people's motives. He remembered the electric carpet sweeper he had purchased for his apartment in Syracuse from a door-to-door salesman. It had cost hundreds more than he should have spent, a complete waste of money. The manufacturer was out of business within a year.

"What was the name of the Chinese company? Was it the Peking Group?" Mort asked.

Clayton shook his head. "No, it was some other foreign name. Rose has the papers. They registered it with whoever they're supposed to. And then we got a separate agreement about the money."

"A separate agreement?" Mort said.

"Yah, and they lived up to the bargain," Clayton said. "The best part is we don't have to pay any taxes. The corporation does. And we're not personally liable if things go south."

"Did you have an attorney?"

"No, he had one who set everything up. We got copies—that's all we needed."

Rose took a document out of her large purse and handed it to Mort. He looked at it and passed it on to Philip McKay who looked at the first page.

"It says that 'Nanking Operations' is the name of the corporation," McKay said. "It lists both of you and Susan Huber as owners along with Nanking Partners, which own 18 percent. Who's Susan Huber?"

"She's their lawyer. She's the one who drew up the separate agreement. Here," Rose said, handing Mort another set of several papers.

As Mort glanced at the second document, he asked, "Where does the money come from?"

"The Chinese, I guess," Rose said. "That young Chinese fellow said they have unlimited money to buy up property, and it's all legal."

"So, they reinvest the bulk of your money for ten years, and make money on it, and give you back 10 percent a year on the original price. You get to farm the land and keep the proceeds from your work, and at the end of that ten years they own the farm," Mort said.

Clayton nodded. "That's the deal. We were one of the first to take the deal, they said. And they kept their bargain."

Studying the second document, Mort said, "This is a lease I think, but I'm not a lawyer. You get to work the farm for ten years and take $20,000. You give them the $130,000 and get a 10 percent return annually on the purchase price for ten years. Am I understanding this correctly?"

Clayton nodded again. "We already got the first payment. We were smart enough to be one of the first around here to sell, and some of the others have been contacting us to make sure it's on the up and up. We got the money, and we told them everything was fine."

"Thanks so much for filling me in. Could I get a copy of these documents?" Mort asked.

"We have a copier here in the office," McKay said.

* * *

Once the Littles had left, Mort said to Philip McKay, "Like I said, I'm not an attorney, but something about their story doesn't ring true. There

150

is no pie in the sky." He held up the copies of the documents. "My wife is an attorney. I'll have her give this a look when I get back to DC."

"This is the first time I heard the whole deal," McKay said. "But if it's all registered and they already got their first payment, it sounds legit, don't you think?"

"Honestly, no. I think there's something in this we don't yet understand."

It was already four thirty, and Mort realized he still hadn't made hotel reservations for the night. It was June, and he didn't want to get shut out.

"Already taken care of," McKay said. "I used some clout, and you've got a room right here at the Totten Trail Inn—authentic Indian Americana—and I'm taking you to dinner at the Devils Lake Casino."

"We share the dinner costs," Mort said. "That's the way it works at the *Washington Post*, but what about Alice? I was supposed to meet her later."

"She's aware of the arrangements. Said she'd touch base with you late tomorrow afternoon, and if you're done with business here you can head back to Grand Forks. If not, she can stay another day."

"The Littles never mentioned Tommy Tang by name. Do they even know he's dead?"

"They do, and they probably know your part in it. Typical Lakota politeness not to mention it."

"How did they find out?"

"Might be a big surprise, but we have television out here. Get programs from as far away as Grand Forks."

"My bad."

"Besides, I know they were contacted by some official from the Forks after Tang was dead—you know better than anyone—to keep them from getting jumpy. I think a deputy sheriff."

Mort rolled that around in his head. Why would an official be notifying the Littles? How would any official in Grand Forks know about the business arrangement with Clayton and Rose? Who was that official? And who was this attorney, Susan Huber? He had some additional digging to do.

Thirty-four

It was now afternoon, and the sun was pushing toward the western horizon when McKay and Mort pulled up to the casino, an imposing, bowl-shaped concrete building, its exterior covered with Indian designs. The restaurant, called The View, was just that. Nestled on the shore of the lake, its guests could enjoy a great view of the lake through enormous windows.

The menu was limited but interesting. Mort ordered a large shrimp cocktail, French onion soup and a sixteen-ounce T-bone steak. McKay ordered the Captain's Platter—King Crab, shrimp and fried seafood.

As the waiter walked away with their order, McKay said, "I've asked a friend to join us. Should help with your investigation. Arthur Chambois is an agrarian, a college guy, but he's really up on anything involving farming in North Dakota. And farming in general. Should be a good source for you."

Arthur Chambois arrived moments later and made Mort feel like a midget when he stood up to shake hands. A beanpole of a man, about six-eight, wearing jeans and a thick wool shirt despite the heat, Chambois had a shaved head and a patch over his left eye. His right eye was the color of the lake.

Noticing Mort staring at the eye patch, Chambois explained, "Fishhook. I should have stuck to farming." He laughed at his own joke.

Everyone sat down and Chambois told Mort, "I know your mission here, and I think it's great that a paper all the way across the

153

country is investigating land sales in North Dakota. Farmland sales, that is. Law doesn't mean a thing to those foreigners, but we got enough of our own buying up farmland too."

"I know about Bill Gates," Mort said. "Are there others?"

"Gates has about 250,000 acres with his Red River Trust, which for my money should be named *mistrust*. But there's another Easterner, a guy named Malone, who has over two million acres of farms, timber and ranchland. Two million acres! What the hell does anyone need that much for? Set up agriculture corporations, corner the market, drive up prices? *Capitalist bullshit!* And then Musk, the Tesla guy—his family is involved too."

"According to what I read, Gates is interested in new methods of farming," Mort said. "In a recent interview he said he owns only one four thousandth of US farmland, and the reason he's into it at all is to make farms more productive and create more jobs. No ulterior motives."

"Right, and I can sell you a bridge in San Francisco. Look, I got my degree from UND, and yes, there are new methods being implemented all the time, and that's good. But shit! We don't need corporations or billionaires running the show—foreign or domestic. For sure, the little guy gets screwed again."

McKay chimed in. "The Chinese already own 400,000 acres of American land—prime timber—and they're looking to build a wet corn milling and processing plant right here. Buying up a lot of land near the Grand Forks air base and building another big plant near Becker in Minnesota for data processing."

"That's what got the locals freaked," Chambois said. "Why China? Why not *us*? Congress looked at the situation and said these purchases were not in their jurisdiction. If not theirs, then whose? The local politicians are finally starting to pay attention. They've been crapping around for years with a bill to restrict sales. But have you seen anything yet? I haven't."

"Still, farmers like the Littles are willing to sell," Mort said. "Doesn't make sense."

Chambois leaned in toward Mort and lowered his voice. "The farmers, they've been struggling. And look around. The Chinese already own America's largest meat processors right here in the West. And the Brazilians have a large chunk of our timber. It's a 'Show Me the Money' proposition. And that expression is probably one of the only good things to come out of a left-winger's mouth. I think it was Obama."

Mort smiled. "Actually, it's a quote from the movie Jerry Maguire with Tom Cruise and Cuba Gooding."

"Whatever," Chambois said, leaning back in his chair.

"I told you he was smart," McKay said to Chambois.

"How come there's no federal law about this?" Chambois asked. "Yeah, I know in a few states they're limited to how many acres of farmland foreigners can purchase, *allegedly*, but that's because the states passed laws, not the feds. Like right here. Talk, but no law. Instead of wasting your time out here, you'd do better to write about our Congress that sits on their fat butts and lets these crooks get away with this. They'll end up with the wheat, and our people will get the chaff—or I should say, the shaft."

"That wasn't my assignment," Mort said. "But I'll mention it to my editor when I get back. What I'm investigating is whether the Chinese are skirting the law with these farm purchases. Whether it's even the Chinese. And I've got more interviews tomorrow, thanks to Phil."

"You'll hear the same thing," Chambois said. "People getting older, the hard scrabble life, and those Asians dangling diamonds in front of their eyes."

"Then why would these locals take the deal and continue working their land?"

"Because then they'll sublease to some poor migrants who probably don't even have papers and who'll jump at the chance to stay in this country, even for pennies. Only ones who come out ahead are the Chinese or the billionaires or whoever else has the money to rob these poor suckers."

"You paint a pretty grim picture," Mort said.

"It is grim. It sucks. And our people can't keep up with all these new farming innovations. They can't afford them, they don't have the know-how, and these billionaires—Chinese or whatever, even

Americans—can virtually steal their land. Have you heard of vertical farming?"

Mort hadn't.

Chambois plunged forward, undeterred. "They build what looks like greenhouses and grow produce in vertically stacked layers. Buy up the acreage, use hydroponic growing methods in less space or on arid land, use less land and less water because it filters down from the top layers, expose it to the sun like a greenhouse and grow all sorts of exotic fruits and veggies, climate controlled. Musk's brother, Kimbal, is into that. *Easy* when your brother is one of the world's richest men."

Chambois was getting wound up. His single eye burned with intensity as he waved clenched fists like weapons. "In Spain they're using agrivoltaics in their vineyards—rotating solar panels that are off the ground. Requires much less land and produces a better crop. It combines solar farming with traditional methods—greenhouses with solar panels above, producing both crops and energy. You think our poor people can even fathom that? No, it's too costly, and now their property is gone, and these vultures can clean up and control the market."

Mort shook his head as if shaking out the torrent of information his brain was taking in. "But if the farmers are getting a fair price for their farms, and most of them will be retired in ten years, what's the harm?" he asked.

"The harm," Chambois continued, "is that they get today's price, give up their property, and then the big buck guys step in, take over and control the future. And there's more. Like seed technology, where they can grow in non-arable, hostile soil. But you need scientists to develop the seeds. You think our poor people can do that? No way. So, they're suckered into these deals for a few years and then they're out on their asses."

McKay joined the conversation. "That's the reality, Mort. It's bad enough that Indians have been screwed over again and again for centuries. Treaties? Not worth the paper they're written on! These new farming techniques—too expensive and too complicated for the little guy. This means the whole country, the whole economy, gets screwed."

Mort held up his hands as if surrendering. "Guys, at the *Post* I'm one of the little guys. My assignment is just to investigate the legality of these acreage sales. What you're describing is a whole new ballgame."

Chambois looked at Mort fiercely. "Nevertheless, see what you can do—what your editor, your paper can do. If we don't do something to protect ourselves, we'll lose this whole new ballgame in a shutout. The damn politicians are only interested in one thing, getting reelected and raising money—until their pants are on fire and then it's too late."

They finished the meal, shook hands and Mort gave Chambois a business card. He promised to stay in touch.

* * *

McKay told Mort there was one more important person to meet. At the other side of the reservation, they stopped at a simple, small, one-story building with a large dream catcher hanging next to the door. Before McKay could knock, the door was opened by an elderly, stooped man, a true stereotype of the American Indian. He was no more than five-foot-two or three and wore a baggy shirt, jeans and moccasins. A silver buffalo medallion hung from a silver chain around his neck.

"Mort, I want you to meet Charlie Wild Buffalo," McKay said, "one of our most respected elders. Charlie, this is Mort Ahrens from Washington. He's writing the story about the people buying up our farms."

Mort stuck out his hand, but Wild Buffalo ignored it and gestured them inside. The sparse living room had a large animal rug, probably buffalo skin, a single wooden chair and a table. The walls were bare except for a native headdress that hung near a closed door. It reminded Mort of a ceremonial setting, not a living room. Wild Buffalo indicated they should sit on the floor and lowered himself carefully, crossing his legs.

Mort felt he had been transported into another world. If this house had instead been a teepee, the illusion would have been complete. He eased into a sitting position.

"Bad medicine," Wild Buffalo said. "The spirits tell me these people are evil. No good will come of these sales. We have lost our land again and again, treaties and promises broken, and each time we have less than before."

"Well," Mort said, "that's what I'm here to find out. Are these sales legitimate? Do these purchasers have ulterior motives? Are they seeking to learn military secrets, find out sensitive material, threaten our democracy? I had my first interviews today."

"People only tell you what they think will benefit them," Wild Buffalo said. "But history tells the story of oppression, even death. My people have been victims for centuries, and what has a good sound often comes from mouths with forked tongues."

McKay said, "Mort is with a newspaper that has won many awards, and he was on a team that won the Pulitzer Prize."

"I know of this man. I read the *Washington Post* online," Wild Buffalo said, indicating the room behind a closed door. "I know he is both brave and honest."

Mort felt humiliated by his earlier assumptions about this simple old man, the simple, traditional home. He was surprised to find this old man was hooked up to the internet and reading the *Post* online.

"You are surprised?" Wild Buffalo said to Mort. "Behind my house you can see what connects me to the world. I wanted to meet you, and if I can help in your mission, I stand ready."

"I am honored," Mort said.

"Come, we will seal our friendship," Wild Buffalo said. "We will smoke." With that he got up and went into the other room.

In almost a whisper, McKay said, "This is a great honor for you. He is very selective about who receives his trust."

Wild Buffalo came back into the room with two pieces of a two-foot-long pipe. White fur hung from the stem. He carefully put the bowl and stem together and took tobacco from a pouch and placed it in the bowl. He struck an old-fashioned wooden match on a piece of flint, held the flame to the bowl, placed the stem in his mouth and inhaled deeply. A wisp of pleasant-smelling smoke curled out of the bowl. He took the pipe from his mouth and handed it to Mort.

"Your people have a tradition such as this?" he asked.

"No, not like this, but we have a tradition where once a year, at the end of the year, we blow from a ram's horn to wash away the sins of the year gone by and to welcome in the new. I'm Jewish."

"Ah," Wild Buffalo said. "Your people also know centuries of deprivation. Smoke."

Mort put the pipe to his mouth and inhaled deeply. Not a smoker, he started coughing and gagging. McKay and Wild Buffalo laughed.

"This is the sacred pipe," Wild Buffalo said. "C*hannunpa*, in the words of our people. It was brought to us in a time of famine by White Buffalo Calf Woman, carrying a message from the buffalo nation. She said that if the pipe was smoked in a time of need, such as famine, buffalo would appear and the needs of the people, and their wishes, would be granted. Then she walked outside, turned into a white buffalo calf and vanished. One day I will walk outside and disappear. But wishes will be granted by the sacred pipe. And so be it."

The pipe was passed a few more times. Mort inhaled carefully but could feel himself getting dizzy. It was a decade ago or more since he had occasionally smoked a joint in Syracuse.

White Buffalo stood and said, "Go, and your mission will succeed. My heart goes with you."

They stood and left. This time White Buffalo grasped both of Mort's hands at the door and held them tightly, staring intensely into Mort's eyes and chanting a few words under his breath. Mort couldn't understand them, but assumed they were in the native Lakota language.

In the car, Mort said, "That was an incredible experience. I'm totally blown away."

"You should be," McKay said. "I've never seen him respond like that to a stranger. It was very spiritual. You have been empowered."

Thirty-five

McKay dropped Mort off at tribal headquarters and gave him directions to the Totten Trail Inn. Walking into the kitchen through the back door, he met the woman caretaker, Shari, who showed him to his room.

The fort was a series of buildings that dated back to the 1870s. The restored buildings had been arranged around a large, wide-open yard. It had been many years since they had housed soldiers and stored their armaments and gunpowder. Most buildings had two stories, and Shari told Mort that the winters were often so harsh that the soldiers would sometimes get frostbite just walking from the barracks to the latrines. He noticed some uniforms on display as he walked around.

It occurred to him that this was an odd place to build a fort because the lake was not within view, but then he realized that the fort existed to control the Native Americans, the Lakota, and not to fend off foreign aggressors.

In his room, he tried calling Danni to tell her about his incredible encounter with Wild Buffalo, but she didn't pick up, so he went over his notes to prepare for the next day's interviews.

His room was like stepping back into the nineteenth century—large, with period furniture and a poster bed, a large rug with Indian designs. He imagined he was in a scene from a Western movie in which a woman in a calico dress was talking to Hopalong Cassidy. As a boy, he had loved the bravado of Westerns. Looking into the mirror on the back of the door, he couldn't resist a quick draw, pulling an imaginary pistol out of a fantasy holster and getting off a couple of shots. A brochure on the table informed him that the inn was a State Historic Site.

At last, he headed to the gift shop, which was still open. While musing through a large selection of Lakota and Native American gifts, his cell phone rang and he answered.

To his surprise, it was Sheriff MacCauley. "How's everything going?"

"Really well, almost magical. This is an extraordinary place."

"What's your projection on time?"

"Well, several more interviews lined up for tomorrow—probably take up the morning—and then we'll head back. I have a lot to digest, a lot of research and digging to do—and a lot of questions."

"Well, plan on dinner here," MacCauley said. "Alice is welcome as well. I have something special for you."

"I don't want to impose, but I do have questions for you."

"Greta insists. And when Greta insists, it's a command. Give us a heads up when you're on your way back so we can figure on the time."

Mort again tried Danni's cell phone—still no answer, so he left a message.

In the gift shop, he was confronted by a multitude of choices—artifacts, replicas, clothing, cups, even miniature pipes—and he browsed the entire shop. He looked at a replica wooden canteen that Danni could carry with her on her jogs, but decided it was too bulky. He stopped at a display of jewelry and fixed finally on a North Dakota Passport—a small, decorated notebook. He paid for it, went back to his room, made more notes for himself and fell onto the bed still reveling in his experience with the sacred pipe. He was asleep within minutes.

* * *

After three interviews the next morning, two of which were similar to what the Littles had reported, Mort met with Nathan Sleeping Horse, a weathered, muscular man in his sixties with a thick, grey ponytail that hung to his waist. He had a weathered complexion from years in the sun, and dark, deep-set eyes over prominent cheeks.

162

Nathan volunteered that his wife had passed a decade ago, they were childless, and his one hundred and sixty acres were becoming more than he could handle, even with help. He told Mort that after talking to others, he had sought out Tommy Tang and got an offer of $300,000 for his farm. Tang had provided names of people who might work the land, leaving him time for a leisurely life he had never enjoyed before. He received 10 percent of the property value—$30,000—and signed the papers a little over a year ago, giving the balance back as called for under the agreement. He had anticipated his first annual payment, but it hadn't arrived, nor had he been able to contact Tommy Tang.

Nathan knew of others who had been offered similar terms, but he didn't know if they had accepted. Describing himself as a loner, he was now getting apprehensive about getting his first annual installment. When Mort told him that Tang was dead, Nathan was shocked.

"What do I do now?" he asked frantically. He had not yet hired any "tenant farmers," as he called them. Mort copied the documents Nathan gave him and promised to follow up with more information as it became available.

Mort said to McKay, "Poor guy hasn't received his overdue first annual payment, which is disconcerting. The more I hear, the more suspicious I get."

Nathan Sleeping Horse barged back in and said, "I forgot to tell you—I was contacted by some sheriff, and when I told him the payment was overdue, he told me to stay calm and he'd check it out. Never told me Tang was dead. Never got back to me."

"When was this, and do you know the sheriff's name?"

"About a week ago. His name—I forget—Richard something, I think."

* * *

That afternoon, on the trip back to Grand Forks, Mort told Alice Whitebird about his conversation with Nathan Sleeping Horse.

"I know him," she said. "Kind of a loner, eccentric, big problem with the demon rum. I'm surprised he remembered that much. He probably drank up the money already."

"Well, I have a copy of his documents," Mort said, "and a lot of research left to do."

Mort mentioned that the MacCauleys had invited them to dinner.

"If it's all the same," Alice said, "I'll pass on that. Too much catching up to do."

Mort remarked how barren much of the land appeared until suddenly a farm would pop up.

"Be a lot more farms if so many of our people hadn't escaped to the cities," Alice said, "or died fighting to hold onto land that was ours by treaty and then taken away by subterfuge or downright savagery. We never really recovered from the War of 1862. And then Abraham Lincoln, the Great Emancipator, gave the order to hang thirty-eight brave Lakota warriors in Minnesota, the largest mass execution in American history. Think about it. Wounded Knee. Little Big Horn. All the treaties and compacts signed with the government—broken one by one. Then gold was discovered in South Dakota on reservation land and our people were pushed right out, treaty or not. And they depleted the buffalo herds as well. Left a lot of tribes starving."

"Dances with Wolves," Mort said. "I loved that movie for its realism. Taught me my only Lakota word—*tatanka*—buffalo."

"Well, you're going back a much more informed man," Alice said. "Not only with language, but very few outsiders have smoked the sacred pipe."

"Now all I have to do is put the pieces together and come to a coherent conclusion."

"Make sure you stay safe while you do that," Alice said.

Thirty-six

"Well, you're not scalped. That's a good sign," Clete MacCauley told Mort. "Did you get what you needed?"

"Had one of the most unique experiences of my life," Mort said. "I smoked the sacred pipe with Charlie White Buffalo, and—"

"That *is* incredible,' MacCauley said. "He's one of the most respected elders. No one ever asked me to join them with the pipe. But then, I have no jurisdiction on native soil."

"Must be my good looks," Mort joked. "The interviews went well. And I have a bunch of questions for you. So, what's this surprise you have for me? Will it make my day?"

"I suspect it might. C'mon into the kitchen."

They walked into the kitchen where Greta was standing at the stove with a mischievous grin. Another woman in an apron over a purple slack outfit was cutting up vegetables for a salad. She turned around with a smile even wider than Greta's.

"Danni!"

Danni couldn't hide her delight at Mort's surprise. "Glad you could make it in time. We've prepared a really nice meal."

For one of the few times in his life, Mort was virtually speechless. But he managed a few words. "How? When did you get here? How did you know who to contact?" He crossed the kitchen floor, wrapped Danni in his arms and they shared a long kiss. A tear escaped from Greta's eye.

Danni finally said, "I know your reputation with women when you're in Grand Forks, so I had to protect my interests." Then she confessed that she wanted to share some information with Mort and pick his brain. She also wanted to see Grand Forks for reasons he did not understand. She remembered how helpful to Mort the sheriff had been, so she did a little research, and two flights later here she was. Clete had picked her up at the airport, and she and Greta had immediately bonded.

* * *

After a pleasant dinner but before dessert, Clete excused himself for a few minutes and Danni cleared the table with Greta, leaving Mort to ponder what Danni had meant by needing to share some information with him. Greta returned to the dining room.

"Another terrific meal," Mort said. "Now I have a bunch of questions for Clete, which I hope he can answer."

"Not tonight," Greta said. "The questions can wait." She walked to Mort's side, leaned over and whispered, "Danni is ovulating."

Mort was stunned. "What?"

"She's ovulating. That's the real reason she came out here. She doesn't want to miss another month. I think it's so romantic."

Mort sat in stunned silence as Clete walked back into the room.

"I guess you both have to get out of here," he said, giving Mort a wink. "I'll see you tomorrow."

* * *

Danni and Mort headed back to his suite at the Best Western. While he was driving, Mort reached out and squeezed Danni's hand. "Just a quick question," he said. "Is there anyone who *doesn't* know that you're ovulating?"

"They're a great couple," Danni said. "Greta and I immediately related to each other, so I shared that bit of news with her. I guess she said something to Clete."

"As long as you didn't take out a full-page ad in the *Herald*," Mort joked.

At the Best Western, Mort stopped at the desk to get a second key for Danni. Reagan was at the desk and glanced in her direction.

"I got to hand it to you," Regan said. "You sure know how to end up with the lookers."

"She's my wife."

"Whatever."

* * *

After showering the next morning, as Mort was drying himself with a big towel, Danni came up behind him and affectionately squeezed his shoulder.

"You were terrific," Danni said.

"Which time?"

"Always the wise guy. I'm ready for a big breakfast. Downstairs?"

"Can't. I've got to deliver a message from Alison to Darcy, who owns a café here. You're invited."

"I just can't get Alison out of our lives, can I?"

He swatted her with his towel.

Thirty-seven

After ordering breakfast, Mort asked if Darcy could stop by their table. She arrived a few minutes later wearing her apron and a questioning look.

"Is everything okay here?" Darcy asked.

"Just fine," Mort replied. "I'm Mort Ahrens from the *Washington Post*, and I'm following up on the story Alison Powers was covering. She asked me to say hello from her and let you know she's doing well."

"Glad to hear that," Darcy said. "She's a nice young woman. Terrible thing that happened."

"Hopefully behind us now, but I'd like to pick up where she left off. By the way, this is my wife, Danni Rose."

"Nice to meet you." Darcy and Danni shook hands. "Send Alison my best, and breakfast is on me."

Danni polished off a heaping stack of pancakes, Mort an omelet.

"I thought you went light on the breakfasts," Mort said.

"I guess you energized me last night."

"Well, you exhausted *me*," Mort said, smiling. "After breakfast I want you to meet Alice at the university library. I need to compile my notes, then visit the recorder's office and check with the secretary of state in Bismarck."

"Danni said, "So I get to meet another of your women."

"You know, I'm surprised *Darcy* didn't say anything about your ovulation."

"Smart ass."

169

* * *

At the library, Mort introduced Danni to Alice, and they headed off together for places unknown in the vast building. Mort returned to the fourth floor with his notes and computer, then called Philip McKay at Spirit Lake. They had exchanged email and phone information.

"Philip," Mort said, "thank you again for those interviews. If you could contact Arthur Chambois for me, that would even be of more help. I'd like to get a list, with addresses, of all the people he knows who sold their acreage—the counties they're in, the contact person who represented the Chinese or whoever the buyer was, the names of their corporations if he knows, and the names of the attorneys who handled the transactions. If any of the sellers had their own lawyer involved, that name as well."

Arthur said, "Wait, let me get a pad and pen. That's quite an assignment." Arthur took down the information and said he would get to work on it.

Mort called Clete MacCauley and told him, "You guys have really been special to me—to us, so tonight we reciprocate. Dinner at the Toasted Frog. You pick the time and make the reservation. Just let me know."

Finally, Mort started compiling his notes. He spent most of the morning and the early part of the afternoon in the library and visited the land records office where he got information about procedures for recording land sales in the various counties. He also contacted the secretary of state's office in Bismarck and obtained the procedures for recording corporations and how he could get copies.

What surprised him was that none of the sales he had researched had taken place in Grand Forks County. He wondered why everything initially had seemed centered in Grand Forks, the home of Earl Raincloud. It had been Raincloud's suspicions that had started the entire inquiry, as far as he knew. Why the *Washington Post*? Why not the *Grand Forks Herald*? The *Chicago Tribune*, or the *Minneapolis StarTribune*? All of those offered impressive investigative reporting.

He would have been impressed to know it was the elder, Charlie White Buffalo, who had initially become suspicious of the transactions and had discussed the matter with Earl Raincloud. It had been Charlie White Buffalo who had recommended the *Post* and reporter Mort Ahrens because of the rescue of Justice J.J. Richter the previous year. Armed with that information, it had been Raincloud who started compiling the information that would be destroyed by arson and had called the *Post* specifically requesting Mort to write the story.

Thirty-eight

When Mort checked his phone the next morning, he found a lengthy message from McKay about his conversation with Chambois, who said he had compiled the requested information before Mort's inquiry and would forward it to his email because it was long and involved. Mort had not brought a printer with him, so he headed back to the Chester Fritz Library to download and review the information.

There were over twenty land sales of farms in and around Spirit Lake in the counties of Benson, Eddy, Nelson and Ramsey according to Chambois's account. In each case, the farms had been converted into corporate entities, with a separate corporation created for each sale—The Nanjing Corporation, with similar designations for Qinghai, Dunhaung, Wuhan, Hangzhou, Jiuzhai, and so on. In each case the formula was the same—the farmers sold their acreage for a fixed amount, had reinvested 80 percent of that amount back into the corporation and had then received 20 percent with the stipulation that an additional 10 per cent would be returned to them each year. During that ten-year period, the original owners could work the land and retain the profits derived from the crops. At the end of the ten years, the corporations would then own the land outright.

What particularly caught Mort's attention was an entity called The Wuhan Corporation, because Wuhan was the city in which the Covid virus had allegedly escaped or was born, leading to a worldwide pandemic. Danni remained with Mort as he compiled the information.

"Those are all names of Chinese cities," she noted.

"And there are different names of the Chinese corporations and investors," Mort said, "each of which allegedly owns only 18 percent of each sale initally, just under the allowed amount for foreign investors and possibly limited by pending legislation before the legislature in North Dakota. Also, the only other person mentioned as an owner, except for the actual farmers, is an attorney from Grand Forks, the mysterious Susan Huber, who represents these purchasers."

He explained the parameters of the transactions, and Danni recoiled.

"Jesus Christ, Mort!" she exclaimed. "This is a massive Ponzi scheme."

"A Ponzi scheme?"

"Yes, don't you see it? They suck these gullible investors in, keep 80 percent of their money, and then claim they'll pay the balance over a period of time. All promises. But they don't follow through. It might start out okay until the money disappears, and the investors get screwed. It's been going on for ages. This kind of scheme got its name because of Charles Ponzi in the 1920s. It starts out great, but then the annual payments dry up. By then, the scammers are gone. We teach about this in law school. How much is involved?"

Mort did a quick calculation.

"Well, the 80 percent from the farms that we know of amounts to about twelve million dollars."

"What about others? The ones you *don't* know about at this point?"

Mort just shrugged. "Who knows?"

"This is a big state. Not a large population," Danni said, "but with thousands of farms. We could be talking about a hundred million dollars!"

"If you're right we've stumbled on a hornets' nest. This sounds like something for the FBI. But I've got to be sure before we make any wild accusations."

They were already in the Chester Fritz Library, so Mort put in a call for Alice Whitebird. About ten minutes later, she joined them on the fourth floor, and he ran their suspicions past her.

"Good heavens," Alice said. "If this is true, these farmers will lose everything!"

"Everything except the property they were willing to sell in the first place," Mort said. "It's not the typical Ponzi, which Danni said involves only money or securities. But these farmers have given up title to their property and signed what I think are mortgages. That alone could lead to long and drawn-out court battles."

Alice grew pale. "And tens of thousands in lawyers' fees, which they don't have."

"We're not sure about this yet," Mort said, "but I already met one farmer yesterday who hasn't yet received his annual payment, which is overdue."

"What do we need to find out to be certain?" Alice asked.

"Well, all these transactions go through a lawyer right here in Grand Forks," Mort said. "She set up all the corporations. Susan Huber."

"I don't know her," Alice said. "But I don't know every lawyer here in Grand Forks. She's certainly not one of the best known."

Mort got on his cell phone again and called MacCauley. "Clete, do you know a local lawyer named Susan Huber?"

"Of course. She has a small office here in the city. Real estate and immigration law. She's married to Richard Comfrey, my part-time deputy. She's a Swiss-American. Why do you ask? Gonna take my suggestion and move here?"

Mort knew he had to move cautiously. Huber was married to Deputy Comfrey, and some of the farmers had been contacted by "a deputy sheriff" after Tang's death. Making allegations that proved false could result in a libel case that could destroy Mort's career and reflect on the *Post* as well. He decided to tread carefully.

"Nothing like that," Mort said, "but her name came up and I have to ask her some questions."

"Give her a call," MacCauley said. "She's definitely the brains of *that* marriage. Not Richard. Hold on, I have her number right here on speed dial." He gave Mort the number.

Mort turned to Danni and Alice and spoke firmly. "Not a word to anyone until I check this out."

Mort immediately placed a call to the North Dakota Secretary of State in Bismarck. After being shifted from office to office several times, he connected with a woman, Sylvia Sinclair, in the corporate division. After explaining his issue, she faxed him the information that she could find for each of the corporations on Chambois's list plus those from the people he had interviewed. All the charges were put on his corporate credit card.

A half hour later, his cell phone rang. "Mr. Ahrens, this is Sylvia Sinclair from the secretary of state's office. This is very unusual, but none of those names you gave me are incorporated here in North Dakota."

"What? Are you certain?'"

"Absolutely," she said. "If they were, they would have to be registered with us. But I found something even more peculiar. I took the liberty of checking further, and each of them is mortgaged here in the state. Could they be incorporated somewhere else?"

Mort was stumped. All the farmers thought they were dealing with in-state corporations. "Sylvia, I really appreciate your intuition here," he said. "Can you possibly send me at least the cover page and the signature page of each of the mortgages? On second thought, one complete set and the rest only first pages and signature pages."

"I can do that," she said.

Documents started coming out of his borrowed printer in the library within a half hour. One by one, as he reviewed the documents, he became more convinced that Danni was right. If this was not a Ponzi scheme, something certainly was amiss. None of the corporations had been registered with the secretary of state, but each had a mortgage registered with the identical information. Susan Huber was the attorney and First Isantanka Trust the mortgagee.

Once again, Alice was Mort's reference point. "Have you ever heard of First Isantanka Trust?" he asked.

"No," Alice replied. "But *Isantanka* is the Lakota word for American. So the name means First American Trust."

"This thing is really beginning to stink," Mort said. "The more I learn, the more suspicious I get. First American—that's you, the indigenous people, the Native Americans. I've got work to do, and quickly."

176

Thirty-nine

Checking for a local bar association, Mort found the Grand Forks County Bar listed on South Fourth Street, not far from the largest cluster of law offices. On its website, he noted that it was the oldest bar association in the United States. He called and was directed to the president, Diane Skol, who had a local law office. He punched in her number, identified himself as a reporter for the *Washington Post*, and received an invitation to meet.

Ms. Skol, a bespectacled brunette who was younger than he had anticipated, greeted him in her reception area. After the customary handshake and cursory introductions, Mort said, "I'm here investigating acreage sales to possible foreign entities and some other matters related to those sales."

Skol nodded perfunctorily and said, "I'm familiar with the kerfuffle, which has even got some of our politicians looking to change the law. I've heard of you as well. You got a lot of coverage in saving your associate a few weeks ago. We'd love to have you as a speaker for our monthly meeting, third Thursday at noon, if you're available."

"Not much of a speaker," Mort said, "and I hope to be back in Washington by then, but if the opportunity presents itself, sure. I just have a few questions about a local lawyer, Susan Huber."

"Susan? By all means."

"How long has she been practicing here? I understand she specializes in real estate and is married to a deputy sheriff."

"Correct. Susan was admitted here about ten years ago, originally from Switzerland but relocated here when she married. I've never met her husband. Susan was admitted on reciprocity without taking the bar exam because she graduated from a good Swiss law school. After the usual bureaucratic stuff, she became a member of the bar. Not active in the local association but pays her dues. I don't think I've ever seen her at a meeting, at least since she first joined. Doesn't attend our functions as far as I know."

Mort thanked her for the information and the speaking invitation and left.

The law offices of Susan Huber, LLC were located on Demers Avenue across the street from the Empire Theatre. Mort noticed the unusual cement-tiled sidewalk. The office had a plaque stating it was registered with the National Register of Historic Places. Most of the attorneys in Grand Forks seemed to cluster their upscale offices either in the downtown area or a little south of downtown. The Huber offices were between those two clusters in a more commercial area.

There were two large glass windows on each side of a plain glass door. One window proclaimed "LAW OFFICES" in large, gold leaf lettering, while the other window had the name "SUSAN L. HUBER, LLC," also in gold leaf. Under that name, in white lettering, was a phone number, email address, and the words "Real Estate," "Immigration," and "Mediator" evenly spaced.

Standing in front of the Huber office, Mort noted the street number. It was the *same number* that he had just seen on the mortgage documents as the address for First *Isantanka* Trust. Looking at the front of the building, however, he could see no indication that the Trust was also located there.

As Mort entered Huber's office, a bell tinkled. He was standing in a waiting room with a few vacant wooden chairs and a small, unattended reception desk with a large blotter but no phone. The walls featured several cheap prints. One door led to an inner office, and another closed door was off to the side near the entrance. He moved forward until he was standing at the desk.

A woman came out from the back room. She was tall, about five-ten, wore a vest sweater over a print dress and had loosely hanging, bleached blonde hair.

"Ms. Huber?"

"Yes?"

"I'm Mort Ahrens of the *Washington Post*. I wonder if I could ask you a few questions?"

She immediately grew suspicious. "About?"

Mort heard the side door open behind him but didn't turn around. Instead, he simply answered her question. "About some of the corporations you've set up involving farm and acreage sales, in which you also seem to be a principal. And about the mortgages. And also about the side agreements with the original property owners. None of these corporations listed in the documents are registered in North Dakota, apparently. I am curious, to say the least. Perhaps you can explain what is going on?"

A male voice came from behind him. "You know, you shoulda stayed in Washington, smart boy. And don't turn around because you've got a .45 pointed at your back."

Huber interrupted. "Richard, stay out of this. I can handle it."

"Not with this sumbitch," he said. "This has got to end right now. They *know* what's going on."

Mort glanced over his shoulder. Richard Comfrey was several feet away with a long-barreled .45 pistol in his right hand. Dressed in jeans with a wide-brimmed hat and western boots, Mort's first thought was that he was in an old-time Western with himself at the point of the bad guy's gun.

"People know I'm here," Mort said, which was the first thing he could think of. "It's not as though this is not going to come out."

"As far as *we* know," Comfrey said, "you were never here. You never got here. Maybe you got lost. With one shot, your next stop is the woodchipper.

Mort dived to his left, a *trap left* move, just as Comfrey fired. Mort spun, and Susan Huber, who was facing Mort, was struck in the chest and driven back as the bullet tore into her.

179

Shocked at this sudden turn of events, Comfrey hesitated a second and then bellowed, "Susan!"

That second was all Mort needed. He executed a right knee strike, grabbed the gun by the barrel—which he didn't realize until later was searing hot—and simultaneously brought his knee up into Comfrey's groin. Comfrey groaned and bent over, clutching at his groin.

Mort torqued Comfrey's wrist down, then punched out and yanked Comfrey's wrist upward and behind his back toward the shoulder in a quick move that put pressure on the man's shoulder. Comfrey screamed in pain.

To Mort's surprise, he had the gun in *his* hand. Almost by reflex, he pushed off with both hands and performed a vertical jump front kick. Comfrey, off balance, was driven backward and crashed through the front window, landing with his head in the street and his body still in the office. A large shard of the broken glass, with the name "SUSAN L. HUBER, LLC," wavered and finally fell, slicing into Comfrey's chest like a carving knife.

Mort was not the best martial arts student, he felt, but the ability to strike and save himself consumed less time than taking several deep breaths.

Clete MacCauley burst in with his Glock drawn and blurted out, "Mort, you okay? Put the gun down."

Mort dropped the gun. Only then did he realize how hot the barrel was.

"I never fired," he stammered. "I grabbed the barrel. His prints will be on the gun. He shot her in the chest," indicating the impaled man.

Mort glanced at the still body of Comfrey then turned to Susan Huber who was bleeding profusely from her chest. She tried to speak, but only bubbles of blood came out of her mouth as she gasped and then went still.

Danni ran in and grasped Mort in both arms.

Mort blinked, clutched Danni and said, "What are you doing here?"

"I had a bad feeling, so I called Clete. We got here a few seconds too late. Are you hurt?"

"I'll be okay, but I suddenly have to pee. And I don't want you ever to make fun of my Krav Maga lessons again."

She leaned up, kissed his forehead and said, "I promise. But you should never have come here alone."

Clete MacCauley felt for Huber's pulse then pulled out his phone and called 911 while he walked to the broken window to check the body of his deputy.

Forty

Within minutes, the Huber law office had more people in it than in the ten years of Susan's law practice. Grand Forks Police Chief Matt Neilson arrived, as well as two squad cars, two ambulances with EMTs and two men in suits who Mort assumed were detectives—he thought he remembered them from the Tommy Tang incident. A crowd of onlookers, curious about all the activity, started collecting in the street.

Mort stood outside the office with his arm around Danni, who was shivering. He realized that he was sweating. Trying to calm Danni, he said, "Maybe we're both in the wrong business. We should open a detective agency."

"Not funny," she said. "We're both professionals, not business people, and certainly not law enforcement types. You just seem to find these situations like some people find stray dogs. I'm just happy you're in one piece."

Mort expanded his chest. "I'm a tiger. Just happy you had a bad feeling and contacted Clete. How did you figure I was here?"

Clete, who was walking up to them, heard Mort's question. "Connected your inquiry with logic, mentioned Huber's office, plus Danni's intuition, and here we are—almost on time."

He looked at Mort and asked, "What's the name of that martial art?"

"Krav Maga."

"I think we might have to hire you as a trainer for our law enforcement people."

"I don't come cheap," Mort said.

Chief Matt McNeil joined them. "The EMTs confirm that both are dead. The detectives are taking photos now and will start processing the scene. Comfrey will *finally* make the front page of the *Herald,* just like he always wanted, if they get a reporter here on time."

"Great advertisement for the law office," Mort said, "except I think they're now out of business."

"The doc is on his way," McNeil said. "If you're both up to it, we can head down to headquarters and take your statements."

Dr. Elijah Cummings, the coroner, pulled up in his dirty, grey Ford Taurus. When he spotted Mort, he did a double take. "I didn't think I'd ever see you again. What'd you do this time?"

"Comfrey was about to shoot me but shot his wife when I ducked out of the way, and he died when the window crashed down on him—after I drop-kicked him through it."

"Your adventures are unbelievable," Cummings said. "But apparently you have a lot of experience." He glanced at Danni, who had separated from Mort's embrace.

"My wife," Mort said, "Danni Rose."

Without a beat, Cummings said, "My condolences to you."

* * *

Mort and Danni drove to the Grand Forks Police Department in a convoy of vehicles that included the sheriff, chief of police, and a car with two detectives. Forensics and additional personnel were arriving at the taped-off crime scene when they left. The modern police headquarters building was the home of the city's ninety-two licensed officers.

Mort was led into an interview room. Over the next hour, he gave his version of events that had led to the two deaths. He felt somewhat shaken, and when he went to sign his statement, he noticed his hands were trembling. Danni and Clete MacCauley also gave statements even though they had arrived seconds after the shootings. MacCauley was able to confirm that the glass from the window fell and sliced into Comfrey's chest just as they arrived.

"Even though we're witnesses," MacCauley said to Danni, "I think we can safely have dinner together. I'm calling Greta at her office." Greta suggested that they eat out, and MacCauley called the Texas Roadhouse and arranged for her to meet them there. Chief McNeil advised that there would have to be a coroner's hearing, unlike following Tommy Tang's death, and that Dr. Cummings said that it would likely be arranged for the following day.

At dinner, Sheriff MacCauley's cell phone rang, and he excused himself from the table while the others continued eating. He was gone about fifteen minutes, and when he returned he was with Matt Neilson who said, "Well, we know a lot more about lawyer Huber and Rich Comfrey than we did earlier today. The detectives found a wealth of material in the law office. So much so that I immediately called the FBI. This thing apparently has international implications, and they dispatched Katelyn Barrington, their local special agent. She was out on a border crossing case but should be here within the hour. I left word for her."

"What can you share with us?" Mort asked, thinking of his story, which was already burgeoning beyond what he had imagined.

"Obviously, I'm limited to providing details about an ongoing investigation," Neilson said. "But there were a ton of files and other materials. They took her computer, which she was apparently using and left on when she was interrupted by Mr. Ahrens. So my guys didn't have to worry about passwords or encryption."

"And?" Mort asked.

"And apparently she had set up some kind of private equity fund in Switzerland, or whatever the correct terminology is. She was the managing partner. I only know what the detectives found, but it was enough to alert the FBI because something is definitely going on here, and it's way beyond us. They found a file that indicated Rich Comfrey has applied for, or was applying for, Swiss citizenship. Looks like they were planning to flee."

Mort sighed audibly. "This thing has more arms than an octopus. What about the Chinese involvement? Where was all the money coming from for the mortgages?"

"That's another weird thing," Neilson said. "There were many individual files for the purchases of the farms, and each purchase had a Chinese corporate name. But there was a file marked "Investors," with percentages and amounts—big amounts, in Euros—and it had... wait, let me look." He fished a notebook out of his jacket and flipped through a few pages. "Had names like Abramovich, and... and Chernyshenko—hope I'm pronouncing it right—and Cherezov, Alekperov, Rotenberg, and so on. Those don't sound Chinese to me."

Mort almost jumped out of his seat. "They're not!" he shouted. "Those are Russians. Oligarchs—every one of them—and sanctioned by the US and our allies because of Ukraine."

Danni had been sitting silently, taking it all in. Suddenly, she raised her hand. "Guys," she said, "this is clearly international. I think the Chinese names were probably just a ruse to confuse everyone."

"A MacGuffin?" Mort said.

"What the hell is that?" MacCauley asked.

"A MacGuffin," Mort said, "is a device which is intended to throw you off. To deceive. Alfred Hitchcock used them all the time in his movies, like *North by Northwest* or *Dial M for Murder*. Here, we've been chasing the Chinese as the bad guys while Huber was apparently working with the Russians, if what the chief's people found is correct."

"Holy shit!" MacCauley said.

"Clete!" Greta admonished.

"Susan Huber was one smart cookie, although Rich didn't finish well in the mental sweepstakes. He was excellent with drunks over the weekends though," MacCauley said.

"Well, I don't understand it and neither did my guys," Neilson said. "Maybe they were waiting until they accrued enough money to live on for the rest of their lives in Switzerland. Just guesswork on my part, but remember—Susan Huber *was* a Swiss citizen."

Now it was Neilson who was interrupted by his cell phone. After a brief conversation, he said, "I've got to meet the FBI special agent back at headquarters, so excuse me. I don't know if we'll learn any more once they've taken the case."

Forty-one

As they cuddled in the hotel bed later, Danni said, "Well, you certainly have a way of finding danger. You're supposed to be an investigative reporter, not an instigative reporter."

"I don't instigate, but it seems to find me."

"Maybe it's just that you're too good. However, as I said to you on our first evening here, there's another reason I flew out to North Dakota. But if you'd rather wait until tomorrow, after the day you've had, I understand," Danni said.

"Well, let's see," Mort said, "today, I was almost killed and then killed the guy who wanted to kill me. No problem. So, what's this other thing?"

Danni rolled to her side and put her arm across Mort's chest, laying her head on his shoulder. This was very welcome by Mort but an uncharacteristic gesture from Danni.

"I think I'm going to go ahead and let Simeon keep that additional portrait of me that he apparently did as long as he doesn't produce a limited edition of it."

Mort sat up straight and almost dumped Danni on the floor. "What!" he said. "After the way you threatened him and carried on? If he painted another, what's to stop him in the future?"

"I did *not* carry on!" Danni said, firmly. "I just didn't want any nude—or semi-nude, as the case may be—picture of me in circulation. But I spoke to the girls, or rather they called me while you've been out here, and Simeon had this terrible falling out with his daughter which

I told you about, and it really affected him, and he's fallen off the edge, gone into a deep depression. On top of that, he's really in a funk because there's only one other likeness of what he calls *The Reluctant Madonna—me*—and when he got my letter, it almost drove him over the edge. It could be disastrous. It could ruin his career if he makes copies, to say nothing of the damage to his mental health. I don't want that on my conscience. So let him keep this new portrait he created so long as there are no more."

"What about *your* career? Doesn't that count for anything? You said this portrait could possibly cost you your job at the law school."

"J.J. was right, as usual," Danni said. "There are over eight billion people on Earth, and the chance of this second portrait ever surfacing to harm me is remote. Especially under the circumstances. I *never* posed. Weighing that against Simeon having a breakdown, or destroying his career, or worse, are chances I'm willing to take. He can keep it in his studio and look at it if that's what he needs to keep his sanity. But you've got to say it's okay with you."

"If that's what you want, of course it's okay with me. You know I feel that every woman has the right to control her body. But if he makes serigraph copies, it could also be very beneficial to Simeon's wallet. Originals? He could make a fortune."

"It's not about money. He doesn't need money. From what they say, his talent has brought him a ton of wealth, and it's just one more portrait, which he'll have to swear to keep in his studio. Money? They say he's been a wise investor."

"Maybe I should contact him for some tips."

"Mort, be serious. Balancing it against his state of mind, I'm willing to take the chance."

* * *

Mort suddenly sat up in bed. The clock said a quarter to seven.

Danni rolled over. "What's the matter?"

"My phone. My phone is ringing. Shit, what time is it?" He pulled his phone off the night table and looked at the time. "Who the hell is calling at this hour?"

It was Steve Ginsberg, Mort's managing editor.

"Steve, what's up?"

"Aren't you in North Dakota?" Ginsberg asked.

"You know we're here in Grand Forks," Mort said.

"We? Who's the *we*?"

"Danni is out here with me."

"Danni? Is with you? *Why* is Danni with you? Is that the reason you missed one of the biggest stories of the year from North Dakota?"

"What are you talking about, Steve? I'm on top of things."

"The FBI just released a statement—practically in the middle of the night. I just got a call from the desk. They broke up what looks like an international securities ring with local law enforcement. A couple of people were killed. That's what I'm talking about."

"Steve, I'm on that one, trust me. I was the one responsible for the ring being broken up. It was a Ponzi scheme, we think. Danni figured it out—hoodwinking farmers out of their land. I was going to put it all together this morning after I testify at the inquest and then call it in. Just need to piece together a few more facts."

"Inquest? You have to testify? Mort, you didn't…"

"I only killed one of them."

"Oh, my God. Can't we send you anywhere without someone ending up dead? And you said something about Danni figuring it out. Why is she with you? I mean, I don't object, but…"

"She came out a couple of days after I got here. Very personal reasons. But she's the one who figured out what triggered everything."

Mort heard Ginsberg's wife speaking in the background. "Dead? Who's dead?" Mort heard him turn to his wife, and say, in a low voice, "It's Mort Ahrens. He apparently got the answers to a big investigation. As usual."

"Anyway, Steve," Mort said, "I was going to speak to you before you saw it on the news. I didn't expect the feds to make a statement so quickly."

"With all the bad news circulating here in Washington—investigations, accusations—I guess they wanted to go with something positive they could brag about. Give me the lowdown."

Mort tried to quickly summarize what had happened, and how a deputy sheriff wound up dead.

"Oy! Do you need a lawyer?" Ginsberg asked.

"No, the sheriff was right there on the scene with Danni. He's a buddy. There'll be an inquest, hopefully later today, and then we'll head back. In the meantime, following the inquest, I'll shoot you as much of the story as I have."

"You know what? Put Danni on the phone."

"I'm right here, Steve," Danni said. "You're on speaker. Everything worked out, but Mort almost got killed. A couple of seconds made the difference. We're fine now."

"I can't wait to hear the details," Ginsberg said, "but do me a favor and wrap him in Saranwrap."

"Will do," Danni said. "And don't forget you still owe us that honeymoon trip from last year that you promised."

Forty-two

The small hearing room for the inquest was crowded with Chief Matt Neilson and two of his detectives, Sheriff Clete MacCauley, Danni and of course Mort all present. Also there was Greta MacCauley, who took a day off from her job to offer moral support and a young reporter from the *Herald*, notebook in hand. The inquest began promptly at ten, conducted by Dr. Elijah Cummings, the coroner, and was recorded on digital audio as well as with a small TV camera. Just as he began to speak, a woman strode in.

Katelyn Barrington was an FBI special agent stationed in the Federal Building. She had arrived at the trauma scene several hours after the deaths of both Rich Comfrey and his wife, Susan Huber. Dressed in a blue business suit and white blouse, Barrington was a lean, five-six African American. She looked around as she entered, and her eyes met Danni's.

"Kate!" Danni exclaimed.

"Danni! What are you doing here?"

Dr. Cummings, clearly rattled by their outburst, cleared his throat. "Can we proceed with the inquest, or would you two like to have time for a reunion?"

"Sorry," they both said in unison.

"Thank you," Dr. Cummings said, and the inquest proceeded. Mort explained what had brought him to Huber's office and the events that led up to the two deaths. Sheriff MacCauley confirmed that Huber lay dying on the floor as he entered and that the glass window had broken free and impaled Comfrey, resulting in his immediate death. Danni confirmed MacCauley's account, and Dr. Cummings entered his findings into the record with the time and cause of death in each case.

A Grand Forks detective, Jasper Franzon, confirmed the identities of the deceased and related some findings from Huber's office, including contents of documents that led to the FBI taking jurisdiction, but only after ascertaining that the only fingerprints on the .45 that killed Susan Huber were those of her husband, Richard Comfrey, although Mort's prints were on the barrel as he had said they would be.

Dr. Cummings concluded the hearing by determining that Huber's homicide death was caused by the gunshot wound from her husband's pistol and that Comfrey's was from the glass shard that had impaled him. He ruled that Mort's actions were justified as self-defense. The hearing concluded shortly after noon.

Outside the coroner's office, the *Herald* reporter sought statements from all the attendees but was met with a unanimous "No comment." Danni and Katelyn Barrington hugged each other warmly, and Danni explained to Mort that they had been law school classmates. She introduced Katelyn to everyone and said, "We lost touch after graduation, and here you are today. Incredible."

At Katelyn's invitation, Mort and Danni joined her for lunch at Ely's Ivy, which was near her office in the Federal Building. As they entered, Mort nodded toward the River City Jewelers store nearby and whispered to Danni, "That's where your necklace came from."

"I'll check it out after lunch," Danni said, smiling.

After their meal on the patio, Mort said to Danni, "I have to get this story out. Why don't you drop me at the motel and spend some time with Katelyn?" He looked at Katelyn and asked, "Does that work?"

"Love to," Katelyn said. "DC flew a team out to take over the case because of the international implications, so I'll have some free time. I can show Danni around."

* * *

Mort spent the early part of the afternoon writing the initial story on the land swindle plus the death of the Hubers, then emailed it to the

Post. Checking flight times, he discovered that the last Delta flight to Minneapolis was only two hours away and decided they wouldn't be ready that soon, so he booked a flight at a quarter past five the next morning. They would still be home in DC by late afternoon.

Two hours later, Danni came in, bubbling after her time with Katelyn and said, with a mischievous twinkle in her eye, "I know things that you don't know."

"I was counting on it," Mort said. "Why do you think I suggested it?"

"I just thought you were being nice," Danni said sarcastically. "Here's the poop—although Kate couldn't say much, of course. We pretty well had it figured out. Except the part with the Russians."

"And?"

"What's it worth to you?"

"Another night here in Grand Forks. *Toujours l'amour.*"

"Sold! Well, we know that Comfrey was renouncing his citizenship to become a Swiss citizen. His wife had apparently set up a Swiss-based private equity fund in a city called Zug—where a lot of financial outfits apparently are based—to buy up the farms. We already knew this. But it wasn't the Chinese, as we thought. It was these Russian oligarchs that she was getting the money from—illegally in most countries, but easy to do under Swiss banking laws."

"And the Russians," Mort surmised, "with all this cash, and under sanctions all over the world, needed some nefarious way to invest it. So, they sign on to this private equity fund. And no one knows they're the real investors."

"Correct, Sherlock," Danni said. "Huber was putting all these proceeds from the farmers into this equity fund after getting the mortgage money from the Russians. The transactions not only built up the fund tremendously but made her look like a genius to the Russians. And we're talking big bucks, at least two hundred million dollars, maybe more. More than enough to live a very good life as Swiss citizens."

"So, this First *Isantanka,* or First American, if you will, Trust outfit," Mort said, "gives out mortgages to these phony Chinese-named corporations and the farmers, and they get the money from Huber, who gets it from the Russians, and they give back 80 percent, and she sends this money overseas to this private equity thing that she set up, and it's now in Switzerland, and after a year or so, this phony trust stops paying, and the farmers are screwed."

"That's about it," Danni said.

"How much money does it take to set up a fund like this?"

"What's the difference?" Danni said. "The Russians are rolling in money—billions—with no place to legitimately invest it because of the sanctions. This deal is perfect for them. It's all under the table so they stay anonymous, except to Huber. Any one of those Russians could come up with twenty-five million or more without blinking an eye. Pocket change for them. Thus, she's sitting on perhaps as much as a quarter billion. She tells the Russians they'll get 7 percent, maybe even 10 percent back each year—with virtually no oversight."

"But the Chinese thing. Just a subterfuge, as we suspected?" Mort said.

"Definitely. Even your Tommy Tang. Or your *late* Tommy Tang. Kate couldn't say much, obviously, but the Grand Forks detectives found a lot of cash vouchers to Tang before the FBI took over, so he was obviously working for Huber and not the Chinese."

"But he was employed for a time by the Peking Group," Mort said. "Maybe as a double agent? I guess that was to put the blame on the Chinese for the land purchases, and maybe to spy on the Peking Group, as well. It was probably Huber and her husband who sent Tang to kill Alison in case she had seen him when Raincloud was killed. As I said, the Peking Group seemed legitimate to me."

"I wouldn't award the Oscar to them yet," Danni said, "although that was not part of my conversation with Kate. Once you told me about the spy balloon, the military drones at the airport, and the Chinese trying to build a facility near the airport—well, they might be legitimate, but maybe not. Plus, we know that you tend to be too trusting to begin with."

"Thanks a lot. I've got to get some of this down." He opened his laptop and then paused, thinking. "But what about the payments to the farmers. The 10 percent a year?"

"That's the likely Ponzi scheme part," Danni said. "That smelled bad to me from the first I heard of it. Sure, they pay for the first year, and maybe even part of the second—though I doubt they'd be that generous—and meanwhile Huber has accumulated a fortune that she has stashed in Switzerland. Then they plan to walk away and live the life of luxury in some cushy but obscure place in Switzerland. The money used for the mortgages came from the Russian investments, but the farmers end up with only a fraction of what they expected to get from selling their farms. Huber got the rest and put it in this private equity fund."

Mort was typing furiously on his computer, then looked up. "Unbelievable. Weren't they worried about being extradited back to the US?"

"I wondered the same thing, so I asked Kate," Danni said. "Based on her experience in the Bureau, and what she had heard, Switzerland is very reluctant to extradite people merely for financial crimes unless the amount is astronomical—like in the muti-billions—or the country where the fraud took place has the clout to raise havoc with the Swiss government. Native American families from the Dakotas, I would venture, would never meet that threshold. Sad but true. Indians have been screwed over for centuries, and the government has broken just about every treaty or compact with them—just as you said, as Alice said, and the people you interviewed on the reservation said. A prime example about non-extradition is the financier Marc Rich back in the eighties."

Mort shook his head. "Doesn't ring a bell."

"Marc Rich, who was very well connected with our politicians, swindled a fortune from hundreds of investors in the US, then renounced his American citizenship and fled to Switzerland, just like Huber's husband was preparing to do. The Swiss refused to indict him because it was solely a financial crime and because he had become involved in Swiss financial dealings and had donated a fortune to Swiss charities. Renouncing your citizenship to take advantage of Switzerland's perks is not that unusual. Tina Turner did it. Charlie Chaplin and Shania Twain as well. Even Sophia Loren renounced her Italian citizenship and opted for Switzerland."

"Let me catch up here," Mort said, his fingers flying over the keyboard.

"The Rich case is taught in every law school. Susan Huber certainly was aware of it. She just figured that she and her husband could survive the scandal the same way. And she was probably right. Rich, by the way, was eventually pardoned by Bill Clinton, which was another scandal by itself."

That evening, they had an early dinner with the MacCauleys because of their morning flight. As they were studying the dessert menu, Greta looked at her watch and said with a knowing smile, "You two had better get out of here and back to the hotel, if you know what I mean."

Danni blushed, and Mort said, "It's nice to have someone watching Danni's cycle." He asked for the check, snatched it when it arrived and said, "I've got this. I don't know how to thank the two of you enough. You've been great."

Forty-three

With several hours of layover in Minneapolis, they had time for a leisurely breakfast and picked up both the *StarTribune* and the *New York Times*. There was a short article in the *Times* about the events in North Dakota, but Mort said, "They don't have the good stuff. Wait till we publish my article."

Mort had taken the opportunity of booking them in first class because of the trauma of the past few days. After the plane had taken off, he leaned over to speak with Danni. "The poor farmers are the real losers, right? I mean they get screwed all around."

"I've been thinking about that," Danni replied. "I think the answer is not necessarily. Huber registered the mortgages, true, but never incorporated the businesses, as far as we know. If she never transferred the titles to the land, the only thing the farmers are stuck with is the mortgage. They got 10 percent of the purchase price, and if they get the land back, it will be like bonus money, except there will have to be a class action lawsuit to get it. But they'll still have their farms."

"What about this private equity company in Switzerland?" Mort asked.

"That will probably be dissolved under Swiss law because of Huber's death. At least I think so. Which means that even the oligarchs will get their money back, if they can maneuver it with the Swiss, or get lawyers who can do it."

"Do you think that she was also planning to swindle the Russians?" Mort asked. "We're talking about a ton of money."

"With all that money to play with," Danni said, "I think she'd just make even more money for herself and the Russians."

"You're probably right. And besides, people who get on the wrong side of the Russians either fall out of windows or die of poisoning."

* * *

They landed in the capital a little after one o'clock and after some shuttling arrived in Travalah to collect Katie and have dinner with J.J. and Chickie. Danni called Lynette and Kimberly that evening and arranged to get together that weekend. She didn't mention her change of mind about Simeon and the second *Reluctant Madonna,* figuring it would be a welcome surprise not only for "the girls," as Mort referred to them, but especially for Simeon.

"How is he doing?" Danni inquired, referring to Simeon.

"In a deep funk," Lynette said. "Just moping around, not painting. We're really worried. We thought maybe one of us should stay with him because he's so depressed."

"Well, let's see what the weekend brings. I think I've got a surprise that will bring him around."

"What?"

"It'll keep until the weekend," Danni said. She wanted to see the expression on his face when she told him she'd let him keep the second portrait as long as there were never additional copies.

After she hung up, Mort was staring at her. "Are you sure about this?" he asked.

"More so than ever after talking with Lynette," Danni said. "I want to see his reaction."

She never had the chance.

***

Two days later, Danni received another call from "the girls" and put it on speakerphone. Simeon was dead.

"Suicide," Lynette said, almost unable to control her words. "No warning, no call, no anything. We can't believe it. Kimberly was with him last night. And now he's gone."

"How?" Mort asked.

"He shot himself. We didn't even know he had a gun." Lynette broke down and handed the phone to Kimberly.

"He's gone—what a waste," Kimberly said, sobbing. "And now we have to plan a funeral. My God, there are so many loose ends we don't know where to start."

"*You* have to plan the funeral?" Mort asked. "What about family? This daughter he was fighting with?"

"What about his brother in Israel?" Danni asked.

"No, he disinherited his daughter, Melanie, in the new will he just signed. She was here recently, and they had what apparently was another huge argument. Must have pushed him over the edge. He was distraught, and we had to go to him immediately. Wednesday. He wrote the new will right there and called his brother to tell him about disowning her. But he never mentioned suicide. *Never.* We spoke to his brother in Israel today, who was very upset and asked us to handle everything. He knew we loved Simeon and that Simeon loved us. So, everything falls to us. We're heartbroken."

"When did all this happen?" Mort asked. He turned to Danni and whispered, "And everything includes the estate, apparently."

"We think on Thursday—yesterday," Kimberly said. "I left him on Wednesday evening. Lynette left earlier, but I stayed late. He seemed somewhat calmer with us here. I stayed, as I said, but..." she started to sob. Finally, she continued, "Then, yesterday, he didn't answer the phone. We called the police when we couldn't contact him, and an officer showed up at our door—we were his persons to notify. The medical examiner ruled it a suicide. Gun, depression, family troubles. Can you offer any suggestions on how to handle things?"

"We'll help, of course," Danni said. "Now I *really* feel guilty because I told Mort that if it would soothe Simeon's mind and help him battle his depression, I was willing to forgive the new painting of me as long as it never left the studio."

"Oh, my God!" they both exclaimed, in unison.

"It's already Friday," Mort said. "Where are you staying? I assume you're not at home."

"We're here at Simeon's. Surrounded by paintings. Hundreds of paintings. In Rehoboth, Delaware."

"We can get there tomorrow morning," Mort said. "You're right on the shore and not that far from us. A couple of hours. I just have to finish up the story I'm working on."

"And I don't have class yet," Danni said. "Where shall we meet?"

The girls gave Danni Simeon's address and said they'd arrange for accommodations nearby.

"You guys are life savers," Lynette said before hanging up.

"I don't think *life savers* is the appropriate expression under the circumstances," Mort said.

"Talk about guilt," Danni replied. "Now I *really* feel like shit. He died never even knowing that I changed my mind. I guess I'll have to live with that."

Forty-four

In his office at the *Post* the following morning, a Saturday, Mort met with Steve Ginsberg to update him on the facts with a fuller explanation of his adventure. The story was slated for the front page of the Sunday edition, another scoop for Mort. What the story didn't contain were the unverified facts, so he had finessed the "rumored" involvement of Russian oligarchs and the "alleged" existence of the Swiss account holding an astronomical amount of dollars or Swiss francs, attributing it to "unnamed" sources.

"You also cannot mention your role in the death of the two criminals," Ginsberg said.

"How can I do that?" Mort said. "I can write that in the first person."

"You can't," Ginsberg said, looking up as Alison Powers appeared in the doorway. "Alison will write a companion story, a sidebar if you will, about our *hero* reporter who solves the big mysteries but always seems to leave bodies behind."

"Steve, that's not fair. I mean, I understand what you're saying, but the 'hero' reporter part... please let's omit that. Besides, it was Danni who figured out the swindle."

"It is what it is," Ginsberg said. "And Alison," he continued, looking at her, "make sure you mention that part about Danni. Give her credit and try not to make our *hero* look too good. His reputation is going to kill us."

Alison smiled. "Well, it's a good thing. I know he saved my life."

Ginsberg said, "As Jack Webb used to say on that old TV show, *Dragnet*, 'The facts, ma'am, just the facts.'"

Alison looked at him, puzzled. "Jack Webb?"

"Forget it, Alison," Ginsberg said. "Before your time."

Mort briefed Alison, gave her copies of his notes, finished his story and was out of the office by eleven. Shortly after noon, he and Danni were on their way to Rehoboth.

* * *

On the way to Rehoboth, Mort was driving and humming "On the Road Again," the Willie Nelson favorite.

Danni interrupted him. "Despite what the girls said, I can't believe that Simeon committed suicide," Danni said.

"It sure sounds like suicide, from what they said," Mort replied. "Depressed, gun at his side, loneliness, big argument with his daughter. It fits the essentials. I will say one thing… he certainly didn't seem like the gun-owning type. Too much the artist."

"Look at you," Danni said. "You don't seem to fit the Wild Bill Hickok profile, but in retrospect, I'm glad you had that gun and showed me how to use the damn thing. But I agree that Simeon seemed too much… well, alive… to consider a suicide. With too much of an ego. I guess we'll know more once we get there. But remember, he was a religious Jew… didn't even pick up a paint brush on the Sabbath. Religious Jews don't commit suicide. They just *don't*. It's considered a sin, and they don't want to leave this life as sinners."

"Well, from what I remember from religious school my parents sent me to three days a week, religious Jews don't believe in heaven or hell either."

"I never heard that," Danni said. "So what do they believe in?"

"I was taught there is an afterlife, *olam habah*, which is the world to come."

"I don't know anything about that," Danni said. "My childhood thankfully omitted imposed religion except for recognition of who we were. I'll settle for this world, with all its blemishes, because that's the only one I can confirm. You're obviously far more Jewish than me. So, how *was* your bar mitzvah?"

"Definitely not worth the six years of after-school Hebrew lessons," Mort said. "And certainly not worth the money my parents laid out beyond their means to impress their friends and the congregation. I did wind up with a couple of thousand bucks and a bunch of *tchatchkes* though."

"Tchatchkes?"

"Trinkets, junk you'll never use."

"I see what you mean. Glad I missed it."

"And then the required speech I had to give," Mort mused. "Today I am a fountain pen."

"A fountain pen?"

"Yeah, well, if people didn't know you well, that was like the obligatory gift. I probably still have some, still unwrapped." Mort smiled. "I put them to use becoming a journalist."

Forty-five

They didn't know what to expect at Simeon's place. Yes, Simeon had been a world-renowned artist, and yes, artists and painters reputedly painted in studios or lofts, but Rehoboth Beach didn't lend itself to the stereotyped description of a community that housed artists' lofts. It was a small, affluent community on the Atlantic where people maintained summer or vacation homes. With only a population of less than two thousand year-round residents, the population surged ten-fold in the summers. The town boasted a mile-long boardwalk along the ocean and claimed to be "The Nation's Summer Capital."

After two hours on the road, Mort and Danni found themselves facing a faded, white Victorian-style home featuring two turrets, both on the same side of the house.

"Creepy," Mort said. "Reminds me of Angela Carter's "*The Bloody Chamber*."

"That was Gothic," Danni responded. "How about "*The Prisoner of Zenda*?""

Mort nodded agreement. "But I guess it made him happy."

"At least until several nights ago."

They were not even to the front door when both Kimberly and Lynette burst out, smothering both of them with hugs and kisses.

Finally, Mort said, "Okay, let's get to it. How can we help?"

"We don't know where to start," Lynette said.

"Well, for starters, is he buried?" Mort asked. "Has the medical examiner or coroner or whatever signed off that it's a suicide? Has there been an autopsy? How's that for a beginning?"

"He's still with the medical examiner," said Kimberly. "They said there are several cemeteries nearby… we just haven't picked one. We were waiting for you."

"Did you tell the medical examiner that he was a religious Jew?" Danni asked.

"No," Kimberly answered. "Should we have?"

"Absolutely," Danni said. "So that's a place to start. We'll call."

Mort interrupted. "No, a place to start would be lunch. I'm starving."

"We can call the SEED," Lynette said. "They deliver. That's what Simeon used to do when we visited."

Danni nodded. "And another thing we can do is get into the house."

Indoors, the questions began and so did answers. Simeon's body had been discovered by the police on the "welfare" check requested by "the girls." An autopsy was necessary because even though it was clearly a suicide in the medical examiner's judgment, Delaware law required autopsies in suicide cases. And then there was the .38 pistol that was still in his left hand.

Lynette and Kimberly had arrived within hours of being called by the police. Lynette reluctantly identified the body and promptly vomited because of the trauma. Kimberly had refused to take part in the identification and waited downstairs. The body had been removed to the medical examiner's facility and was still there.

"I don't see why they need an autopsy," Kimberly said. "The officers and medical examiner all said it looked like suicide. Why can't they let the poor soul rest in peace?"

"Has there been any notice in the papers?" Mort asked. "What about comments by neighbors or friends?"

"We haven't seen the papers," Kimberly said, "and he was pretty much a loner. Anyway, most of the year the town is deserted. A neighbor, a lady, did stop by when she saw the police cars, but this is a pretty large piece of property, not many neighbors. We spoke to her, and she was very sympathetic. But we haven't heard from her since. She thought we were his daughters because she's seen us here before, but she didn't even know Simeon was a famous painter. She left her name and number if we needed any help, but we called you right away."

Mort took out his phone and opened a browser. A half-minute later he exclaimed, "Aha!" He explained that he was curious why there had been no notice in the local paper, nothing picked up by the wire services, daily papers and TV. But he had discovered that the *Cape Gazette News,* which served Rehoboth Beach and several other surrounding communities, only published on Tuesdays and Fridays. If Simeon had died on Wednesday and the body was not discovered until Thursday, the first publication would have been on Friday, which was today. They would have to get a printed copy and see what the local press had written. Probably nothing—it was likely too late to make that edition.

The girls were so upset that they hadn't even contacted the art gallery that sold his art, or his agent. They were seated in the living room, which was furnished lavishly with antiques and thick, blue cotton drapes that blocked out the light. A rolltop desk sat in a corner with a Tiffany lamp sitting on top.

"He kept all his records in the desk," Kimberly said. "There's a bunch of them. He had a checkbook, but apparently lived by credit cards. And a bunch of records of his investments. A lot of them. Had a broker in New York. His assets totaled in the millions, I'm sure, which is probably not unusual for a world-renowned painter. And then there's this house, and whatever we haven't discovered in it yet. The art gallery, which also operated the gallery on the ship, still owes him a lot of money, according to his notes. And he has a safe deposit box at a bank in Philadelphia. Who knows what's in there? What are we going to do with all that money?"

"We?" Danni said.

"The new will— thought I told you when we called. After the fight with his daughter, she left him a letter that would curl your hair. She must have stormed out of here, written it somewhere local, and stuck it in the mail slot in the door. There's mail, bills and what looks like checks that we didn't open. He gave the note from his daughter to Kimberly to hold onto."

"This thing is getting really involved," Mort said. "It sounds like you're going to need really good legal counsel."

"We know Danni is a lawyer, a law professor," Lynette said. "Could you do it?"

"Far beyond my pay scale, from what you've said."

Mort told them, "We know some good attorneys."

Suddenly, the doorbell rang, or rather intoned the famous first four notes of Beethoven's Fifth Symphony.

"Appropriate," Mort said. "That must be the food." He walked out of the room and a minute later returned with two large bags marked "SEED Eatery."

"I see that he's got an alarm system," Mort said. "And what looks like a video doorbell, or at least something where he could see who's at the door."

They took the food into a large kitchen that had been modernized with a large center island accommodating six chairs. They sat around the island, and Lynette got glasses out of one of the cabinets.

"You obviously know your way around," Mort said.

"We've been here often."

I'll bet you have, Danni thought.

Forty-six

After lunch, Mort took out a small notebook and said, "Okay, let's do this systematically to make sure we touch all the bases. First, I didn't see a computer anywhere."

"He didn't have one," Lynette said. "Didn't believe in them. He communicated by his cell phone though."

"So, where's the cell phone?"

"The police took it but said we can get it back sometime."

"Next," Mort said, "we should see the rest of the house and then contact the medical examiner and see about burial or cremation."

"No cremation," Danni interrupted. "Against the beliefs of religious Jews."

"No cremation?" Mort said. "Seems like the sensible way to go."

"Religious Jews feel that the body is the property of God, and you can't defile it by burning," Danni said.

"For somebody who had no religious training, how come you know all this stuff?" Mort asked.

"I read a lot. And I did take a course on Judaism in college, just to find out what I was missing."

"Not much," Mort said. "And somebody should have told Hitler about that no burning bit." He took a deep breath. "Okay, burial then. We'll have to find out where to do that. Who to notify—"

A faint ringing sound came from another room. "My cell phone," Kimberly said, getting up and moving quickly to the living room. She had been unusually quiet.

209

"Where were we?" Mort asked, looking down at his notebook. "You said he wrote a new will. That will have to be probated. You guys have it, I hope?" Mort asked, looking at Lynette.

"Yes," Lynette said. "And that terrible letter from his daughter."

Suddenly, they heard Kimberly shouting from the adjoining room. "She has *no say* in this!" She's *disowned*! Out of the picture. She told him to go fuck himself! That bitch is probably responsible!"

Kimberly stormed back into the kitchen holding her cell phone. "That was the medical examiner," she said. "That bitch of a daughter called and said she's the only heir and wants the body released to be cremated. I told her we'd be right over with the will."

"Houston," Mort said, "we have a problem. Does it seem strange to any of you that the daughter knew about her father's death even though there has been no announcement about it?"

* * *

It was less than twenty miles to the medical examiner's office on Patriots Way, in Georgetown. Chris Knoblachy, an investigator, met them at the front door. "I don't know what's going on here," he said, "but we don't want to get in the middle of any family squabbles. This woman who called wanted to know how soon the body could be cremated."

Knoblachy looked at Kimberly and Lynette and said, "I know the two of you from yesterday. You seemed nice enough, but now I don't know who is in charge."

Kimberly waved several pages in front of her.

"We have Simeon's will right here," Kimberly said. "Melanie, the daughter, has been *disowned,* and *we* are his heirs."

"Well, we can't get involved with something like that," Knoblachy said, "so it's probably going to end up in chancery court. This thing is turning into a mess."

"Can I view the body?" Mort asked, which took everyone by surprise.

"I don't think so," the investigator said. "We don't do public viewings. And he's been identified."

Mort whipped out his press credentials. "The deceased is a world-famous artist, and if he committed suicide, that is definitely news for the public record. I'm a bureau chief in investigations with the *Washington Post*, and I've got to verify the ID before we write the story."

Mort took his notebook out of his shirt pocket, and said, "Let me make certain that I have the spelling of your name correct for the story."

The investigator hesitated, then nervously spelled his name. "For the paper? Well, if it's all right with them," Knoblachy said, indicating Kimberly and Lynette, who nodded assent. "I guess it's okay, but it still looks like it's going to end up in chancery court. Follow me."

As Mort passed Danni, she whispered, "Boy, you've got balls." Mort just smiled.

The mortuary room was appropriately grey with two large autopsy tables on wheels in the middle. The room had an air vent and overhead fan but still reeked of chemicals.

Knoblachy slid out one of four refrigerated drawers and lifted the white covering. It was Simeon, face-up, not that Mort had any doubt that it would be. Mort bent over to examine the bullet wound in the head. He noted a small hole in the skull above the left temple but didn't see an exit wound on the other side.

"For God's sake, don't touch anything," Knoblachy warned.

"That was the furthest thing from my mind," Mort said, "It's Simeon, all right."

Forty-seven

As they settled into the car for the trip back to Rehoboth, Kimberly handed a document to Danni. "This is the new will," she said. "We actually saw him write it and then we all went to a real estate office where the guy was a notary, and we signed and swore to it in front of him. The notary said it was as good as gold, said it was self-proving, whatever that means, and then we left. I think the guy might also have been a lawyer."

"This is all written in longhand," Danni said. "Cursive writing but pretty easy to read. If needed, a forensic handwriting expert could confirm it's his writing. And signature. I'll have to check that out." She flipped through the pages and said to Kimberly and Lynette, "You two are the only beneficiaries, except for a bequest to his brother. But you're *also* the witnesses. That might be a big problem."

"I hope not," Lynette said. "This is starting to get very complicated. We just want to bury the poor man and move on."

A lot richer, Mort thought.

Danni took out her phone and started scrolling. She was silent for a couple of minutes and then said, "Damn. A holographic will *is* good in Delaware, and believe it or not, the witnesses to the will *can* also be the beneficiaries. That's a new one on me."

"What's holographic?" Kimberly asked.

"Handwritten."

"Simeon said it was all good," Lynette said. "And so did the real estate guy."

Danni picked up the will again, reading a passage out loud. "'My entire estate, both real and personal, except for a bequest to my bother Mordecai, I leave to my dearest friends, Lynette Gilette and Kimberly Sims.'"

Lynette explained. "He was copying from his other will, which he tore up later because the realtor said to get rid of prior copies."

"Come to think of it," Mort said from the front seat, "I never knew your last names. You were always just Lynette and Kimberly. Or 'the girls.'"

"Let me get back to the document here," Danni said, reading again. "'I specifically omit and exclude my daughter Melanie Gold, as she had made it clear that she despises me and wants no part of me in her life, so I want no part of her in my death.'"

"That seems pretty specific," Mort said. "I never knew Simeon's last name either. He was always just Simeon. Do you think this will hold up?" Mort asked.

"Probably, if everything conforms to the statute. But it's very unusual," Danni said. "I've never seen a will where the beneficiaries were also the witnesses. Handwritten to boot. And even if the daughter's entitled to some share, by statute, the bulk of his estate will certainly go to the two of you."

Mort shook his head. "I guarantee we haven't heard the last of this, especially after that call from his daughter. I did ask the investigator about a Jewish cemetery, and he said the closest one he knows is in Dover. That's about sixty miles. I'm assuming the ME will release the body right after the autopsy, probably in a day or two."

Back at the house, Mort called the cemetery in Dover. When he clicked off, he said, "Jesus, dying Jewish is expensive. Oops, there's an oxymoron for you. Anyway, the plot will cost about five grand, plus the fee for opening and closing the hole, and then there's the casket and the expense of a hearse to Dover, and whatever other charges they can think up. I don't know who pays for an autopsy."

"*Que sera, sera*," Kimberly said. "Let's just get the poor dear buried as soon as possible. If that bitch tries to interfere, well…"

"*Que sera, sera*, whatever will be, will be," Mort said, "From *The Man Who Knew Too Much*, a 1956 Hitchcock film with Doris Day and James Stewart. Loved it."

"He's so smart," Kimberly said, holding her hand over Mort's head. "He knows so much."

"Almost a genius," Danni said, derision hanging with her words.

* * *

At Simeon's home, Danni and Mort were finally given a belated tour of the rest of the house. What previously had been a dining room off the kitchen had been converted by Simeon into his bedroom, and the first-floor guest bathroom had been expanded into an *en suite* with a double-sized shower and bidet.

Danni said, "A bidet? Obviously planned for the comfort of *guests*."

The king-sized bed was covered with a heavy silk duvet and multiple pillows, and the windows were covered with thick maroon drapes. The closet doors were made of hand-fashioned mahogany, and the walls were covered with paintings of Simeon's undraped models.

"I feel like I'm in a bordello," Mort said.

"And how would you know what a bordello looks like?" Danni asked.

"Kimberly never made it to the bedroom walls, but there is one of me," Lynette said, pointing to a portrait.

"Pity," Danni answered.

"Lynette was always his favorite," Kimberly said.

"Oh, that's just your imagination," Lynette replied. "He liked us both the same."

They moved to the second floor, led by Lynette. Kimberly opted to stay downstairs because she couldn't bear to look at that scene again, she said.

Lynette replied, "Again? You didn't go upstairs with the police when I did the identification."

"I just couldn't bear to see him dead," Kimberly said.

Simeon had removed most of the interior walls on the second floor except for structural beams. What remained was a huge studio with easels, paints, brushes and dozens of paintings, many finished, stacked against the walls. There was also equipment for silk-screening and a large collection of decorative pillows, several chairs, mounts upon which models could pose, rolls of canvas, stretchers, and a few frames of varying sizes. Prominently displayed on an easel near the center of the room was another *Reluctant Madonna* in oils.

"You look sensational," Mort said. "Even better than the first."

"Stow it," Danni said.

The wooden floors were paint-splattered in many places. In the center of the room, in a spot that had few paint splatters, was a chalk outline of a body.

Lynette choked up and wiped her eyes.

Mort went over and knelt by the chalk marks. He took off his glasses, wiped them clean and then bent over the spot that would have been Simeon's head.

"Almost no blood stains," Mort said. "Very odd. I've read that the head usually bleeds profusely from a wound. Did they wipe up this spot?"

"I think the technician took some samples," Lynette said, "but it was so upsetting I couldn't watch and went downstairs to Kimberly. She was really upset—jumpy. She worried me."

"Let's go back downstairs," Danni said. "Lynette's right. This place gives me the creeps, knowing that he was alive here just a few days ago."

Forty-eight

Back in the living room, Mort took out his phone and hit speed dial. The call was picked up after the second ring and Mort said, "Travis? Mort here. You guys got any plans for the weekend?" A short pause.

Travis Anderson had become Mort's close friend the previous year after Mort had saved Travis's life. Travis and J.J. had been close friends for over a decade, and Mort had become a beneficiary of that relationship.

"Mort, where are you calling from?" Travis asked. "I heard you were in the Dakotas."

"That adventure's over, I hope," Mort said. "Danni and I are in Rehoboth Beach, Delaware, and we'd like to offer you a few days on the beautiful Atlantic."

"That sounds tempting. What's the occasion?" Before he was named the head of the Supreme Court Police with a big assist from J.J., Travis had been chief of the thirteen-hundred-member police department in Montgomery County, Maryland.

"Just friendship. Plus, I just finished an important story," Mort said. "Join us on the seashore, you and Michele. With the Court term over, you probably need a break."

Mort could hear Travis apparently talking to another person, probably his wife.

"Where did you say you are, Mort?" Travis asked.

"Rehoboth Beach, Delaware," Mort said. "Just a couple hours away."

"Michele says yes, so it's a go!" Travis finally replied. There was a little more conversation back and forth, directions were given and Mort said, "Great!" and clicked off.

Mort turned to Danni and said, "Tomorrow, I want Travis to check this place out. And now, another question, ladies. No suicide note? No last words?"

"That's another strange thing," Lynette said. "Nothing. Gone without a word."

"What was his mood after the fight with his daughter? And who is she? Where is she?" Mort asked.

"He was seething," Kimberly said. "But more depressed than ever."

Lynette added, "His daughter, Melanie, is a chemist, lives in Kentucky. Something to do with the Kentucky Derby, or horses—something like that. Louisville, I think. Apparently insisted that she was getting married whether he liked it or not. I mean, she's not a kid—in her thirties, for sure. We have her phone number and all."

"Why did this upset him so?" Danni asked. "Loss of parental control of a daughter in her thirties? That would be odd."

"Her boyfriend, or fiancée, or live-in, or whatever, apparently has something to do with the horses, or the track. But what freaked Simeon out is that this guy has a criminal record. Assault, violent crimes, covered in tattoos, from what Simeon said. He thought the guy was taking her for a ride. Probably after her money. She wouldn't listen and left in a screaming fit from what we understand, then slipped that awful note in the mail slot. And then Simeon just lost it. Lost it completely."

"You said you have the daughter's note. Can we see it?" Mort asked. Kimberly left the room and returned with what looked like a photocopy of handwritten writing on a page of notebook paper.

"The police took the original and made us a copy." Kimberly handed it to Mort. Danni moved next to him and they started reading.

"This is pretty brutal," Danni said after a minute. "It certainly flies in the face of her calling the medical examiner like a concerned daughter and wanting to handle his funeral."

She read from the pages. "'It's always about you and what you want, isn't it? It's always been that way and sadly it will always be. I am done, and I'm guessing this is the last time we will ever communicate but I'm okay with that. I want no part of you. For now and forever, Fuck you.'"

"That leaves little to the imagination," Mort said. "But it also raises a lot of questions. Let's wait until Travis gets here tomorrow and I'll ask him."

* * *

The girls had booked Mort and Danni a room at the Boardwalk Plaza Hotel and prepaid for two nights. The Boardwalk Plaza was an imposing, Victorian-style structure right on the ocean. Mort and Danni rose up to their room in a glass-enclosed, ocean-view elevator. The spacious room featured reproductions of Victorian antiques, a king-sized bed, and a balcony overlooking the sea.

"Not too hard to take," Mort said.

"It's lovely," Danni said, "but are you really going to let them pay?"

"Damn right. They booked us for two nights, and I'll pick up the tab when they meet us here for dinner later. Also want to get a room for Michele and Travis, which *we'll* pay for. It was my invite. How about a little stroll on the boardwalk before dinner?"

"Maybe after dinner, in the moonlight."

"Sounds romantic."

* * *

Michele and Travis arrived slightly after noon the following day, Sunday, and drove straight to Simeon's. After introductions and bringing the new arrivals up to date on Simeon's demise, Mort asked Travis to check out the studio. "The chalk marks are still there."

"Ah, the ulterior motive for getting us up here," Travis said, grinning. "I knew there was a catch!"

"Hey, just because you're now with SCOTUS, you can't let your other talents dry up."

219

Travis smiled. "By the way, I brought you a present. Today's *Washington Post*. You've done it again. The lead story on the front page about your North Dakota adventure, as you called it, and a side story about you and your reputation for solving these things but always leaving bodies behind."

"Wonderful," Mort said. "I could have done without that last bit. Must be the story written by Alison."

"Well, she made you out to be deserving of a congressional medal. Even mentioned that you, Danni..." he looked over at her, "were the one who figured out the Ponzi scheme and came up with the Russian theory. Also has quotes from the local sheriff extolling Mort's brilliance."

"So let's deal with the problem at hand," Mort said, changing the subject.

They went upstairs and Travis inspected the floor. "Very little blood stain, as you said. If he was holding the gun to his head, and fell where they found him, I'm pretty sure there would be substantially more blood."

"That's what I thought when I first looked," Mort said.

"What does that mean?" Lynette asked. "Couldn't he have walked to that spot and fell?"

"If he shot himself in the head?" Travis asked. "Improbable he did any walking. At most, staggered a step or two. It might mean that the body was moved after he was dead, or..." and he paused.

"Or?" Danni asked.

"Or he was already dead when he was shot in the head. Once a person dies, the heart stops pumping out blood. But... this is only speculation," Travis said.

The went back downstairs, and Lynette asked Kimberly, "What was the last thing he said to you when you left on Wednesday? You got home after two in the morning—I was getting worried."

Kimberly paused, stared up at the ceiling, then wiped her eyes and said, "He said, 'I love you, and I always want you to remember that.'"

"Why didn't you tell me that?" Lynette asked.

"I was so upset leaving him, I don't remember what I said," Kimberly replied. "I still am. It was... was so devastating to see him so depressed. But he assured me that he'd be okay."

The women went into the kitchen. Mort and Travis remained in the living room.

"You said you inspected the body?" Travis asked Mort.

"Yeah, not a pleasant experience. I don't know why I did that."

"Which side of the head was the shot?"

After a pause to re-create the scene in his head, Mort said, "Left side, about here." His index finger indicated a spot right behind the temple. "But I didn't see an exit wound on the other side."

"Unless it was a high-powered round, the bullet is probably still in there," Travis said, "which is a good thing. If he stuck the gun in his mouth, his brains would be all over the place. Was he right- or left-handed?"

"I don't know."

"I'm going to have to train you better," Travis said. He called into the kitchen. "Hey, was Simeon right- or left-handed?"

A voice from the kitchen answered, "Right-handed. Why?"

"Just curious," Travis said.

"Where do we go from here?" Mort asked.

"I'd like to see the CSI forensic photos."

"Do you think the local police would have 'em?"

Travis scrolled through his phone and made a call. He talked for a few minutes in a low voice, then turned to Mort. "We're in luck. There's only one detective on the local force, nineteen patrol persons in all. They called in the Delaware State Police."

"And... that's lucky? Why?"

"Because the colonel, the chief of the Delaware State Police, is an old buddy," Travis explained. "Deb Boller and I went to the FBI National Academy together about a decade and a half ago. She's really good people. Worked her way from the ground up just like I did in Montgomery County. In fact, she recently invited me to a hundredth anniversary party here for the state police. Small world."

After several more calls, Travis said, "She's making arrangements for me to view the crime scene photos. We'll have to go to Georgetown."

"That's only twenty miles," Mort said. "That's also where the ME is located. When you say 'we,' does that mean I'm invited?"

Travis nodded. "And you can tell me all about your latest great case on the way there."

Forty-nine

The Delaware Department of Justice was a two-story, Colonial-style brick building fronted by six white pillars with a central entrance. When Travis and Mort arrived late in the afternoon, they found that Deb Boller had left instructions for Travis to view the photographs and any other forensics her detectives had gathered. They were ushered into a small interrogation room to study the evidence.

In one photo, Simeon's body was sprawled on his back, legs straight out, with a revolver a few inches from his left hand, arm bent at the elbow. He was completely naked. His eyes were open, staring vacantly at the ceiling, his right hand under his buttocks. His face looked contorted in pain.

"Holy shit," Mort said, "he's naked. Nobody said anything about him being naked."

"Maybe he wanted to go out the way he came into life," Travis said. "Seriously, though, I think that's very unusual. Plus, a peculiar position—gun in the non-dominant hand, but I guess you never know."

Travis pointed out the powder burns on the left side of the head. The investigative conclusion was death by gunshot. The report also indicated no exit wound. The photographs showed the weapon was a five-shot .38 revolver, with the chamber empty and four bullets remaining in the cylinder. Travis referred to it as a "Saturday Night Special."

"He must have had that gun a long time," Travis said. "I don't think they even make that type anymore."

The report noted that there was no registration requirement for pistols or rifles in Delaware. Mort looked at the report and said, "Another good Second Amendment state. And by good, I mean anything but."

The crime scene investigators had done a good job with measurements, but that data didn't lend anything to the suicide investigation. Since the apparent cause of death was suicide, and the weekend had intervened, an autopsy was scheduled for the beginning of the week.

* * *

On the trip back, Travis said, "Feels like we're missing something."

"Me too, but what?" Mort said.

"If I knew, it wouldn't be missing. How far away does the daughter live?"

"Kentucky, near Louisville, I think."

"What does she do?"

"Something to do with the Kentucky Derby."

"You don't know what?"

"She's a chemist, but I don't know what she does at the track."

"A chemist," Travis said thoughtfully. "What if she didn't go home after the blowup with her father? What if she hung around here in Delaware, or came back and returned to the house? Did she have a key?"

"She was the *daughter,* Mort said. "Only child, I think. Pretty *sure* she'd have a key."

"What time was he found?" Travis asked and then looked at the report, which gave him the answer. "A little after two on Thursday afternoon. Indications are he died sometime Wednesday night, according to the medical examiner. What time did what's her name—Kimberly—say she left that night?"

"I think she said around nine or so."

"So, maybe sixteen hours until he was found. Nothing seemed disturbed, according to the report, and your friends—who identified him several hours after the police got there—said everything seemed to be intact, including his credit cards and a little cash."

"But how does that explain the head wound, which apparently occurred postmortem if the lack of bleeding is a true indicator?" Mort asked.

"Maybe it was just an attempt to throw the ME off track," Travis replied. "You said the daughter was a chemist. Suppose she, or her significant other, poisoned him—maybe with some obscure poison they use on horses—thinking that an apparent suicide would negate any toxicology investigation. I've seen things like that during my career. Or suppose she somehow administered a drug that brought on a heart stoppage? This is far beyond my area of expertise, but possibilities abound."

Mort smiled and patted Travis on the shoulder. "You, my friend, have just opened up a huge can of worms. You know, Danni pointed out that he was religious—that he would never have committed suicide, even depressed as he was, because it would be considered a sin and prevent him from an afterlife. And then there's the lack of blood. Was he already dead when he was shot in the head?"

"Okay, another problem," Travis said. "We were told he was right-handed, yet the gun was found inches from his left hand, the non-dominant hand, and the bullet wound was on the left side of the head. Surely his daughter would not have made *that* mistake."

"Unless..." Mort said, "unless it was the boyfriend who pulled the trigger and didn't know Simeon's dominant hand."

Travis sat back and closed his eyes, thinking. "Unlikely, unless the daughter wasn't there, and the killing was done by the boyfriend."

Now it was Mort who paused in thought as he stared ahead at the highway. "Also unlikely," Mort said, "because I can't imagine she left him alone to fake the suicide, especially since she knew the layout of the house and he probably didn't. Or maybe she didn't think he was bright enough to handle it without her."

"Okay," Travis said, "let's suppose she slipped him some sort of poison— there are several that can affect the heart—and probably some that can put a horse down that we don't even know about. So she gave the boyfriend the house key, knowing her father would be dead by then, and had him fake the suicide, and figured she could trust him enough to handle a phony suicide, especially thinking that her father's state of mind and the traumatic events of the final argument between them would be enough to throw the investigators off. No autopsy was necessary."

"A possibility," Mort said, "especially if she didn't know that Delaware mandates autopsies in cases of suicide. I wonder what the law is in Kentucky where she lives. I'll have Danni check that out. And then, of course, there's the fact that the daughter had no way of knowing that he had immediately changed his will and left the bulk of his estate to Kimberly and Lynette. That must have come as a shock, thus the call to the medical examiner saying she wanted the body cremated, which was a way to get rid of the poison evidence quickly. Imagine when she found out that the girls, as I call them, had replaced her as heirs."

"On the other hand," Travis said, "how did she know he was dead if no announcement had been made? Even Kimberly and Lynette didn't know until after the police called following the welfare check. I'm also curious about why Kimberly didn't get home to Maryland until after two in the morning if she left at nine and the old man was okay, or said he was. That's five hours for a trip which should only take half that long."

"Maybe she was just distraught about the events that had gone down."

"But if he was still alive, and said he was okay... How well do you know these two?" Travis asked.

"We met them on our cruise. When I got sent to North Dakota, Danni spent a lot of time with them, so she knows them much better than I do. Why?"

"An estate possibly worth a fortune is a mighty big temptation if you know you're the beneficiaries."

"Hard to imagine," Mort said as they arrived back in Rehoboth. "They seem to be just a fun-loving and happy couple, interior decorators by trade. Danni had a great time with them, she said, which took a lot of pressure off me for having to leave."

"What do you know about their finances?"

"Me? Nothing. I don't think Danni does either."

"You know what the Bible says. 'The love of money is the root of all evil.'"

Mort looked astonished. "Since when are you quoting from the Bible? That's a side of you I never saw."

"All those Sundays back in Detroit when my mother made me go to church," Travis said. "I'd like to think I retained something."

* * *

The porch on Simeon's home wrapped around the entire front and side of the building. Strangely, there was no furniture on the porch—no chairs, no recliners, nothing for a person to rest on or relax. Clearly, Simeon was not one to lounge on the porch.

Travis sat balancing on the banister, a phone pressed to his ear. "Deb," he said, "thanks again to your people in Georgetown for the heads up. I looked at the material and have some observations, if you don't mind."

"Glad to hear your thoughts," Deb Boller said from her backyard as her husband was preparing to barbeque. "I also spoke to the investigating detective for his thoughts. When we got the call, I don't think we realized we had a world-famous artist at the center of it."

Deb Boller and Travis had met while training at the FBI National Academy in 2008, when both were officers from their respective police forces, Travis with the Montgomery County Police in Maryland, and Boller as a patrol officer with the Delaware State Police. They had bonded and remained fast friends yet had never shared a case as they rose to the top of their respective departments.

"Really nice HQ you have there," Travis said. "Do you get a lot of action from Rehoboth?"

"Most stuff they can handle locally. We get maybe a few serious calls during the year. Not necessarily cases that require an autopsy though."

"Noticed a lack of blood at the scene of the alleged suicide," Travis said.

"My guy is on it. He plans to do further investigation at the scene and ask more questions of that woman who was apparently last to see

227

the deceased alive. Unusual as well to find the deceased naked. We'll have the autopsy probably tomorrow. Should give us some more info."

Travis nodded even though Deb couldn't see him. "A good friend says that as a religious Jew, the deceased would not ever have contemplated suicide."

"That's yet another aspect for us to factor in," Boller said. "And if he was already dead when shot in the head, the can of worms opens."

"There's a family angle," Travis said, "a rather severe argument with a daughter right before his death, and apparently an estate of some size."

"The estate situation is a matter for the chancery court," Boller said. "They're welcome to it. I'll be satisfied if we put the cause of death to bed, if you know what I mean."

"I'm with you on that," Travis said. "Truth is, I *thought* I was just invited down here for a weekend on the shore."

"Enjoy it while you can. I'll keep you in the loop."

Fifty

As Mort, Danni and the Andersons prepared to leave on Sunday evening, Kimberly asked, "Will I be all right talking to that detective tomorrow without anyone here?"

"Thanks a lot," Lynette said. "You know I'll be here, right?"

"You *know* what I mean. But I'm nervous."

"Just tell the truth," Travis said. "I'm sure it will be okay. He's just tying up the loose ends. The autopsy will probably answer any questions."

"Whether Simeon would like the autopsy or not," Mort said. "I'm sure that God makes exceptions when it's mandated by law. By the way, did you know he was stark naked when they found him?"

"Naked?" Lynette almost screamed. "Why would he have been naked?" She looked at Kimberly, questioning.

Kimberly closed her eyes and shook her head.

Once she was alone with Kimberly, Lynette asked, "Why *did* you get home so late? It was long after I got back. I was really getting worried."

"Maybe I left later than I thought," Kimberly said. "That whole thing with the daughter, and his state of mind… I don't know. It was all so upsetting."

* * *

Roland Fitzgerald set a tape recorder on the large island and opened a notebook with his pen ready. A sergeant with the Criminal Investigations Unit of the Delaware State Police, he was about forty, handsome with thinning hair and dressed in civilian clothes. He sat in Simeon's kitchen with Lynette and Kimberly, accompanied by Janet Nowicki who was in her trooper's uniform. Danni and Mort were not present.

"Can I get you something to drink?" Lynette asked.

"No, we're fine," Fitzgerald answered for both of them. "I'd just like to tie this thing down as quickly as possible with a few more questions. You were both pretty shook up when we were here last week."

"I'm still pretty rattled," Kimberly said. "We talked about one of us staying over with Simeon, but he insisted he was okay, so I left a few hours after Lynette."

"You said somewhere around nine or ten?"

"Well, I might have been wrong about that," Kimberly said, "because Lynette told me I didn't get home until sometime after two. I drove slowly because I was so upset. It still would only take about three hours to Timonium."

"Maryland, right? So, you might have left later?"

"I guess so. It's been an upsetting few days."

"And the gun?" Fitzgerald said. "Did you know he had a pistol?"

"No, we had no clue before that horrible evening," Lynette chimed in.

Fitzgerald turned to her. "If I could just ask the questions of Ms. Sims," he said, "because she is apparently the last person who saw him alive."

"Excuse *me*," Lynette said.

"Well, we didn't know about the gun before that last night," Kimberly said, "but when I offered to stay over, especially because the daughter was apparently involved with an... a rather unsavory character, he told me that he had a gun and showed me where he kept it. I told Lynette about it when I got home."

"So you saw the gun?"

"Yes. I don't know anything about guns, and it looked like a toy to me, so I asked Simeon about it. He said he'd had it for years, and it was loaded but he'd never used it. But he said he knew how if he had to, and I suggested that he keep it closer than in the desk."

"What did he say?"

"He laughed at me and said I was being overcautious. It was the first time I had heard him laugh in days because he'd been so upset."

"But was he upset enough to commit suicide? You said he assured you he was okay when you left."

Kimberly choked up and tears started down her cheeks. She turned to Lynette and said, "Could you get me a tissue, love?"

Lynette left the room.

"Was he clothed when you left?" Fitzgerald asked.

Kimberly snapped. "Of course he was dressed. What are you inferring?"

Lynette returned and handed Kimberly a box of Kleenex. Kimberly extracted one and wiped her eyes.

"No inference intended. Just trying to get everything straight. It would seem that for a famous painter at the top of his game, it would take more than just a family argument to push him over the cliff, even if he was so upset with his daughter that he drew a new will. We're trying to piece it all together," Fitzgerald said. "Didn't anyone mention that when he was found he was naked?"

"No one told us that," Lynette said. "He was covered with a sheet when I identified him, but they only showed me his head. Why the hell weren't we told? *Why* would he have been naked?" She turned and looked at Kimberly, "Did you have any idea?"

"Of course not," Kimberly snapped. "Why would that poor man have been naked? Did someone come in after I left?" She dissolved into tears.

"I'm sorry about that," Fitzgerald said. "I didn't intend to upset you, but what about other pressures he might have been under?"

"Well, he did have other pressures," Kimberly said. "There was that foul-mouthed note from the daughter where she told him that she never wanted to hear from him again."

"But that was at least a day earlier, right?"

Lynette raised her hand like a student in a classroom. "Can I say something?"

In a flat tone, Fitzgerald said, "Yes."

Lynette leaned over the counter. Her ample breasts practically rested on the counter, and Fitzgerald did not miss the opportunity to observe them as she spoke softly. "There had been some business problems that were upsetting him as well. A woman we met on the cruise he felt would be the perfect model for him, the model he had been searching for, for years, and he painted a marvelous portrait of her. It sold right on the cruise for a lot of money. He wanted to do others of her, but she didn't even pose for the original. She's a friend and we believe her, but she threatened him with a lawsuit if he ever painted her again. She's a law professor, and he was very upset that he couldn't replicate—I think that's the word—what he called his *Reluctant Madonna.*"

"That's true," Kimberly said. "I didn't think of it, but it really depressed him. It was like his *Mona Lisa,* but there was only the one original, and the world would never get to see it. But he painted another and had it up in his studio. Wanted to make serigraphs. But she was adamant."

"As far as I know," Fitzgerald said, "there's only one *Mona Lisa* too."

"But millions of copies," Lynette said. "And if Simeon made copies of this portrait, he could be sued, embarrassed, maybe even bankrupted. You know how those things are. And the publicity... he was very upset. The really sad part is that Danni, the woman in the painting, changed her mind about the one upstairs in the studio, and was letting him keep it, but he never knew that."

"He was already dead," Kimberly said, then burst out crying again.

Lynette went to her and put her arm around her, but Kimberly shook her off. "If only I could have told him the threat was gone," she said. "It might have been inspiration to keep him alive."

Lynette said, "He did paint this other portrait of her—for himself, I guess. It's upstairs in the studio. He became obsessed with Danni.

The one in the studio was better than the first, her husband said. Then, we covered it up. Do you want to see it?"

Fitzgerald paused and looked at Janet Nowicki, the patrol officer, and shrugged. "I'm at least curious," he said, "although it's outside our investigation."

Nowicki shrugged back, as if to say *Why not?*

In the studio, Lynette undraped the portrait. Kimberly said she couldn't bear to go into the studio and waited downstairs.

Fitzgerald stared at it without speaking.

Nowicki said, "Hell of a painter all right."

Fitzgerald looked around and stopped at a portrait of Lynette resting on an easel. He did a slow turn and asked Lynette, "Is that you?"

Lynette smiled coyly and replied, "We posed for him, and he gave us paintings."

"Both of you?"

"And others, but we don't know them."

"Well, I think we should figure out who they were and contact them," Fitzgerald said, "We need to determine if he was shot *after* he was dead, as the ME suspects now, which confuses our investigation, or if it's just one of those things that can't be explained. Weird. And the house was locked?"

"The daughter, the chemist, had a key. Check her out," Kimberly said.

"The daughter, yes. She called the ME before the news was out about his death. We will definitely follow that one up," Fitzgerald said.

Kimberly and Lynette said they would try to locate information about Simeon's other models. After a few more questions, the officers left.

Fifty-one

Travis Anderson was back at his desk in the Supreme Court on Tuesday. Behind his desk were two computer screens. On the desk were photos of Michele and his two children and another of Travis and J.J. Richter at one of their annual Law and Order presentations. One of his two desk phones signaled a call.

"Travis," Col. Deb Boller said, "it was great to spend time with you over the weekend, although I'd rather it wasn't under those circumstances. I have the results of the autopsy from the ME, and I can share her conclusions as well as shoot you a copy."

"Great, Deb," Travis said. " That was quick."

"Autopsy yesterday, report today. She's very efficient. I'll just read the pertinent portions to you. 'Death was the result of a myocardial infarction. Blood clots in the arteries, and scar tissue as well as the presence of cholesterol, indicative of cardiomyopathy and prior damage to the heart muscle. Deceased, age sixty-eight, had an enlarged heart. The heart weighed 362.6 grams.'"

"Well, that's pretty good proof that he was dead by the time he was shot in the head," Travis said. "The question now is why would you shoot a dead man?"

Boller replied, "To confuse the investigators would be my first guess. Or perhaps to avoid an autopsy. Not every state requires an autopsy in a suicide, although they should," Boller said.

Travis added, "And maybe to hide the fact that death was caused by some sort of a drug."

"We're not done with the autopsy report," Boller said. "I told you, Dr. Barksdale was very thorough. Here's what she said about the head injury, reading from the report. 'The brain, which weighed 1442.3 grams, was autopsied by the usual deep cut into the scalp from behind the right ear and over the crown. Skin and soft tissue were peeled back to preserve the wound on the left temple, and a cut was made through the skull. Based on suspicion by the investigating officers, the lack of substantial blood loss was due to the fact that the subject was already deceased when a bullet was fired into the left temple. There was no evidence of neurodegenerative disease of the brain. Upon dissection, a gun cartridge was removed from the soft tissue of the right cerebral hemisphere and has been turned over to the forensics division for analysis.'"

Boller continued. "They sent out samples for a forensic toxicology report on the blood, urine, liver, heart, kidneys, spleen and hair to check for illicit drugs or poisons—and some material for DNA testing. The ME said some of the DNA scrapings from the body of the decedent were very unusual. She said the lab was somewhat hampered by the five-day delay in performing the autopsy, but positive results can be expected back within a week to ten days. I'll keep you in the loop. And I hope you can make our centenary party. It'll be a good time for us to catch up."

"Deb," Travis said, "I can't thank you enough. I'm going to check on autopsy requirements in Kentucky, where the daughter lived, although I'm sure you're on that already. And yes, I'm going to make every effort to be there for the one hundredth."

* * *

After they disconnected, Travis called Danni in her office. "I just heard from Delaware with the autopsy results," he told her. "He died of a heart attack, not the gun shot. Question is—was he poisoned before the heart attack, and if so, by whom? The daughter, perhaps?"

"I'll let the girls know," Danni said. "They already called to tell me that the daughter already has retained a lawyer who started a procedure in chancery court to contest the will."

"As they say, follow the money."

"By the way," Danni said, "I already checked on the law about autopsies in Kentucky. While all sudden or unexplained deaths have to be reported to a county coroner, section 72.025 mandates an autopsy *when the death of a human being appears to be the result of suicide.* However, there is some indication that the coroner can defer an autopsy if enough facts leading up to the suicide are known and can be verified and supported by a pre-existing medical condition. The girls verified Simeon's mental state, his depression, his agitation with the daughter, and he had a history of prior coronaries. The daughter might have figured that Delaware MEs had that same sort of discretion and they could avoid an autopsy—which is not the case. And remember, she also wanted him cremated right away. Cremation would destroy any evidence in the body."

"Of course, this is all speculation," Travis said. "The daughter is innocent until convicted. But if they find drugs were involved before Simeon was shot, I'd say a prosecutor would sit up and pay attention."

* * *

Danni reported the autopsy conclusions to Lynette and Kimberly and let them know the police would be asking for DNA samples from both of them. They had very different reactions to the news.

"If I was a betting person," Lynette said, "I'd bet the toxicology report comes back with some weird poison in his system. If it killed him or brought on a heart attack, the staged suicide would throw the investigation off track."

Kimberly asked, "What kind of DNA? Our DNA is all over that house. What do they think DNA is going to prove?"

Danni told them. "In the meantime, we have to be ready to mount a case in the chancery court. I'm going to do a quick study of that court and its rules. Unless you want to get local counsel."

"Does that mean you're going to represent us?" Lynette asked excitedly.

"We'll see," Danni said. "I'm not admitted in Delaware, and it would mean a *pro hac vice* admission, which is a procedure where an out-of-state lawyer from another jurisdiction can be admitted for one particular case, but let's see what I find. I'll check with Mort to get his thoughts."

"No," Lynette said. "We trust you. We know you. We stick with you if you can work out permission to handle the case in Delaware."

Kimberly agreed.

A half hour later, the detective who had interviewed them at Simeon's called to ask the girls if they would come to Georgetown the following day to give DNA samples.

Danni discussed legally representing Lynette and Kimberly with Mort that evening. They decided that if she was going to get involved, she should be with them during the procedure, so Danni decided to meet the two in Georgetown, Delaware.

Fifty-two

The day dawned with the capital enveloped in heavy smog that filtered down from record-setting Canadian wildfires. It took Danni longer to get to Georgetown than she had anticipated. When she arrived, Lynette and Kimberly were waiting in Lynette's car outside the police station.

Once they were seated in the interrogation room, Danni was introduced to officer Fitzgerald as their friend, their attorney, and the woman in the portrait on the easel in Simeon's studio.

"Will you be representing these ladies, or is this more of a show of support?"

"I don't know that they need representation here," Danni said, "but I will be exploring admission for the chancery proceedings."

"Well, I'm glad you're here with them," Fitzgerald said. "There are some questions that need to be answered. And as an aside, I don't think the portrait did you justice."

Danni blushed at the unexpected compliment.

Kimberly was fidgeting and said, "What kind of questions? And why do you need DNA from us?"

"We have to tie up all possibilities in a death case, even an apparent suicide," Fitzgerald explained. He called in the medical tech who administered an oral buccal test to each of the women by inserting something resembling a Q-tip into their mouths and taking a swab from each. He placed each swab into separate, marked glass vials, noting the name of each and the date and time of the swab.

"Now Ms. Sims," Fitgerald said, "you said that you left the deceased around nine o'clock in the evening. Am I correct?"

"I said I might have been wrong about that," Kimberly said, her eyes darting to Danni. "It might have been later. I already said that."

"But he was alive when you left, right?"

Kimberly raised her voice. "I told you all that, dammit! What's going on?"

"I don't understand this line of questioning either," Danni said.

"I told you as many times as I'm going to tell you," Kimberly shouted. "He said he was fine, and I left. I had a long drive ahead of me."

"Did he make any phone calls before you left? Specifically, did he call his daughter?"

"I *told* you," Kimberly shot back angrily. "I don't know if he called *anybody*. Not before I left. I don't know who he might have called. He was distraught about her. He disowned her. She wrote that despicable letter to him. You have it. What is this all about?"

"Yes," Lynette said, "why all these questions?"

"Well, frankly," Fitzgerald said, "we reached out to his daughter, Melanie. She received a call about eleven that evening and recorded it on her phone. The call was from a hysterical woman screaming that Simeon was dead and she hoped that the daughter was now happy because it was her conduct that had killed him, but she'd never see a penny of his estate."

Kimberly jumped up and started out of the room. Officer Nowicki blocked her from leaving.

Lynette turned to Kimberly and said, "Kim, did you call her? How would you have known he was dead?"

"Come back into the room, Kimberly, and sit down," Fitzgerald said, raising his voice.

Danni told Kimberly, "I don't think you should answer any more questions until we find out what the story is here."

Fitzgerald raised his hand and motioned Kimberly to sit back down. "This case has taken some unusual turns," he said calmly. "It's clear that Mr. Simeon, or rather, Mr. Gold, died of a heart attack. His daughter said that the call was very shocking to her, and her anger at her father dissipated with her grief. That's why she called the medical examiner the next day to make funeral arrangements. We've listened to the call and verified that it came from Simeon's home—but not his phone, which we have in our evidence room. The question is, did you, Ms. Sims, make that call, and did you know he was dead before you left that evening?"

Lynette looked at Kimberly and said, "Kim?"

Kimberly burst into tears and threw herself into Lynette's arms.

Lynette said, "Kim, what is it? Tell us."

"You don't have to say anything," Danni said.

Kimberly tore herself loose from Lynette's grasp and shouted, "Yes! I killed him. I loved him and I killed him!"

Danni said to Fitzgerald, "Can you give us this room? I'd like to talk to my client."

"No!" Kimberly yelled. "It's all gonna come out anyway. I killed him—I killed him with sex. And his heart gave out. It was me, it was my fault, and now he's gone." And with that she started wailing uncontrollably.

"I'll wait outside," Fitzgerald said.

"No!" Kimberly said. "It's all gonna come out. It might as well be now. Turn that thing on," she said, pointing at Fitzgerald's recorder.

"Kimberly," Danni said, pleading.

Kimberly pointed at the recorder again. "Turn it on, I said. Danni, I know you mean well, but I killed him, and now I have to pay."

"He died of a coronary," Danni said.

Kimberly choked back her sobs. "He said he was all right when I was ready to leave, but I could see he was depressed, so I said to him, 'Simeon, I'm gonna make you forget about everything tonight,' and I stripped off my top. I pushed him onto the pillows in the studio—we were in the studio. I don't wear a bra and I know he loved my breasts. But he loved having sex with Lynette more than me."

"Kim, that's not true," Lynette said.

"Yes. It. Is. And you know it. I have better tits, but you were always more relaxed, more natural. You *know* it. He even said it himself. I was never that relaxed with a man. Simeon or any other

241

man, since I was raped as a teenager. But I was going to give him a night to remember."

Glancing at Fitzgerald, who was open-mouthed, Danni thought, *You can say that again.*

"We made love," Kimberly said, "and I tried to throw all my inhibitions aside, and it was wild, and passionate, and he loved it too. He was sweating and smiling and he said 'one more time.' And I said 'You ain't seen nothing yet, buster,' and we made love again and we were both sweating and panting and he said 'I've never seen you like this.' And he was kissing me and holding me, and I said 'One more time.' He told me 'I don't think I have it in me.' And I said 'I want it in *me*,' and then we were making love again and suddenly he clutched his chest and gasped and moaned 'My pills, get my pills.' I ran downstairs to the medicine chest and got his nitro—he always called it his nitro— and when I came back he was in the middle of the floor on his back with eyes open, and I screamed. I screamed so loud I scared myself. I screamed and I started pounding on his chest and I started mouth to mouth, but he didn't move. Just laid there with his eyes open. I listened for his heart. I didn't hear anything. I put my ear to his chest. Nothing! I didn't know what to do—I so was terrified."

Danni handed more tissues to Kimberly, who grabbed a handful and swabbed her face.

"I stood there naked, for I don't know how long," Kimberly continued. "It seemed like hours, but it was probably only a few minutes. I was sobbing… I was shaking, I got down on my knees, and I begged him to wake up but he didn't. He was dead. I was sure he was dead and I killed him."

Lynette said, "Kimberly, you *didn't* kill him. We knew he had a bad heart. And if he died having sex with you, he died happy. Because he loved the sex. Stop blaming yourself. It happens… death happens."

Kimberly turned to Lynette as if no one else was in the room. Danni and Fitzgerald just stood there, silent observers.

Kimberly stopped crying but focused now on Lynette. "I was so scared. I was scared because we had always had sex together, the three of us. I was scared because I saw a side of me that I have never seen before—the aggressor, the insatiable one. I was scared because I didn't know what to do. But most of all..." she reached out to Lynette. "I was scared because you would be angry with me, and you'd stop loving me and leave me, and I could never endure that."

"Kimberly, I love you," Lynette said softly. "I love you and there is nothing to forgive. I might have done the same thing. You are here, we are here, and we will be here forever."

Kimberly burst into tears again and folded into Lynette's arms. They clutched each other tightly and hugged and kissed and cried together.

After a minute or two, Fitzgerald interrupted. "I don't want to be a downer," he said, "but the gun, the suicide, where did that come from?"

Kimberly untangled herself from Lynette.

Danni stood by, speechless.

"I was so scared that I had killed him and Lynette would leave me," Kimberly said, "that my mind started to think of ways to make it look more, I don't know—believable. His state of mind, his depression. So, I got dressed—well, more accurately, I threw on my clothes. And then I remembered the gun conversation which we just had, so I went downstairs and got the gun. I don't know anything about guns, but I held it with a tissue so I wouldn't leave fingerprints. And I remembered he said it was loaded, and I went back upstairs and put it in his hand and squeezed the trigger with his finger. And the noise was incredible—like an explosion—and I couldn't even look. I haven't been able to step into the studio since that moment. And he looked so sad, but I went out to my car and left. I was still crying, still shaking. So I drove real slow."

Lynette said, "That explains why you got home after two."

"And that explains, in your confused state of mind, why the gun was in his left hand, not his dominant hand," Fitzgerald said. "But what about the call to the daughter?"

"I don't remember making it, but I must have. I was hysterical and needed someone to blame, so I must have called her. Her number was downstairs, so I must have called on my phone. I don't remember."

At this point, Danni joined the conversation. "Well, if you did call her, and it certainly appears that you did, it will be on your phone. That explains how she knew he was dead. You might as well surrender your phone now to Sergeant Fitzgerald." She turned to Fitzgerald, and said, "Can I speak to you outside for a few minutes?"

Danni and Fitzgerald went into the hall. Officer Nowicki remained outside the door.

"Will you be charging her? What with, if anything?" Danni asked.

"At the moment, I am rendered numb," Fitzgerald said. "That is the most incredible story I've ever heard, and I've heard quite a few. Or should I say confession? But to what? She certainly didn't commit homicide. Disturbing a dead body? Giving a false statement? A gunshot to a dead man? I'm going to have to discuss this with my lieutenant. Whatever it is, it's not homicide, although we were pretty certain there was something wrong with her story. We were just waiting for the forensics."

"Because?"

"Because, if you'll forgive me for being graphic, the ME noted there were abrasions on his, uh, member—his penis. So, they took what appeared to be pubic hairs for analysis. I'm now pretty certain they will prove to be Kimberly's."

"Hearing what we just heard," Danni said, "I wouldn't be surprised. Are you going to charge her with anything now?"

"We know where to reach her. I'll follow it up quickly. Why don't you arrange to get admitted to the bar here in the meantime so you can represent her? Or get a public defender. We're certainly not looking at jail time."

"I don't know if I'm ready for criminal law," Danni said. "My specialty is the environment. I think there were several times just now that I should have intervened, but I wasn't sure. Not good in a criminal case."

"You couldn't have done much. She had to get this off her conscience, and that's how it went down. Better now for her sake than when the forensics came back. Look, if I can help you in anything except a criminal case I'm working, feel free to give me a call."

Fifty-three

Kimberly was issued an appearance ticket, the same low-level notice to appear that one would receive for a traffic violation. Fitzgerald checked with his superiors to see what, if any, charges would be coming down. Kimberly left shortly after noon, gratefully hanging onto Lynette, bound for Rehoboth. The will contest with Melanie still remained, regardless of any possible criminal charges. They thanked and hugged Danni, who headed back to DC.

Danni called Mort in his office. "You won't believe the morning I just had."

"Fill me in," he said.

"You don't have time to hear all the details. Unbelievable. I'll tell you at dinner. Don't forget we have dinner with my mother and J.J. tonight in Travalah. Got to hear all the plans she has for his Labor Day bash. It'll have to hold until then. Pick me and Katie up around five."

"You've really got my curiosity up," Mort said. "Is anybody in jail?"

"Nope, but I am questioning my ability as a criminal lawyer."

* * *

The table was set for five. Lupe was preparing to serve a Mexican roast from a recipe she got from her mother years earlier. She was always uncomfortable when seated at the dining room table with the family, but Chickie had insisted because she was laying out all the plans for the Labor Day fete, and Lupe, queen of the kitchen, would be supervising the caterers.

"I heard from Travis earlier today," J.J. said, looking at Danni. "I already told Chickie, but that stalker you shot escaped from rehab earlier today. Travis was going to call you, but I told him you were in Delaware, so he's probably calling later."

"My God," Danni said. "Do I have to start worrying about him again?"

"He only wanted to *capture* you," Mort said, "but he wanted to *kill* me, if you recall."

J.J. said, "He slipped his ankle bracelet and got out of the rehab facility, but he's still recovering from his wounds, and they were pretty serious, thanks to Danni. Travis said they have a good line on his whereabouts, and it's only a matter of time before he's back in custody."

"Well, I'll be looking over my shoulder until then," Danni said. "What can we do?"

"We can get you federal marshal protection if you want," J.J. said, "but that's up to you."

"Hey, I'm the one who was shot," Chickie said.

"Collateral damage, my love," J.J. teased.

They discussed defensive possibilities for the next few minutes and learned that Travis had advised J.J. that the US marshals plus the FBI and all local law enforcement had been alerted. The consensus: there was no immediate threat. Danni did not want the offered protection, and there were marshals still stationed outside the Travalah residence because of the earlier threats regarding the Supreme Court. J.J. didn't like it, but Travis had insisted on maintaining protection at least for the present time.

"I repeat," Mort said, "I'm the one he wanted to kill. What about me?"

"Just use your Krav Maga skills, or whatever you call them," Danni said with a smirk. "They seem to be very effective."

"If he come here," Lupe said, "I use my frying pan." That broke the tension.

246

As they were eating, Danni relayed the events of the morning with Kimberly and Lynette. Katie was under the table waiting for handouts from Mort, and Connie was asleep on the floor near J.J.'s feet as usual. Danni described not only her shock at Kimberly's story but her displeasure at not having stopped the "confession" before it got started and her unhappiness with her own performance as a criminal attorney.

"That's why there are specialties in law," J.J. said. "You can't just jump from one area to the next without proper training. A good lesson for all. But I do admit, I have never heard of a case being resolved like this one. A suicide is draped in mystery, suspicion of foul play from the daughter and possible poisoning, and death by copulation and a weak heart. That's a new one."

"In his own way, Simeon was a stalker," Mort said. "He preyed on women who fawned over his talents, probably seduced them with the promise of a painting or ended up in a trifecta like he did with Kimberly and Lynette. He certainly tried his damndest, like a lecher, to get Danni to pose."

"What can you say when a man dies like that, too young—still in his sixties," Chickie said.

"Live by the sword, die by the sword," Mort said.

"Mort!" Danni admonished.

"I no understand," Lupe said. "He die by a sword?"

Fifty-four

The week began peacefully. Mort returned to the *Post,* content to catch up on his emails and compose a follow-up article on his North Dakota adventure. He checked in with Clete MacCauley to update himself and gather additional information, had to answer or ignore numerous emails about the Russian involvement plus deal with congratulations for having solved a topic of national concern. He even urged the MacCauleys to come east for J.J.'s Labor Day event. He held several meetings with his small unit of reporters as they awaited their next investigative assignment, relishing the quiet of the down time.

Danni returned to her office and was disappointed to learn her summer class had been canceled due to low enrollment. Summer classes were always an "iffy" proposition, and she was not terribly upset. In fact, she was looking forward to a few weeks of relaxation before the new term and the opportunity to spend time with her mother planning J.J.'s postponed July 4th fête—now scheduled for Labor Day. Travis was just as happy with the postponement after the threats to the justices and felt that things would quiet down with the court out of session.

Chickie was planning a much bigger affair than usual, with over a hundred guests, including the justices and Court personnel, plus the reporters who covered the Court. She hired a caterer, and speculation was rife that the occasion would feature an announcement by J.J. that he was retiring from the Court as he reached eighty.

Danni kept her eyes open for an unwelcome appearance by Devon McCarthy even though she was assured by Travis and the authorities that it was unlikely. Nonetheless, she was figuratively looking over her shoulder, unconvinced that two bullets would dissuade him in his pursuit of her.

"You should be flattered," Mort said. "You've got one guy who was ready to kill me to steal you away, and another one who fantasized your body and made you his 'Reluctant Madonna.' All within a few weeks." Danni made it clear that she did not appreciate that kind of attention.

On Wednesday, Danni received a call from Lynette and Kimberly. "We've been served with a paper called a 'rule to show cause' by that bitch-daughter Melanie in the chancery court to set aside the will. It names both of us and our home address, but we were served here so she had to do some digging for our names and all," Lynette said. "What do we do now?"

"Read it to me," Danni said, and Lynette read the entire contents. Rather than a summons, it was actually a motion seeking more immediate relief instead of the usual preliminaries and trial. It was returnable in two weeks and required an answer before an event that was described as a "hearing date."

"Will you represent us?" Lynette asked.

"I said I would, and if I can get admitted there, I will," Danni said. "Did Melanie mention anything about her father, or the fact that he's still not buried and residing with the medical examiner?"

"Not a word," Lynette said. "She doesn't give a shit about anything but the money."

"That may be a good point for the hearing," Danni said. "I'll get to work on getting admitted. By the way, and more important, how is Kimberly doing?"

"She's still not herself—shook up and convinced that I'll leave her—and now this court thing has thrown her for a loop. Plus, she still has to answer that appearance ticket. In other words, she's a wreck."

"Well, I'll contact Fitzgerald and see what we can do about that. Maybe kill the proverbially two birds with one stone."

"Bad analogy," Lynette said, and Danni agreed.

"By the way, who's the daughter's attorney?" Danni asked.

"Didn't list one," Lynette said. "It was just in her own name."

"I guarantee you she didn't author a rule to show cause on her own," Danni said. "That was probably to make you think she's doing it on her own. But two can play that game. Go down to the court, ask the clerk for help and put in a general denial to the charges. I'm sure the clerk will give you an assist, and I'll get on it from this end. Shoot me a copy."

* * *

Danni called Mort and brought him up to date.

"I want to help them, but I really don't feel too qualified," Danni said.

"I have an idea," Mort said. "Let me call Ron Ciresi."

Mort had met Ciresi during J.J.'s kidnapping. He was a well-known criminal attorney and had represented a man accused in a triple killing, which was solved when Mort determined the killer was actually a twin brother of Ciresi's client. Mort and Ron had become friendly, and Mort had even written a feature article on the wrongly accused man.

"Timing is everything in life," Ciresi said to Mort when he called back several hours later. "Next week I'm starting a two-week teaching stint in DC for NITA—the National Institute for Trial Advocacy—to teach young attorneys and law students how to try cases. Danni can sit in, and after a week she'll know enough to make a good presentation in that Delaware court. There's really no trick to it, just the ground rules, the rules of evidence and self-confidence. If I wasn't teaching this course, I'd try the case in Delaware myself. I still owe you for last year."

Professor Danni Rose was going back to school.

* * *

Ron Ciresi was an imposing sixty-year-old with a flowing grey mane, who had the reputation of being one of the best—and toughest—

criminal attorneys in the East, if not the nation. Like so many circumstances in Mort's life, their friendship had blossomed as a result of J.J.'s kidnapping, and Ciresi was taking time off from his practice to spend two weeks tutoring students in trial practice for NITA. The course was scheduled over the coming weeks at Howard University School of Law in the capital. Howard was only a little more than a mile from American University Law School, where Danni was an assistant professor. Some of the best trial attorneys in the country volunteered their time to NITA.

Danni showed up early for the course in jeans with her hair pulled back into a ponytail. Ciresi dressed casually, his short-sleeved, flowered sport shirt and beige slacks a far cry from his usual courtroom appearance.

"Danni," Ciresi said, "I would never have recognized you. You look like a teenybopper."

"That's the idea," Danni said. "I want to be as anonymous as possible. In fact, if you'd list me as Mrs. Ahrens, instead of Danni Rose, it would be most appreciated."

"And I was all set to give you a big intro," Ciresi said. With that, he gave her the course materials, which included a book of practice materials, the Rules of Evidence and a pocket-sized copy of the Constitution, then introduced her to the two other attorneys who would be teaching with him.

Five minutes later, he ddressed the students and lawyers in the auditorium. After a brief overview of the class, he wrapped it up with, "By the end of two weeks you will be well on your way to a rewarding and aggravating career. Keep that copy of the Constitution with you always. You will appear in front of judges, many of whom are political appointees who know a lot less than you will know about trial practice when you leave here. You will also appear in front of some of the best jurists in the nation, and Pay them great heed. The learning process is unending."

A hand went up in the gallery and a student asked, "How do we know the good ones from the rest?"

"From the bruises to your ego. Mostly, you'll be in front of men and women who took an oath to respect and follow the Constitution, and who bend over backwards to do just that. But there are some, and I assure you that you'll quickly recognize them, who know less than you do but think they know it all. Those are the ones to do battle with. And, if you're right, you'll prevail, if not in their court, then on appeal."

The first week was to go over the ground rules of trial practice. The second week was slated for actual moot court cases against an adversary, many with a volunteer jury of high school or college students. Even though it was summer, there was never a shortage of prospective volunteer jurors. Unfortunately for Danni, week two would be trial by fire in the chancery court in Delaware.

The days were spent in lectures and practice situations, question and answer sessions, and on trial practice in general. Toward the end of the week, Danni was startled when Ciresi singled her out and said, "Mrs. Ahrens, you have an adversary on the stand, and you're convinced that he has information that is crucial to your case but you're not sure of his answer. What do you do?"

"Well, we're taught never to ask a question when we're not sure of the answer. But if your gut tells you it's crucial, you take a shot and go for broke." She raised her hand with fingers crossed and got a laugh.

"Very true," Ciresi said. "Dangerous, so use sparingly."

Fifty-five

Lydell Hendrickson, the fifty-year-old realtor with a shaved head who had notarized the signatures of Lynette and Kimberly as witnesses to Simeon's will, was an attorney admitted to practice in the chancery court. He liked "the girls," was a big fan of Simeon's and was more than willing to move Danni's admission for the will contest case.

Chancery court in Georgetown was located on The Circle, which housed the Department of Justice and several other courts. When Danni saw the colonial-style building, she felt a tinge of nervousness. Was she up to this task? Could her one week of preparation possibly have readied her for the task of defending her friends? In law school, she had shied away from trial practice. Criminal cases were, in her opinion, for the yahoos and more outgoing members of her class. Now she found herself as one of them.

The large, wood-paneled courtroom featured a raised bench flanked by American and State of Delaware flags. On the walls hung portraits of former judges and a large electric clock. In front of the judge's bench was a recessed platform with four chairs for court personnel and a stenographer. Facing the bench, separated by a wide aisle, were two tables, each with three chairs, for the opposing parties and their counsel.

Lydell Hendrickson, in a blue "Sell with Lydell" shirt, looked across the courtroom where Melanie's attorney was standing. "Don't worry. You're up against a doofus. He's a good ole boy who needs a can of Bud in his hand to function."

Clem Green, fortyish with unkempt hair and an overbearing attitude, walked over to Danni and said, "*I* would've moved your admission. No need to bring in the *king* of the real estate world." He turned to Hendrickson and said, "You ever been on the inside of the courthouse before?"

Hendrickson ignored him. When the case was called before the Honorable Beatrice Burr, Hendrickson said, "Your Honor, I move the admission for this case of Danielle Rose, a member of the District of Columbia and New York bars, and an assistant professor of Law at the American University School of Law in Washington."

"A *professor*?" Green said. "I should have checked her out. Now I'm intimidated."

Judge Burr scowled, then peered at Green through oversized glasses with black frames and asked, "Do you consent, Mister Green?"

"Absolutely, Judge. I can't wait."

"Just a yes or no, Mr. Green," the judge snapped. "Save the gratuitous remarks. If you're ready, you may proceed."

Melanie Gold sat at the bench on the left of the courtroom. She fidgeted with her hands, looking very uncomfortable. Lynette and Kimberly occupied two of the chairs on the right, looking nervous but intense.

Green called Melanie to the stand and went through her life history, her professional credentials as a chemist, and the fact that she was an only child who "loved her father dearly," admitting that they had had some differences, only to be shocked to find that he had handwritten a new will only days before his death. She had always been told, she said, that she would inherit the entire estate.

Danni sat quietly and did not object to any portion of Melanie's testimony or any of Green's questions, which ranged far afield. Several times Judge Burr looked at Danni, anticipating an objection, but it was not in her game plan.

"Cross examination?" said Judge Burr.

"Thank you, Your Honor," Danni said, pushing back her chair to stand. "Ms. Gold, do you own a home?"

"Objection!" Green shouted from the counsel table on the left.

"Mr. Green," the judge admonished, "when you seek to object, in this court you do so on your feet. What's the nature of your objection?"

Green pushed himself to his feet. "It doesn't make any difference if she owns a home or not."

The judge looked at Danni, who fumbled her notes while nervously searching for an answer.

"Subject to connection?" the judge interjected, looking at Danni. She had thrown Danni a lifeline.

"Yes, your honor," Danni said, relieved. "I can connect it up."

"Objection overruled. Proceed."

Befuddled, Melanie answered, "Eight years ago."

"And isn't it true that the money for the down payment, around forty thousand dollars, came from your father, the late Simeon Gold?"

"Yes, but…"

Danni interrupted. "And four years ago, didn't your father give you ten thousand dollars as a loan to pay off some debts for the man who is now your fiancée?"

"He gave it to me, yes. Ronnie had run up against some problems."

"Was it a loan, a gambling debt, or money lost betting on horses?" Danni asked. In the tempestuous period before his death, Simeon had shared with Lynette and Kimberly much of his background with his daughter.

Melanie stammered, "He owed money, and I asked Dad to stake me to a loan."

"And how much of that money has been repaid?"

"Well, none of it… yet. The pandemic and all… you know."

"No, I don't know," Danni said. "That's why I'm asking."

Green was on his feet. "Objection. What's this got to do with a will contest?"

Danni learned fast. "Subject to connection, Your Honor."

"Overruled."

"And you recently had a falling out with your father, isn't that so? A rather serious argument?"

"Families have squabbles and differences all the time," Melanie said. "It had nothing to do with loving him."

"But weren't you once again asking for money, although you haven't paid back anything from four years ago?"

"I wanted the money to get married," Melanie said. "I'm pregnant, and I wanted the baby to be legitimate."

"Is this the same fiancée whose debt your father paid off?" Danni asked.

Melanie nodded yes, and Danni asked, "Is that a yes?"

"Yes."

"And does that man have a criminal record? Isn't that why your father objected?"

"Years ago, he had a few minor problems. He paid for them and straightened out his life. He's even licensed to work at the track. They don't give licenses to criminals."

"But your father objected, right?"

"He was being unreasonable, pig-headed."

"And isn't it true that your father objected to your fiancée because of that background?"

"My father didn't *know* him. He met him once and they didn't hit it off. He was being unfair."

"But will you concede that your father had the right to leave his estate to whomever he chose?"

"I'm his daughter! His only child! His estate should be mine. All those years before my mother died, he was carousing around, running with other women. He was far from perfect. But he didn't know what he was doing when he changed his will. Those two whores buffaloed him."

At this point Melanie started crying, and the judge called for a short recess. Ten minutes later, they resumed.

"I'm going to ask that the witness's last answer be stricken, Your Honor, and that she be directed not to volunteer material," Danni said.

"The last sentence will be stricken," Judge Burr said. "How far are you going to go with this line of questioning?"

"I'm moving on, Your Honor," Danni said, turning back to the witness. "In the last four years, how many times have you called your father... except to borrow money?" Danni asked.

"Objection!" Green shouted, as he jumped to his feet.

"You can answer," Judge Burr said.

"He's on the road so much, with art shows, or on cruises where he sells art, or at studios all over the world…"

"So," Danni said, "how many times?

"I don't know. A few."

"It was recently Father's Day, Ms. Gold. "Did you call him or send him a card or contact him by email?"

"I never know where he is," Melanie said.

"But you manage to find him when you need money," Danni said.

"Objection."

"Sustained. Just stick to questions, Ms. Rose."

"My apologies, Your Honor," Danni said. "I just have a few more in this line of questions."

The next questions determined that Melanie had not sent Father's Day greetings or cards, nor any birthday cards or similar recognitions over the last decade.

"He's won national and international awards," Danni said. "Have you acknowledged any of those?"

"It's impossible to keep up with his career. He moves around so much."

"I think this would be a good time for a bench conference," Judge Burr said. "Counsel, would you both approach the bench."

Fifty-six

The judge quietly conferred with the two opposing lawyers. Because of the configuration of the courtroom, the judge actually left her seat and stepped down to talk to the attorneys at the side of the bench.

"Before we go any deeper," she said, "is there any chance we can resolve this matter?"

"We didn't institute the case," Danni said, turning to Green.

"We think that Mr. Simeon—I mean, Mr. Gold—was very upset when he changed his will and that he wasn't thinking straight," Green said. "We think he was misled by these two women who exerted undue influence on him, so much so that he lost it and committed suicide."

"He didn't commit suicide," Danni said. "He died of a coronary."

Green was shocked. "A coronary? I thought he shot himself."

"You thought wrong—confirmed by the medical examiner."

"But he certainly wasn't acting rationally when he handwrote this supposed will and left everything to these two... two gold diggers, if I might say—who he didn't even know that well."

"We don't need denigration of the parties," Judge Burr said harshly.

Green didn't apologize, just nodded that he understood.

Danni said, "Actually, the deceased had a loving relationship with these women. He knew them extremely well. The women spent a lot of time with him here in Delaware, and they even went on some of his tours and to his art presentations. They became the daughters that your client wasn't."

"I was just hoping there might be some middle ground," Judge Burr said. "I hate to see a child cut out of the parent's estate if it's avoidable. Mr. Green, do you have any other witnesses?"

"No, Judge, I'm ready to rest our case. But I intend to do quite a job on those two when I cross examine," Green said, "to show undue influence and how they twisted his thinking."

"Then let's proceed," Judge Burr said.

Danni called Lydell Hendrickson, the realtor, and qualified him both as a lawyer and licensed real estate broker. She then asked how well he had known Simeon.

"I knew Simeon well… for over a dozen years," he said. "When he bought his house from me, and over the years he purchased several other pieces of property in Rehoboth which he rents out. We actually became friends, had dinner several times, and he gave me two of his paintings."

That last bit of information came as a surprise to everyone in the courtroom.

"On the day he came to you with Ms. Sims and Ms. Gilette to have you witness their signatures on his new will, do you have any opinion as to his state of mind?"

"He was—Simeon," Hendrickson said. "Very serious, and he explained to me that he was writing a new will—"

Green jumped to his feet. "Objection! Hearsay."

Danni moved on. "Without telling us what he said were his reasons, did he appear lucid and competent?"

"Definitely."

"In control of his functions, whereabouts, and what he was doing?"

"Absolutely."

"No further questions."

Green cross-examined but got nowhere in attempting to show that Simeon was incompetent at the time the will was executed. He asked, "Didn't you think it was strange that he came in with a handwritten will, and that it was being witnessed by the beneficiaries?"

"I thought it unusual," Hendrickson said, "but holographic wills are valid here in Delaware, and I never actually read it to see who the beneficiaries were or what else was in it. That was none of my business. I was just acting as the notary."

Green, clearly frustrated, had no further questions.

"I'd like to recall Melanie Gold, Your Honor," Danni said.

Green jumped up. "She's already testified, and you had your shot at her."

Danni turned to the judge. "It's just a few questions, Your Honor, and she *is* still here in the courtroom. The relevance will be obvious."

Melanie was recalled and reminded that she was still under oath.

"May I approach the witness, Your Honor?"

Her request was granted.

Danni reached into her briefcase on the counsel table, removed several papers, and handed one to Melanie.

Danni asked, "Do you recognize this and is it your signature?"

Green was on his feet again. "I object," he said. "I don't know anything about this!"

Clearly taken aback, Melanie looked down and pushed the papers away.

"This goes directly to the relationship between the witness and the deceased," Danni said, "and to the question of credibility." She handed a copy to Green, who read it.

"I knew nothing about this," he said, waving the papers and turning to Melanie. "Did you write this?"

Melanie nodded and sat silent.

"Would anyone care to share this with me?" Judge Burr said.

Danni handed a copy to the clerk, who handed it to the judge, who looked down and read it.

"I'd like to offer it as an exhibit," Danni said.

"I still object," Green said, "whether she wrote it or not."

The judge turned to Melanie. "Did you write this?"

Melanie offered a weak, "Yes."

The judge handed it back to the clerk. "Mark this as Defendant's One," she said.

Looking at Melanie, Danni asked, "Ms. Gold, did you write, 'I am done, and I'm guessing this is the last time we will ever communicate, but I'm okay with that. I want no part of you. For now and forever, fuck you.' Did you write that and is that your signature?"

Melanie started to cry but said, "Yes."

"The defendants rest, Your Honor," Danni said.

Green was on his feet again. "Rest? But you didn't put them on the stand," he said, gesturing toward Lynette and Kimberly.

A good trial lawyer quits while ahead. If Danni had learned no more than that from her NITA course, all the experts had drilled it home.

There was a discussion at the bench with the judge, and Green spoke briefly with Melanie, followed by a wagging of heads. But the case concluded. Danni gave a very brief summation, pointing out that the burden was on Melanie, the plaintiff, to show that the will was invalid. Green said it was clear that Simeon had executed the will under duress and without a clear head, influenced unfairly by the defendants, and that the new will should be invalidated.

Judge Burr said, "I see no point in requesting briefs or prolonging this decision. I'm ready to rule from the bench. Mr. Green, Title 12, chapter 9, section 901 of the Delaware Civil Code clearly gives the right to a parent to disinherit a child. I'm not saying that I like it, or that I agree with it, but it is the law. And while it's highly unusual to have a holographic will, let alone one in which the beneficiaries of the will are also the witnesses, that is what is provided in Title 12, Chapter 2 and has been sustained by case law. Under the circumstances, the will is valid. There has been no testimony of incompetence or undue influence. The Rule to show cause is dismissed. This case is concluded."

* * *

It all happened so fast that Lynette and Kimberly were not sure what had occurred.

Danni leaned over to them and said, softly, "That's it. It's over. We won."

The two women could hardly contain their joy. They embraced, and Melanie Gold stalked from the courtroom followed by her sulking attorney. Judge Burr started off the bench but waited until Melanie and her attorney had left the courtroom and motioned for Danni to approach the bench.

"Ms. Rose," she said, "you did a commendable job. I find it hard to believe that this was your first trial experience."

"I did get some help from a NITA course your honor, but I admit I was quite nervous."

"You hid it well. What I said about not favoring parents who disinherit children was true, and even here, you might consider speaking to your clients to work out some kind of a settlement with the daughter if the estate warrants it."

"I will suggest it to them, Your Honor, and I appreciate your remarks and the way you handled the proceeding."

Once outside the court, "the girls" practically mugged Danni. "How can we ever repay you?" Lynette asked.

"Just send us a bill. You were wonderful," Kimberly said.

"I didn't do it for a fee," Danni said. "I did it for friendship. But we're not quite done yet. There's still that outstanding citation against Kimberly in the Court of Common Pleas to be taken care of, and most importantly, I think you should get to work on funeral plans for Simeon once the medical examiner releases his body."

* * *

A phone call to Detective Fitzgerald by Danni resulted in a short conversation in which he explained that he had discussed the case with his lieutenant. Under the unusual circumstances, they were willing to resolve the case with a plea to disorderly conduct, a fine of three hundred dollars and forty hours of community service by Kimberly. He explained that she did shoot Simeon, although he was already dead, and had touched the body by putting the gun in his hand, plus she had made a false statement to the police. But under the peculiar circumstances of the crime, they thought this would be a fair resolution. So did Kimberly, and they made arrangements for her to make an appearance and enter a plea.

Simeon was buried a week later at a Jewish cemetery in Dover. In attendance were Kimberly, Lynette, Mort, Danni, Lydell

Hendrickson, John Lock from the art gallery, and Simeon's agent. A Rent-a-Rabbi suggested by the cemetery and hired by Lynette and Kimberly offered a prayer and a few innocuous words. The girls were in tears. Mort stepped forward and threw the first shovel of dirt when the coffin was lowered.

Fifty-seven

About ten days later, FedEx delivered a large package addressed to Danni. Mort said, "I bet I know what's in that box."

They carefully unwrapped the only other *Reluctant Madonna* in existence, beautifully framed with an effervescent note from Kimberly and Lynette.

"I think we should hang it in the living room," Mort said, tongue in cheek.

"Over *your* dead body," Danni said. "It's a gorgeous portrait, more attractive than the subject. But I don't think it will ever see the light of day."

"Doesn't hold a candle to the model. How about my office?" Mort suggested.

Danni swatted at him, and they settled on the storage area, discreetly covered.

* * *

Danni divided her time between preparing for the next semester and occasionally helping her mother with advice for what was called "J.J.'s July 4th Barbeque, to be held on Labor Day." The summer was slipping away. Notwithstanding assurances from Travis and the authorities, Danni was still being very cautious of her surroundings, fearing that Devon McCarthy might suddenly surface.

Mort and his team were looking for the next mountain to climb. He was intensely scrutinizing the movement throughout the country to ban books from libraries and schools and pitched a proposal to have his team do an extensive investigation on the practice and its sources. He was certain that there was something nefarious involved for there to be such widespread activity in so many states in such a short period. They were awaiting approval to forge ahead.

Chickie, with Lupe at her side, continued preparing for the Labor Day fete. The guest list, exclusive of the other justices and Supreme Court personnel, had grown to over a hundred, and provisions had to be made for seating, a buffet with copious amounts of food, the location of the bar, and all the other requisites of a stellar event. A guitarist was hired for soft music during the afternoon, and the only thing they couldn't plan for was the weather.

J.J.'s marriage to Chickie the previous year and his recovery from a kidnapping had taken the planning out of his hands. He constantly complained about how "that woman" had changed his life. He actually loved every minute of it, but his Harley was now gone, he no longer got to man the grill for the barbeque, the gardeners inevitably didn't do as good a job as he claimed he had done on the lawns, and he could not get used to the idea that two Secret Service agents were always present for his safety. In addition, the Montgomery County Police planned to locate a team at the entrance to the property to check visitors on the day of the barbeque.

"Who do they think we expect?" J.J. complained. "El Chapo is in jail, Dillinger is dead, and we've got enough guns around here to start a rebellion."

* * *

Labor Day arrived with the sun shining. A heat wave that had ravaged the East Coast for two weeks had ended in a barrage of thunderstorms and hail, which had eased the temperature into the low eighties. When everything appeared ready, a small bus with the caterer's logo on its side arrived just before noon, was waved in by the police guarding the entrance, and unloaded a dozen servers and chefs clad in white slacks and blue jackets.

"I feel like I'm a character in the Macy's Day Parade," J.J. grumbled. The guests started arriving at around two, including: J.J.'s close friend, retired Justice Anthony Battaglia; Justice Julius Gallagher, whose life J.J. had saved after suffering a heart attack, and his wife; Kimberly and Lynette who had been invited by Danni; Sheriff MacCauley and his wife Greta from Grand Forks, who had been invited by Mort; Travis and Michele Anderson and Steve Ginsberg and his wife.

By five o'clock they had mingled, imbibed, eaten heartily, and were preparing for cake and dessert. Lupe, dressed uncharacteristically and uncomfortably in a beige pants suit, towered over most of the guests and the caterers. She closely watched and directed all the activity in the kitchen while the food was being set out, with some prepared under her surveillance. The caterers were circulating among the crowd, taking last minute drink orders.

A table near the microphone featured a large sheet cake. The curious wandered by and checked it for a message about J.J.'s rumored retirement from the Court, but found it featured no more than a decorated figure of the Greek Goddess Themis, better known as Lady Justice.

J.J. made his way to the microphone, tapped to see that it was on, and prepared to address the group. The guitarist played a loud chord to get everyone's attention. J.J. was flanked by Danni and Mort.

"First," J.J. said, "I want to thank you all, family and friends, for making this a memorable occasion. Especially Chickie, who made all these marvelous arrangements. Next..."

An older woman caterer stood just off to the side of the table where J.J., Danni and Mort were standing. Suddenly, Lupe was behind her pulling a large garbage bag over her head, shouting, "No!" Every eye spun toward Lupe as she tightly clasped the elderly woman, now encased by the bag, and pinned her arms.

"What the...?" J.J. started to say, as a bronze Sig Sauer 9mm pistol with a 30-round extended magazine fell to the ground with a clattering sound.

"She no caterer," Lupe bellowed. "She a killer!"

Within seconds, Travis was at Lupe's side, and Secret Service agents were racing from the back of the crowd to the bagged woman.

"I've got her, Lupe," Travis said. "What the hell is going on?"

Lupe tore the top of the bag open, exposing the head, and a grey wig fell out of the bag.

"She a *he*!" Lupe snarled.

Locked in Travis's grip, the man spun toward Lupe and snarled, "You son of a bitch!"

Mort kicked the gun away and Danni cried, "Oh, my God, it's Devon McCarthy."

* * *

After an hour of mayhem, a semblance of order was restored. FBI agents, ten of them, had arrived in screaming black SUVs. Montgomery County Police had unleashed a SWAT team, and McCarthy had been cuffed and led to one of the FBI vehicles. Although his crime had taken place in Montgomery County, Maryland, it involved a threat to a Supreme Court Justice and his family, so FBI jurisdiction was quickly established.

Travis asked Lupe how she had anticipated McCarthy's actions.

"I see she not serving like the others. She moving close to the front, and her hair is on crooked. Crooked hair. Not her real hair, so I stay close. And when she move, I move," Lupe said. "I not know that she a he."

The senior FBI officer wanted to take statements from the witnesses, but J.J. put the kibosh on that request, insisting that the witnesses would be available at any time but no one, not even the FBI, was going to further interrupt his festivities.

J.J. returned to the microphone, with Danni, Mort and also Chickie now joining him.

"Where was I when we were so rudely interrupted?" he said to relieved laughter.

"We couldn't decide on entertainment," he said, "so we asked Lupe to improvise something. She never fails, but I didn't anticipate fireworks." More laughter, and applause. J.J. pointed to Lupe, who was now standing in the rear of the gathering clearly embarrassed.

"And now," J.J. said, "the announcement that I know many of you have been waiting for. And no, Julius," he said, pointing to and looking at Justice Gallagher, "I won't be stepping down this year." Applause. "I've got to stick around until I'm sure you get it right."

Laughter.

"No, the big announcement, I am happy to share with friends and family, is that Chickie and I are going to be grandparents. Danni and Mort are having a baby." Wild applause. With that he handed the microphone to Danni, who pushed it away with her hand, but J.J. insisted. As usual, J.J. prevailed.

"I really don't know what to say," Danni said. "We're very excited, and I really want to thank my husband, Mort, without whom this announcement would not be possible."

Laughter.

Mort spoke without the microphone. "My first reaction was to look for a bright star in the east," he said, to more laughter, "and when I didn't see one, I knew this was for real."

Danni continued, "If it's a boy, we've decided to name him Dakota." That remark went over the heads of almost everyone present except Greta MacCauley, who leaned over, smiling, and pinched her husband Clete's arm, kissing him on the cheek.

"A special thank you to you, Lupe, for your quick action today," Danni said. "Some of you are aware that Mort has been studying martial arts for some months. Did you see the way he kicked away that gun? What technique! Mort, save your money and take lessons from Lupe."

Steve Ginsberg leaned over to his wife and said, "Now I understand what Danni was doing in North Dakota."

Afterward

It is gratifying to see that legislatures are finally acting to protect Native landowners and farmers from foreign ownership. In July, 2023, the US Senate voted 91-6 to block Chinese businesses or entities from purchasing farmland in the United States. In North Dakota, the legislature passed a law which bans "foreign governments and adversaries" from owning land in the state, thwarting construction of a corn milling plant near the Grand Forks Air Force Base.

Acknowledgements

I am indebted to close friend and retired banker Bill Raker, who not only served as first reader, but lent his expertise to those portions of the manuscript which required knowledge of banking and securities transactions. My wife, Sharon Miller, is always a keen first reader, and sacrificed many hours of our marriage as I toiled before the computer. My son Peter and grandson Peter Theodoratos lent their expertise to certain technical questions.

Charles Lipcon, Esq. of Lipcon, Margulies and Winkleman, a law firm in Miami, gave unselfishly of his time on questions of maritime law, as did Evan Guthrie, Esq. on questions of Delaware law.

Dr. Jay Cohn, a universally respected cardiologist and author, and Dr. Owen Middleton, of the Hennepin County (Minnesota) Medical Examiner's Office, were instrumental in their discussion of heart-related and cardiac issues. Capt. Matt Wayne, of the Dakota County (Minnesota) Sheriff's Office, offered valuable advice in areas of policing and procedure. Friends and family have been a source of strength and support throughout.

I cannot say enough about Chang Wang, Esq., a Chinese-American attorney, author, and media personality for his expertise in all things Chinese and the language and translations which are part of the manuscript, as well as the late John Williamson, whose publication on the Lakota language was invaluable.

Avi Meshar, a master of seven languages and a computer genius, spent dozens of hours undoing my technical shortcomings, and patiently correcting or restoring them when I had inadvertently hit "delete."

There were numerous others who contributed to my efforts, including Shawn Clapp of "The Toasted Frog" in Grand Forks, North Dakota, along with others in Grand Forks, Spirit Lake, and Fort Totten, North Dakota, who prefer to remain anonymous, and to all of them, my sincere thanks.

David Housewright, the Edgar Award winning author, gave unselfishly of his time and offered blistering critiques which I hope I incorporated accurately.

Finally, the staff at Calumet Editions: My editor and cover designer Gary Lindberg, publisher Ian Graham Leask, Josh Weber, who placated my many annoyances, plus super copy editor Rick Polad. Truly, it takes a village.

About the Author

Alan Miller began his love of journalism early in life, and it carried through to serving as editor of his high school newspaper, writing the senior variety show, and becoming sports editor of the local village newspaper at fifteen, which led to a sports reporter position at *Newsday* at sixteen. Since then, he majored in journalism and political science in college, became an attorney, worked on several other newspapers, and taught in colleges, universities, and law schools as well as for the National Institute for Trial Advocacy. As a weekly columnist for a Long Island, New York, newspaper, he won a first-place designation from the New York Press Association, as well as a best column in Bowling magazine, wrote for the late Joe Franklin's magazine, and began appearing on television on Franklin's nationally televised program as a guest. For the last quarter century, he has been the host-producer of an award-winning local access TV program, "Access to Democracy," now networked in thirty-five Minnesota cities and recently created a new local access TV program in Minnesota entitled Writers Corner. He resides in Minnesota with his wife Sharon, and a springer spaniel rescue named Katie.

Made in the USA
Monee, IL
24 August 2023

41514560R00166